Right away he spotted the table squatters
in a dim corner, sucking down foamy dark
beer and eyeing the other customers with a
discreet but distinctly predatory eye.

Not to mention the way their very presence
raised his hackles.

He took a step toward them.

Or he meant to.

Almost instantly he froze. He froze with *fear*. In
disbelief, he tried to shake it off—literally tried to
shake it off, a body memory of shaking snow off his
fingers.

Fear.

Angel™

ANGEL™

fearless

Doranna Durgin

**An original novel based on the television series
created by Joss Whedon & David Greenwalt**

SIMON PULSE

New York   London   Toronto   Sydney   Singapore

Historian's Note: This book takes place just before the third season's "Waiting in the Wings."

First Simon Pulse edition October 2003

SIMON PULSE
An imprint of Simon & Schuster
Children's Publishing Division
1230 Avenue of the Americas
New York, NY 10020

The text of this book was set in New Caledonia.

Printed in the United States of America
10 9 8 7 6 5 4 3 2 1

Library of Congress Control Number 2003108167
ISBN 0-689-86431-0

Acknowledgments go to Lucienne, Lisa, Micol, and Lisa (that wasn't a typo!), and John Ward and Katherine Lawrence—all of whom contributed in their own way, some more demonly than others. And again, thanks to Jennifer (a.k.a. Red Pen Woman) and Amy with her Angelometer.

To family, both born and acquired.

CHAPTER ONE

Cordelia Chase contemplated the enemy.

It stared back, unblinking, a red-and-white floating eyeball of a target.

Someone had drawn a smiley face on it.

Her gaze slid over to Angel; he looked oblivious.

He did it, she decided.

"It would be more impressive if it were one of those hovering target droids from *Star Wars*," she said, eyeing the hapless fishing bobber dangling from a basement ceiling pipe beside the black, worn workout bag. "You know, dodging my own personal light saber. I could do a number on demons if I had a light saber. I wonder what color blade . . . ?" *Maybe a nice peach . . .*

"So far the target's pretty safe, even without the dodging feature." Angel crossed his arms, looking mighty Irish this evening in a black cable-patterned sweater. Something substantial enough to fit in with

1

warm-blooded humans, and yet not so bulky as to hamper the movement of a vampire who didn't get cold anyway.

No, not bulky at all. Just right.

If you like the centuries-old, vampire-with-a soul look, Cordelia told herself.

At the moment, she didn't. She didn't like it at all—no matter how it suited the gloom of the Hyperion Hotel basement. Plastic flowers—*her* plastic flowers—could hardly compete with the soldierly lineup of industrial mops and buckets under the stairs, the unpainted block walls, the randomly stacked furniture rejects under yellow incandescent lighting. She gestured abruptly at the fishing bobber. "I'll never have to defend myself against something like *this*."

"Maybe not," he said. "Or then again . . . who knows. But you need the precision practice either way."

She couldn't argue that. It only made her crankier, and she didn't like the feeling. She aimed a little of it at him in a scowl and tried to decide how to distract him from this particular training exercise.

Turned out he was distracted all on his own, lingering noticeably closer to the exit of the hotel basement. Or rather, closer to the exit, leading from this initial cavern of cement block and pipes and wire grates through the strange passages beneath the hotel and finally out into the sewers. He met her inquiring gaze and said, "The locals are getting restless."

"That's never good." Cordy checked the short, saucy ponytail gathered high at the back of her head and found it still secured to her precise satisfaction. "Especially when I'm pretty sure you mean local *demons*." She slanted a look at him.

Angel didn't answer, which didn't bother Cordelia at all. Sometimes he did that. She returned her attention to the inevitable. The happy-faced bobber. *No*, she decided. *The leering bobber*.

She'd warmed up. She'd done her stretching, along with every other thing that would put off the inevitable: facing her complete lack of . . .

She turned, planted a foot, chambered her other leg and let fly a perfect side kick, missing the bobber completely.

. . . precision. Control. Ability to hit the bad guys where she *wanted* to hit them.

"You're trying too hard," Angel said. He stalked around the basement, absently tapping the bobber with a quick one-two flick of a punch. He hit it, of course.

"Trying too hard at what?"

Cordy glanced up with surprise, finding the rest of the gang—Wesley Wyndam-Pryce, Charles Gunn, and Winifred Burkle—lingering near the top of the aged wooden stairs that ran down the basement wall and waiting for the answer to Wesley's question.

Well, most of the gang. Angel's infant son Connor slept under the watchful gaze of his anagogic empathy demon nanny, Lorne.

Angel glanced up with no surprise at all.

No, of course not. Not with that vampire hearing. But he could have warned her.

"Never mind 'at what,'" she said. "Let's talk about the restless locals."

"Yeah," said Gunn. "I noticed that."

"Noticed what, exactly?" Fred asked. Having come out of hiding to prove herself as one of the gang, not to mention actually painting over the hysterical scribbles that passed for a journal all over her room's walls, she still didn't venture out quite enough to be on the forefront of demony action.

Cordelia told her, "Noticed that you look like the Brady Bunch lined up on the stairs. Which is reason enough to move, if you ask me."

Gunn must have thought so too; he made a hasty descent into the basement. But he didn't waste repartee; he looked at Angel with that slight lift to his jaw that meant business and said, "Demons on the move out there. . . . They're running from something."

"We're all running from something," Cordelia heard herself mutter, but quickly hushed as Wesley looked in her direction. It would be hard to explain her mood when she didn't entirely understand it herself.

Just . . . too many changes. In her life. In *her*.

Angel said, "I'm going hunting. Anyone with me?"

"Yo," Gunn said, straightening his shoulders under his orange long-sleeved tee and indigo vest. "Let's see what's got these demons all antsied up."

"Later, perhaps," Wes said. "If you're still out. I'm in the middle of a tricky bit of research."

"Later," Cordelia said, and did not add *I'm in the middle of a tricky bit of mood.*

"Later," Fred said, tugging a little at one of her usual too-small tops, one with just a little lace around the capped sleeves and highly scooped neckline. The girl must do all her shopping in the junior department; Cordy thought it was about time for a woman-to-woman on that subject. But then Fred threw Cordelia a desperate kind of look and Cordy understood: she saw the fear.

Fred wasn't quite ready for the kind of hunting expedition Angel and Gunn had in mind.

And looking at Fred, Cordy also saw herself. Saw her very own conflicted mood and recognized it with a little shock.

Fear.

Fred trailed Wesley back into the lobby. She discovered that Cordelia trailed her, still wearing the strange expression she'd acquired as they all spoke in the basement.

Fred liked the basement. But then, she had a

5

certain fondness for the sewers, too, leftover from the time in her cave sanctuary on Pylea. To her, such places meant safety and a space to hide. And because Fred was so familiar with hiding, she was also familiar with Cordelia's strange expression. As Wes retrieved a book from the hotel's curving green reception counter, walking absently to his office as he read, Cordelia crossed behind him to snag a coffee mug and the Mr. Coffee carafe that was snugged in behind the counter.

Fred sat on the first tier of the split stairway that led to the second floor, hugging her knees in a gawky way. In honor of the late fall season, the courtyard doors behind her were closed, but she really needed to find a sweater to ward off the chill that had snuck in. She looked at Cordelia and said, "You're awful quiet tonight."

"Better than just being plain awful," Cordelia said, but her heart wasn't in the comeback. She left her coffee on the counter, untouched.

"It's okay, you know," Fred said, wisely.

That got Wesley's attention; he looked up from the book. He'd only made it as far as the grayish upside-down mushroom of a seating arrangement. It was the only gray thing in a luxuriously spacious lobby of an old-copper green, and dark burnt-orange color scheme broken only by living green plants and silver-scrolled torchère lamps.

Some of the lobby chairs, tucked away with ottomans and lamps into the oddest corners, tipped closer to red than to burnt orange, creating a combination that hurt Fred's eyes. Everyone else seemed to take them for granted. They'd come with the hotel . . . ergo, they belonged here.

"And what would that be? The thing that's okay?" Cordelia asked, her lips thinning.

"Being afraid," she said. "Some of the things that go on with us, you'd have to be crazy not to be afraid." She rubbed her knee and added thoughtfully, "I've been both, of course. Y'know, at the same time. But here, not so much. Anymore."

Cordelia admitted to nothing. "But are you?" she said, making it a challenge with that one arching eyebrow.

Fred gave a little laugh, genuinely amused, and fiddled with one of the long, wavy ponytails fastened behind each ear. "Sure," she said. "You'd think not, what with being rescued from Pylea and facing my folks and you know, just in general actually admitting to myself that everything that happened, happened—so's I can put it behind me. And what with not being a cow here in this dimension, and not being chased for being an escaped cow at that. But you and me and Wesley and Charles and Angel . . . we know more than most folks ever dream of when it comes to what's out there in this world. We know exactly what there is

7

to fear. And we face it every day." Then she thought of how she'd declined to join the night's prowl and looked down at her hands and added, "Well, some more than others. With the facing part of it, I mean."

"What makes you think I'm afraid?" Cordelia said, and now both eyebrows were raised as she finally took a sip of coffee.

Fred was not to be deterred, not in this thing about which she knew so much. "'Cause you're pretending you're not."

"Come now, Cordelia," Wesley said, breaking into the conversation, although of course he automatically put a finger in the book to save his place. "We're all afraid of something. And things around here *have* been especially hairy of late. It hasn't been so long since we almost lost you."

Cordelia shrugged, and the loose, cropped T-shirt she wore slipped over one shoulder. "But you didn't, did you?" she said. "As it happens, I am just fine. Finer, even, because you know there's a big pre-holiday blow-out at Fred Segal's, right? It starts tomorrow, and boy am I ready. Everything I own seems to have gore stains on it." She put her coffee mug down. "Now where's Connor? I need baby-time."

She said it as if the conversation were over, and Fred pointed mutely up the stairs, meaning Angel's rooms—as if Cordelia hadn't known that in the first place. But Fred knew the conversation wasn't over, that being afraid was never over. And that you couldn't run from it, that the closest you could get to stopping it was to turn around and run right at it.

Screaming.

CHAPTER TWO

Fear.

Angel left Gunn in his wake in spite of the flashlight Gunn snatched up on the way out of the basement. Long strides, vision that swept the dark tunnels unimpaired . . . he walked as though driven.

Was driven.

"Hey, man, you got some kind of demony bug up your butt?" Gunn asked, taking a few quick steps to catch up.

As a matter of fact, yes.

Angel was his own demon.

He was a demon with a son who shouldn't have been conceived, a son whose nature he didn't understand . . . a son he didn't truly know how to protect or care for.

Not in the smaller sense. In the smaller sense, he knew exactly how to love Connor. He had only to look at the baby—*his* baby—and it all but knocked him off his feet. But when it came to the bigger picture, the part about guiding Connor through life . . . and specifically through the life Angel's haunting past had given him. Now it was easy enough to feed and cuddle and clothe the baby, and if nothing else, Angel could be certain that he himself wouldn't die of old age or heart attack or cancer or any of those human woes that would leave Connor on his own.

But what about the first time Connor asked why Daddy couldn't go out in the sunlight? And what about the first time one of Angel's enemies tried to reach him through his child? His only child, his impossible child, his . . .

Connor.

And Angel was terrified.

Bad vibe.

Gunn followed Angel's shadowed form through the sewers to whatever junction had been inspiring murmurs and whispers throughout the denizens of this dank, smelly place, and all the way to Angel's ears. *Bad vibe.* Gunn didn't like it when the big guy gave off a bad vibe. No telling when all that lurking evil might quit lurking and start rearing up.

But . . . that couldn't be the cause of Gunn's uneasy feelings. Not by far. The lurking evil thing he was used to. And when it came right down to it, so

11

what if Angelus did make a play? Gunn knew how to stake a vamp.

He even knew how to stake a vamp who wore a face he loved, and Angel's didn't come near to being that.

So his restlessness, this need to trot off and behead something, had nothing to do with Angel. . . .

Except that it did. It was about Gunn waiting for Angel to do the wrong thing, say the wrong thing, *become* the wrong thing. Which would make it absolutely clear that Gunn had made the wrong choice, throwing in with a vampire instead of sticking with his own gang. Sure, Rondell had lost the mission—but what if Gunn hadn't gotten distracted by the excitement of working with Angel Investigations, going to the source of demon troubles instead of nibbling away at individual vampires and demons, been lured by the thought of playing in the big leagues? What if Gunn had been with his boys all along, not driven away by his memories of Alonna and the way he'd failed her?

Maybe they would have kept sight of the true mission and not turned into the kind of people who killed for the fun of killing and called it righteous because the victims were demons. Perhaps harmless demons, but Rondell and the not-at-all-dearly departed Gio had no longer been able to see those shades of gray.

So maybe he'd failed them after all.

12

And maybe in the end he'd fail his friends at Angel Investigations.

Bad vibes.

A demon lurks.

A small demon.

A cautious demon.

A demon on the perimeter of disaster, tucked away in a safe little sewer nook, its lumpy, ill-defined body squeezed and distorted and contorted into safety. All unaware, it has stumbled onto the death throes of a Gavrok spider, and the creature that has slain it. The little demon knows the Gavrok spider didn't belong here. . . . But it also knows the six-legged spider would have done this particular creature no harm. Not with all those claws on all those arms beneath all those teeth . . .

But the big creature seems to harbor an obsession with killing the demons it encounters. Another fresh kill is smeared across the curving concrete, and not long ago the little demon had come across a pack of small scavengers industriously cleaning the site of yet another recent kill. They scattered before it, perhaps sensing its hunger.

Now it has more than hunger on its mind. Now it knows what's behind the recent massacres in an underground population that generally coexists with little more than the occasional squabble. It wants badly to escape this frightening scene it has stumbled upon, but is wisely afraid to move from cover—especially as the creature before it lifts its heavy, taller-than-wide head as if detecting the little demon's presence.

But there is a scuffle in the tunnel in the opposite direction, and human voices. The creature whirls in that direction with amazing speed. While normally the little demon finds humans in the tunnels to be of great interest and possible resource, this time it is not even tempted. Keeping itself as low and flat as it possibly can, it scoots out of its cranny and scurries away. Driven by fear, it makes a new resolution: It must acquire new survival skills. It found itself not the least inclined to be picky, or to follow its usual precautions. Any skill that caught its attention, that pleased it, it would acquire.

As many as it could, as fast as it could.

We're all afraid of something.

Wes watched Cordelia retreat up the hotel stairs, noting the rigidity of her shoulders beneath her tummy-revealing shirt, her refusal to glance back at them. He was right, and she knew it. *He* knew it—deep in his bones, where it counted. Deep in his abdomen, where the gunshot wound of not so terribly long ago still twinged at odd moments, making him wonder if it would ever heal.

Bringing home to him each time, with a profundity of awareness he could scarcely fathom, how close he'd come to death. How *easy* it was to do that.

To die.

Fear.

Cordelia bent over little Connor, humming softly as she smoothed his little baby shirt over his soft baby tummy. Connor gurgled in an unfocused way, sleepy and ready for his bottle.

Or maybe for some projectile vomiting. *'Cause, you know—babies . . .*

She glanced up and found Lorne regarding her with a strange look, bottle in hand and clashing, oh so badly, with his deep purple disco-ready shirt. Not that the shirt didn't already clash with his lime-green complexion and the red horns and eyes he sported—not to mention *just a little eyeliner*, as he'd once confessed to Fred's father. No, the bottle just added a whole other dimension to the unique look Lorne called his own.

But the expression he wore . . . a disturbed expression—one with lurking sympathy and complete understanding to boot.

"Oh," Cordelia said in sudden realization. "Oh, damn. I was humming. Damn."

"Not the best way to keep those thoughts to yourself around me, hunny-bunny," Lorne said, not without admonishment.

Like he'd removed her finger from the dike, those thoughts came bursting out. "When does it *stop*?" she asked. "I was scared when I got here, no money after all those years of having everything. And then living in that disgusting roach-infested one-room apartment. But then I found Angel, and I found my new place which I love"—okay, so that came with the ghost of Dennis Pearson attached and had involved no little scariness until they'd evicted the spirit of Dennis's nasty mother—"and then I got these visions that happen to come with migraines, and I got sent to your home dimension where I was sold as a *cow*, and when we actually made it back home, the visions tried to kill me, except now I'm part demon and what does that *mean*, anyway? Does anyone here know what it means? How I've changed? What it'll do to me before this is all over—assuming I live that long?"

Lorne gave her both raised eyebrows. "I'd applaud, but my hand is full of Junior's bottle. Nice catharsis. Very nice indeed."

"Yeah, right," Cordelia said sourly. Her tone didn't translate into her gentle touch as she put Connor in his bassinet and tucked his blankets around him, but when she straightened to put her hands on her hips, it was all over her face. She could feel it there, sardonic and even a little bitter. "Except you can't fool me any more than I can fool you. I did go to school, you know, and did quite

16

well. I remember drama class. And I remember that catharsis means getting it out of your system. One great big emotional burp."

"And I thank you so much for that image." Lorne handed her the bottle, and she held it for him as he gathered the baby up, a tiny bundle of soft wrappings against his intensely purple shirt. Already the room had that milky baby smell. A soothing smell.

It didn't do much for Cordelia. Not this time.

She said, "Well, that wasn't catharsis. Because it's all still inside me."

"No, princess, you're right. *That* was recognition. Sometimes it has to come first," Lorne said. "In any event, it's all perfectly understandable. Just try to deal with it all before it passes burpville and becomes volcanic, will you?"

As if. She thrust the warm bottle at him with a scowl. He took it, making cooing noises at the baby until his expression turned to satisfaction.

Lorne turned back to Cordelia and would have said something, but Wesley's appearance in the open doorway distracted them both. He leaned in as though he only planned to be there for an instant, one hand hanging on the door frame.

"Angel just called—"

"*Angel?*" Cordelia interrupted with some skepticism. "On his cell phone?"

"Gunn did the actual calling," Wesley admitted.

"But it was at Angel's behest. They need help—apparently they've found the cause of the problems down below." And he would have disappeared, if Cordelia hadn't stopped him.

"Problems?" she demanded. "Say more."

He hesitated. "I'm not yet sure. The description could fit a dozen different demon species."

She put her hands on her hips, rife with impatience. "Just tell me if we're arming up to hack something big, or if this is a chase-and-stomp."

"More of the former than the latter, I'm afraid," Wesley said.

"Whoa there, buckaroo," Lorne said, with no trace of a whoa-there-buckaroo drawl. He shifted Connor in his arm, adjusting the bottle. "Former, latter . . . I can't keep those straight unless I have diagrams."

"Huge," Wesley said simply. "Mucus-laden. Pulsing."

Cordelia looked at him with distaste. "Mucus?"

"Let's just hurry, shall we? They're holding it at bay. If we're too late we'll end up chasing it down again—unless we're *really* too late, in which case we'll be making another hospital run."

"The way you're going through emergency rooms lately, someone's going to peg us as a big bad co-dependent group of Munchausen's by Proxy," Lorne said.

Cordelia shot him a look. "You scare me sometimes,"

she said. "And don't think I won't look that up when we get back."

This time Wesley did disappear from the doorway. "Fred's gathering up some weapons," he called back down the hall. "Let's not waste any more time!"

"Fred?" Cordelia said in surprise. If they'd asked Fred to join in . . .

It wasn't good.

I can do this. Again. So what if she wasn't much into the fighting, she'd focused on the customer relations and the phone answering and creative research. . . . But things changed. *She* had changed. And anyway, she'd been training. And spending more time in the field.

"I am strong," she reminded herself under her breath, reciting the words to a Helen Reddy song that was older than Cordelia herself but sure did have legs. "I am invincible, I am . . ."

She sighed. "Not Reddy."

"Pumpkin!" Lorne said with delight. "That's *my* kind of joke!"

Wesley's voice floated down the hall, possibly even up the stairs. "Cordelia!"

"Coming!" she bellowed back, then winced as Connor gurgled and made the hiccuping sounds that meant he was cranking up for a good cry. "Sorry."

"Shoo," Lorne said, gesturing with his formidable chin in lieu of his full hands. "Go on, grab a sword and go take care of this thing. It's not like you're not leaving me with all the hard work."

And as Connor's wail filled the room, Cordelia wasn't sure she could disagree.

Angel looked down at the blood on his hand. The blood was his, and it ran.

The hand trembled.

On the other side of the creature trapped near a three-way storm sewer junction, Gunn . . . giggled.

Between them, the demon snarled something juicy sounding. Not intelligence—nothing of this creature spoke of anything but the dimmest intelligence. Bright eyes swiveled, chameleon-like, near the top of a head that looked like a thick flying saucer set on edge. Its tiny little arms would have been amusing—had there not been so many of them. And had not each arm been equipped with six razor sharp claws.

Angel bled.

The demon crouched on two thick legs, using an equally thick stump of a tail for balance when it lashed out with those gnarled, long claws.

Its agility had taken Angel by surprise in their first clash—ragged slashing wounds scored his arm . . .

And still they bled.

"Hello," he said, looking at his own torn flesh through what used to be a favorite sweater. "Vampire here. Heal already."

Gunn laughed like Angel had said something terribly witty. Combined with his own inexplicably bleeding and painful self, facing a demon the likes of which he'd never seen before . . . Angel's head spun.

Or maybe that was just the way he'd hit it when that lightning fast kick slammed him up against the concrete of the storm sewer wall. Like his wounds, his head, too, should have healed.

It hadn't.

The demon snarled again, exposing approximately a kazillion needle-sharp little teeth, and as it whirled to face Gunn, the pulsating boils on its back and shoulders glistened in the dim light.

"Ooh," Gunn said, singsongy. "What big teeth you have, Grandma."

What big teeth you have?

"Gunn?" Angel said in utter disbelief. A glimpse of Gunn beyond the demon revealed that Gunn, too, had been hurt, but not badly. Just enough to show a little blood and some strategically torn clothing. But if Gunn didn't drop out of that swaggery street pose and put that battle-ax to work, he was going to need more than a Band-Aid. Angel narrowed his eyes, recognizing a strange dreaminess in Gunn's behavior and torn clothes. Vaguely familiar, blast-from-the-past flower power and over-sized bell bottoms and . . . well, the mini-skirts had been okay. "You're giving me a bad sixties flashback," he told Gunn, shouting over the drooling snarl of the posturing demon. And really, with the sixties, once was enough.

He was going to have to hurt Gunn if the giggling didn't stop. But they weren't far from the hotel. . . . Regardless of Gunn's strangely altered status and Angel's failure to bounce back from the first painful exchange of blows—all they had to do was stall the demon long enough for the others to arrive.

For there was little question the beast was the inspiration of the underground's restlessness. A fresh new batch of mayhem—streaks of demon blood and demon gore, and lumps of demon bodies—had led Angel almost directly to the beast. It must have a lair around here somewhere, but he had no intention of cornering it there. Even the most dim-witted of creatures turned wily and extreme in its own lair. And this one was enough trouble right here.

"Watch it!" Angel snapped as the demon sprang on Gunn, closing what had seemed like a safe distance in one startling move. Gunn merely grinned, with no alarm whatsoever, twirling the ax in a lazy way that might, if he was idiotically lucky, accidentally carve off some tiny bit of demon flesh.

It's not right. . . . None of this is right. . . .

But even as the true wrongness of the entire situation hit him—*not healing, Gunn's gone gooey—*

Angel saw clearly enough that the demon was about to drop kick Gunn across the sewer at the end of those gnarled grizzly claws. He abandoned his staggering and bleeding, and launched himself at the demon, drawing on every bit of vampire speed and strength and letting his face loose while he was at it.

"Niiice," Gunn said, nodding in appreciation as the beast whirled away from him with only inches to spare, clawing at its back with all its many little arms in an attempt to dislodge Angel. Angel clung to its glistening skin, scrabbling for a hold on the slick round boils, hacking at it with barbaric style.

One of those thick, bent hind legs raised up, reversed itself with a crunching noise that made Gunn wince with exaggeration, and took direct aim at Angel. He threw himself aside but not fast enough, not nearly fast enough.

The gnarled foot caught him in the hip and punted him across the short space to the concrete wall, where he slammed so hard against it that he seemed to hang in place. . . .

No, wait, it was the broken ladder rung he'd been impaled on.

"Damn," he said, gasping reflexively. "This is gonna hurt."

Already there.

As Gunn foolishly pestered the demon to distraction, Angel shoved himself away from the wall with a grunt of effort and agony; when he hit the ground he just kept right on going, crumpling into something that really, more than anything, simply wanted to whimper for a week or two. With darkness edging in around his vision and his body curled around itself in a dark nook beside the broken ladder, Angel found his thoughts going back to those times of his greatest endurance . . . his greatest torture. Those unending hours in the barn with Holtz and his sanctimonious accomplices in Rome; here in L.A. when Spike had paid a vampire named Marcus to acquire information about the Gem of Amarra; a hundred or so years in hell, courtesy of his lover's gentle sword.

Always he had the knowledge that there was nothing they could do to him that wouldn't either kill him outright . . . or quickly heal. Always he had the wherewithal to eventually stumble away, batter his way free, or even, when Angelus, run like a dog, laughing as he gained strength with every step.

Hidden in his shadowed nook, Angel knew without looking, without uncurling himself to check out his wounds and pains, that the impossible was happening. Or, *wasn't* happening.

He wasn't healing. He also wasn't dying, no more than ever . . . but neither was he healing. *At all*.

A furious, gargling roar echoed through the tunnels. As one, Cordelia, Wesley, and Fred stopped their hurried jog to exchange a glance. Fred swallowed visibly and readjusted her grip on the machete-like *dao* she held.

"Gosh," Cordelia said brightly. "D'you suppose that's what we're looking for?"

"If it's not, we're in trouble," Wesley said grimly, so obviously not in the mood to play along with her sarcasm. From his forehead shined a cyclopean light, directly into her eyes. "We can hardly handle two such creatures at the same time."

Cordelia squinted and waved fiercely at him, and he adjusted his stance so his light moved off her face. Whereas Cordelia had a sturdy—and waterproof— industrial size flashlight, one of the square-ish ones that sat nicely on end to bounce light off the tunnel ceiling when it was time to convert skulking into fighting, Wesley wore his recently acquired head-lamp. Cordelia was about to kick him in the shin and snatch it away as he bent over the offended leg.

"It's set on L-E-D," he told her, anticipating her commentary. "It's a very mild light."

"It's set," she told him archly, "To shine down-ward."

"Yes, naturally."

"Well, duh! Guess who's shorter than you? You know—*downward*?"

"Maybe the headlamp is best for single-person excursions," Fred said tentatively. "Or if we were all the same height. . . ."

"I see your point," Wesley said, but not without regret. He adjusted the light briefly. "Is that better? It's hardly as effective to light one's path—"

Cordelia interrupted with a firm voice. "Yes, but now we can see when you happen to look at us. I think that's a good thing when we're headed to do demon battle together, don't you?"

"Right," Fred said, trying to sound confident . . . and not. "I may not be very good with this thing, but at least now I can be sure I'm aiming at the demon and not one of us."

At that thought, Wesley looked like he might be considering dumping the headlamp altogether. Instead he nodded, cyclops eye bopping, and said, "Very well, then. Shall we proceed?" Except his words were almost entirely obscured by another angry sound, this one low and snarly and crawling along the tunnels like a warning.

They exchanged another look, and they began to run.

Wrong direction, Cordelia's legs tried to tell her. *Run away! Turn around!* But no, they ran right for the angry sounds of battle, although as they drew closer those sounds didn't entirely sound angry at all. She heard a giggle.

A giggle. She was sure of it. A *masculine* giggle.

So it was no huge surprise when she rounded a tunnel corner just behind Wesley and discovered Gunn, bent over his knees and laughing, sword in hand but hardly in a grip or posture that could do Gunn any good.

"Charles?" Fred said, on Cordelia's heels, and sounding as uncertain as Cordy felt. "Are you—"

"Sane?" Cordelia finished for her, planting her flashlight on end near the corner, and noting they had the bonus of a distant maintenance light as well.

"Possibly not," Wesley said, as serious and intent as ever. "I suggest we step in."

Awkwardly—but not possibly as awkwardly as Fred with her fancy machete—Cordelia lifted the short blade she'd brought. *It'd be nice if this were longer—a lot longer—but there's no room. . . .*

Fred gave a short shout that might have been fear bursting out, or might equally have been a determined war cry, and she rushed at the demon, taking Wesley by surprise. He hastened to join her, and Cordelia hesitated only long enough to pull Gunn out of the fight.

Another surprise: He didn't resist her. Still kind of . . . giggling . . . he obligingly followed her tug, and she got more assertive and pushed him against the wall, out of the way. "Stay here," she said, giving him a wary look as she turned back to the demon. But he only waved her on, an inexplicable see-for-yourself gesture.

She took an instant to assess the demon, with all its little *Tyrannosaurus rex* arms, its thick mutant-kangaroo legs, and that weird head . . . those horrible glistening boils . . . all those teeth . . .

A shiver of cold fear ran from head to toe and back again, raising goose bumps and the hair along the back of her neck and down her arms . . . turning her legs to jelly. She took a deep breath, muttered "Too bad," at herself, and jumped into range, using the momentum to swing at the thick stumpy tail on which it leaned back for balance.

An instant later she bounced off the wall, the sword knocked from her grip and her wrist slashed and bleeding. *Who'd have thought those little arms could be so quick?* Quick enough to slap Fred right out of one of her war cries, scoring her cheek. Quick enough to literally snatch Wesley off his feet, several arms working in unison, their claws digging deeply into the skin of his upper arms. With fierce determination he brought his wicked Bowie knife up to strike, his headlamp knocked askew until the artificial moonlight of the lamp fell across the creature's eyes.

It gave a high, girlish scream and tried to clap its hands—all its hands, even the short-armed ones that couldn't begin to reach—over its bulgy, independently swiveling eyes. Still screaming, it lashed blindly at Wesley and then barreled through Fred, abandoning the fight it had so clearly been winning.

Fight, hell. It was more like the ant people taking on Godzilla. Not that it was that big, but those ridiculous little arms . . . that absurd head . . . that ugly, stumpy tail . . .

Cordelia heard herself laugh. It was a spare parts demon, that's what it was. Spare, discarded, unwanted, uglified parts, all stuck to it like a Mr. Demon Potato Head.

Wesley, bleeding from a dozen deep puncture wounds, hooted after it in a most uncharacteristic way. "I scared it off! Me! It took one look into my heroic features and ran for it!"

"Maybe it was your breath," Fred suggested, and then froze in the act of wiping blood from her face as if surprised by her own words. Then she let out a great snort of laughter, a gigantically unlikely noise. Cordelia looked at Wesley, who looked at Gunn, who looked back at Fred, and they all burst out into laughter at once. Cordy's wrist no longer hurt, and when she thought to glance at it, she realized it hadn't been hurt that badly after all. Just a cut. Or wait. . . . Was it even bad enough to call a cut? A scratch, that was it. After all, she'd been training. She knew how to fight this demon—she knew how to fight any demon.

And win.

Wesley drew breath, making a monumental effort to get out a few sober words. "Where's Angel? Isn't he supposed to be here?"

Gunn shrugged elaborately. "Don't see him."

"Maybe the demon ate him," Fred suggested,

wiping tears of laughter from her eyes, revealing a nearly healed scratch on her face.

They considered this thought in a moment of silence, and again burst into laughter all at once, leaning against each other, staggering with mirth as opposed to pain and making their way toward the hotel in lurching, clumsy progress.

The tunnels echoed with roars of laughter instead of demon anger, and if anyone happened to groan quietly beneath it, to call out for help, why then . . .

No one heard.

The tiny, shivery sound of ratlike claws against concrete filtered through Angel's awareness. A pause . . . they skittered closer. *Great. Now the rats.* Drawn by blood, no doubt.

His blood. Still bleeding. Still not healing. Though . . . like any wounded thing, perhaps not bleeding quite so hard as once.

Running out of it, probably.

He tried to glare the rat—or rat-thing—away, but failed by virtue of not even getting his eyes open.

They had left him.

Like Gunn, they'd all turned improbably foolish, and they'd roared with laughter.

And then they'd left him.

From what he'd seen, like Gunn, their slight

wounds didn't match the badly torn clothing, the sluiced blood. Of course, that had been when Angel had still been able to open his eyes.

Guys—I could use a little help here.

It seemed like too much to hope that they'd return before the rats got bold enough to start nibbling, given that they didn't even have the wits to notice he was missing. If he hadn't heard the distinct crunch of the cell phone during the fight. . . . *Damn thing, the one time I actually* want *to use it*—he might even give them a desperate call.

Although he had the feeling he'd get nothing but giggling on the other end of the line.

Impossibly wounded or not, his keen hearing had not abandoned him; he heard the faint, light footsteps some distance away. Too light to be anyone from Angel Investigations, even Fred. Soon the footsteps faltered, and noises of dismay filtered through. Eventually those footsteps turned the corner, and stopped altogether.

"Tsk!"

Angel flinched at the sound, discovering he could still do at least that. The rat gave an un-ratlike squawk of fear and ran for it.

"Such a mess!" the being muttered. Even without looking, Angel knew it wasn't human. No human's voice resonated with that double-vocal-cord effect— one that came from not very high off the ground, especially for a creature with a male timbre.

Angel hoped it didn't have a stake. Hell, a splinter would probably do the trick at the moment.

The creature bent over him, bringing with it a whiff of strangely stale cantaloupe. Angel tensed, unable to help himself . . . so damned vulnerable . . . and groaned at the wash of pain it caused.

"Shh," said the creature. "Oh, this is abominable. I can only be grateful the others aren't here. Had I only been just a little faster . . ." Then it stopped its fretting, and gave a few conspicuous sniffs. "Not human . . . you can't be, if it left you in this condition." Another deep inhalation, a pondering pause, and it said softly, "Vampire. But . . . still . . . a soul?" Then it did the last thing Angel expected; it patted him gently on the shoulder. "Peacefulness, fanged one. Stay quiet in your hiding spot. You are the one who can help me, oh if anyone can, and I will return."

Just get here before the rats.

CHAPTER THREE

Fred, glancing across the Hyperion lobby with a soda to her lips, found Wesley Wyndam-Price sprawled against deep green tile with rusty orange ribbons of color, flapping his arms and legs to make snow angels. She clapped her hand to her mouth, but not before cola spewed everywhere.

"Oh, dear," she said, and pulled up the hem of her blood-stained shirt to wipe her chin. Then she hesitated, giving the shirt a puzzled stare. "Where'd this blood come from?" She scrubbed at it with one sticky hand, but it was good and dry.

Charles looked up from his Game Boy, thumbs still flicking at the controls; he sat in one of the dark rusty chairs sequestered by the split stairs, his feet up on an ottoman. He said without concern, "Yup, you're all over blood, woman."

"And—ew, what's this? It looks like dried old

snot!" Fred pulled her shirt away from her stomach in disgust.

Behind the reception counter, Cordelia removed the spoon from which she'd thoughtfully been sucking the last atoms of Ben & Jerry's and glanced down at herself; she gave a cry of surprise. "Look at me! My shirt is ripped and—"

"We're all bloody," Charles announced with some cheer. "See?" He gestured at his own bright orange pullover, where the clashing dried blood was stiff enough to hold up against a poke of his finger. "No big deal, Fred."

"In fact," Wesley said, sitting up so abruptly that his head seemed to magically appear above the gray roundchair, "This conversation sounds oddly familiar."

"That's just *déjà vu*," Fred said, still looking at her shirt with the impulse to pull it right off her body.

"No," Wesley said, looking tremendously thoughtful for someone who had a dust bunny in his hair, "I don't think it is. There's *something* . . ."

"Don't care," Charles said. "It's a good night. I feel good. I feel damn near invincible. Just for once, I don't want to worry about any damn *something*."

Fred smiled fondly at him. That was her Charles, all assertive and . . . and orange. She giggled.

"That's right," Cordelia said. She burst into sudden song. "I am strong! I am invincible!"

Distracted from his thoughts, Wesley joined right in. "I am woman!"

The lobby fell silent.

"Mm," Wesley said, wincing. "I think my timing was off, there."

"Your timing was just perfect," Lorne said, making an appearance on the staircase behind Charles. "Your pitch, on the other hand, could use some improvement. Children, what on or off earth is going on down here? Do you know how late it is? Do you know"—he stopped, gave them a blatant double-take, and finished with words Fred didn't think were exactly what he'd intended—"what you *look* like?"

"Oh, we're fine," Fred assured him.

But Cordelia gave a little shriek. "Look at my shirt! Where'd all this blood come from?"

"That's not Cherry Garcia, chickadee," Lorne said. "Shouldn't there be a first aid kit around here somewhere? Plainly in evidence?"

"That's it," Wesley said, a voice of profound excitement. "We need evidence!"

"Looks to me like you've got plenty of that." Lorne came the rest of the way down the stairs, revealing the fluffy chartreuse slippers beneath his sea foam bathrobe. "It's all over you. The thing is, I see the blood and the sartorial damage, but you're—"

"Just fine," Charles said. "Though let me tell you, I am *not* woman."

"Notes," Wesley said, jumping to his feet with vigor and intent. "We need to make notes. Quickly. We need to figure out what happened tonight, and we need to write it down. On each other."

"Follow the evidence," Fred said happily. She snagged a notebook and marker from the curving green reception counter, reaching directly across Cordy and her abandoned ice cream with no thought to the rudeness of it.

"Clearly, we were in some sort of fight," Wesley said, stalking across the floor like Perry Mason in a courtroom.

"Clearly," Lorne said with a dry irony.

"Apparently, we prevailed."

"Or ran away," Cordelia said. She pointed at Fred with her spoon. "Write that down too."

"The condition of our clothing indicates we may have been wounded." Wesley looked down at his shirt, then stuck his head inside the neck of the button-down like a turtle examining its own insides. Without emerging, he added, "But if we were, we also seemed to have healed."

"Seem to have healed," Fred murmured, writing in big blocky letters suited to the marker.

"Are you getting this?" Wesley said from inside his shirt.

"Every word," Fred promised.

Charles put his Game Boy aside for the merest moment. "Did I mention, I am *not* woman?

You be sure to write that down too."

Fred wrote.

A cold and tangy liquid trickled down Angel's throat, rousing him. *Blood. Lovely, lovely blood.* He swallowed eagerly—too eagerly. Thick dribbles ran from the side of his mouth down to his chin. He choked, and a calm, vibrating voice murmured something soothing and withdrew the offering— but only for a moment.

After that Angel was more careful. He drank slowly . . . and he drank long. And though the pain didn't diminish and the wounds didn't heal, he felt a tease of strength return. Enough so when the supply—the snipped corner of a blood bank bag?—withdrew again, he finally opened his eyes.

The creature before him was wizened and stout, and Angel wasn't sure if its wrinkles came by na- ture or age. He thought it had a faintly green cast, but the fading orangish nature of the flashlight's glow made it hard to tell; it would have been easier in complete darkness. The creature wore shapeless robes and carried a carved and decorated staff that seemed to be as much prop as necessity. The dome of its broad skull sported wispy white hair; its ears flopped, doglike, at the side of its head.

Angel had never seen anything like it . . . and yet he had. He just couldn't think where. Didn't mat- ter. He was lucky to be thinking at all. He looked up at the creature, who seemed quite pleased with itself, and asked, "Why . . . ?"

"I bear the responsibility for what was done to you." The being twitched a robe into place, but its satisfaction faded as it looked around the tunnel juncture and the evidence of the demon's earlier havoc. The stench of earlier victims, the smell and splash of human blood—Angel couldn't detect it over his recent meal, but he knew it was there.

"I don't understand." With great effort, he sat more upright. A rib grated audibly; his teeth ground together nearly as audibly. "My friends, they . . ." *They turned into idiots*. Hmm, perhaps not the best way to start. "It's your fault?" He gave the creature a sudden wary look. "You're not *it*, right? The thing I fought? You're not going to turn into it?"

The creature smiled at that. It had a remarkably wide mouth, with small even teeth. A good dental plan. "No," it said. "I certainly won't. But . . . the matter is complex. It might be that you can be of some help to me, once you recover. Although I warn you . . . your recovery will take much longer than you're used to."

"Yeah, I was getting that." Angel took a hand from his side, looking at the glistening palm. He wasn't leaking blood at an alarming rate anymore, but it still flowed. No doubt if he had more of it, it would flow even faster. "You don't happen to have more—"

"Later," the creature said. "I'll escort you to your lair. You'll need it then, if I don't miss my bet."

"Hotel," Angel corrected him absently, wondering if there was any point in trying for his feet, or if he should just crawl all the way. Hell on his pants if he did. "That lair thing . . . not really classy anymore, you know?"

"I understand. Slowly, now." It held out a short-fingered hand—three fingers and thumb, with wispy white hair on all of them. Angel hesitated, and the creature gestured impatiently. "Come, come," it said. "You are too vulnerable here."

Angel took the proffered support, surprised to find the grip warm and substantially stronger than he'd expected. Carefully, the creature drew him onward, until eventually Angel was on his feet, if not actually upright.

"Angel," he told the creature. "Thank you."

"I am Kluubp," the creature said. "And I doubt very much if you'll be thanking me when you learn what's going on here. But for the moment I accept your gratitude. Now—in which direction is this hotel of yours?"

Angel gave the best gesture he could manage, which was more wishful thinking than gesture at all. But it seemed to have been enough. Kluubp pressed his staff in Angel's hand and let himself be used as a prop on the other side. "Slowly," he said. "As long as I am with you, the Giflatl will not be back."

Slowly.

Very slowly.

The stairs in the basement were the worst, just steep enough that Angel couldn't quite lift his feet as high as he needed to. Kluubp quite matter-of-factly lifted each foot to the next step, humming with a double-throated reverberation. Nothing seemed to have taken him aback during their long, quiet journey back to the Hyperion, one punctured more by gasps and grunts of pain and effort than any few words of conversation.

Nothing, until they reached the first floor.

Lo, the missing companions.

They sprawled around the lobby in various attitudes of sleep—though none that looked actually comfortable. They were covered with their own blood and dried mucus from the demon Kluubp had called a Giflatl, but none of them showed any sign of injury. Nor did they stir as Angel took a few tottery steps on his own, unable to understand what he saw. Cordelia, face down on the counter. Gunn, sprawled in a chair by the split stairway. Fred, curled around the center hub of the gray roundchair. And Wesley . . . on the floor in front of his office. They looked as if they'd simply laid down on the spot when the urge to sleep took them, not minding where that spot might be. Cordy was her curvy, dark-haired, dark-eyed self, not quite as tanned since she'd started working Angel Investigations nights; Wesley still a lanky pale Brit with gray eyes that could grow unexpectedly stormy; Fred remained a petite Southern white girl who'd been stuck in a cave too long; and shave-headed Gunn wore one of his typical loud shirts contrasting markedly with his rich brown skin. As diverse a collection of humans as one could hope to find—and the one thing they all had in common was a blissfully idiotic expression.

"Ah," Kluubp said. "Your friends from the fight."

Angel gave him an absent nod, swaying in the middle of the lobby. "Cordy—," he started, but Kluubp raised a quick hand.

"Let them sleep," he said. "It's better for now."

"It's better for now if I understand what's going on," Angel growled, a hint of his usual self-command coming through.

"It's *best*, for now, to get you to whatever room you call your own," Kluubp insisted with a hint of impatience.

"The elevator," Angel said, feeling a sudden wave of *tottery* coming on. Tonight, he'd skip the stairs. As he turned, though, something caught the corner of his eye. A piece of paper, caught between Gunn and the chair, with just enough visible to read the words:

CHARLES IS NOT WOMAN.

"Come," Kluubp said, tugging Angel just enough to trouble Angel's precarious balance. In the light of the torchère lamps, the short creature did indeed have a definite green cast—nothing like Lorne's intense hue, but more on the order of pale, overcooked peas. His sparse, coarse hair was all the more obvious . . . as was his displeased expression. "These papers will mean nothing. I'll clean them up on my way out."

"Not such a good idea. You don't want to get caught creeping between them after a night like this. And hey, you're—" *Going sideways . . .*

"No, it is you who tilts. Now *come*. I will take care of myself."

Angel obediently followed Kluubp to the elevator. Once inside, he retreated to a corner and slid gracelessly to the floor, smearing his way down even as the elevator rose. The buzz from the blood he'd gulped trickled away, and he allowed his eyes to close. *The elevator's not so bad. Maybe I'll just stay here. . . .*

He gave an offended yelp when Kluubp prodded him with the staff. "Hey! Don't go poking the wounded vampire, right?"

"This will be complicated enough to explain," Kluubp said, with no attempt to make himself clear as they arrived on the third floor and the elevator doors slowly opened. "Best if you're found in bed. Less commotion. We're going to have commotion enough, I guarantee you of that. What with your friends healing, your own failure to heal . . . if only they hadn't put up such a staunch fight. Rarely does any human receive such a dose of—" He cut himself off short to give Angel a sharp look, blocking the doors from closing with his staff. The look itself was somewhat of a failure, since his features were gathered together so closely in that broad face so as to look whimsical instead of imposing, and those puppy dog ears didn't help a bit. But with both voices deepening in displeasure, Kluubp's point was made.

And Angel was too tired to fight.

At the last minute he remembered Connor, asleep in Angel's bedroom. And Lorne—possibly in there with him, or else sleeping not far away. Angel directed Kluubp to the door next to his own, and literally crawled into the half-made bed.

"Here, then." From within his robes Kluubp produced a pint of blood, neatly packaged.

Angel nodded at the dusty bedside table, unable to muster the energy even to drink. A few moments of lying here, every wounded spot shrieking . . . if he'd been human, he'd be dead. He wasn't used to categorizing wounds anymore. Receive them, heal from them. No need to sort them out in the meantime, not usually.

"Mmm," Kluubp said thoughtfully, reverberating

deeply in the process. "There is much for you to learn, but now is not the time. Until then . . . it is best, far for the best, if you do not tell your friends about me. Do not tell them about what happened this night—for I can assure they won't remember. That is for the best, also."

That got through to him, rousing him to open his eyes just long enough to narrow them at Kluubp.

"Do not," Kluubp insisted. "At least until I can return to discuss this more completely so you have an understanding of that against which we fight. There is recipe for disaster in this very night, if you refuse to follow my lead. Do you understand at least that much?"

"I understand," Angel grumbled, though he closed his eyes and let his head sink into the skewed pillow at the head of the bed, "that I don't understand any of this."

"Precisely."

As parting words they were hardly soothing, but Angel was beyond soothing. Like any ordinary human, his body demanded rest so it could heal, and extracted an agonizing price for moments of resistance. Angel let it have its way with him, and Kluubp, when he went, went unnoticed.

Early morning at the Barrington Recreation Center. Carefully cultivated sports fields, soccer among them. A small group of teenage boys gather to kick a ball around, showing off various levels of skill in the brisk fall morning. One of them outshines the rest, their leader by acclamation. Off the field, a quiet young man, struggling with math and sciences. On the field, a developing genius.

In the long shadows of morning, between a utilitarian storage building and a trash bin, there lurks a small gray creature that resembles nothing so much as an overcooked lump of oatmeal blobbed upon the ground. Hard to judge its expression . . . but its eyes blink greedily as it observes the soccer players. It raises itself to its feet, exposing short stumpy legs. Experimentally, it kicks at a stone. The stone makes no effort to dodge, but the creature misses it anyway, and nearly falls on its shapeless posterior.

It takes a moment to pout. Then it fastens its gaze more firmly on the young soccer star. The hapless young man fails to notice.

A moment later, the young man stumbles badly. He trips over his attempted kick, and when he recovers and tries again, he misses the ball entirely.

He laughs it off; they all laugh it off. They decide to find a Starbucks and suck up a little caffeine.

The talented young man never plays soccer again.

Just past early morning at the edge of the Calabasas Landfill, a lumpy gray demon skips along in search of prey. If it could hum, it would, but it can't so instead it grunts happily. After a moment it pounces—not a pretty picture—and emerges from a mound of garbage bearing a small scavenger demon tightly curled into a protective ball. With an expert flick of its doughy wrist, it sends the pill-bug demon into the air, dribbles it between its feet, and boots it on ahead at just the right angle to bounce off a solidified lump of garbage. Before the pillbug demon can spin to a stop, unroll, and make a run for it, the lumpy new soccer expert is again upon it.

For half an hour, the gleeful demon bounces its victim around.

Then it kicks the pillbug up into the air, opens its heretofore undetectable but suddenly immense mouth, and swallows breakfast on its way down.

Fred gazed into the bathroom mirror, looking at her cheek. It was just Fred's cheek, fair and faintly flushed skin beneath chocolate brown eyes. Un-blemished.

She ran her fingers over it. She could have sworn she had a memory—not of looking at herself injured, but a body memory of the injury itself. Slashes of pain across her cheek. The impression of many tiny flailing arms suddenly much more dangerous than she'd thought they'd be.

But she hadn't been in a fight. Not just because

she didn't tend to leap into the fray, but also because she certainly didn't go out alone to pick fights with demons and such on her own—and in spite of the nasty state of their clothing this morning and their inexplicable mutual decision to bed down in the lobby, quite obviously none of the others had been hurt either. And they were all too jolly to be believed, carefree and . . .

Fearless. Unconcerned about much of anything—including the fact that no one had seen Angel. Not even Lorne, who emerged briefly to give them all a very Lornish eye, but would say nothing more than a token good morning before he retreated to check on Connor. He, too, knew Angel hadn't returned. Only he was more worried than the rest of them.

But still Fred looked in the mirror, touching her cheek. Not quite believing it was whole.

At least she was one of the lucky ones. She still lived here at the hotel; it would be easy enough to change out of the disgusting clothes she still wore.

Outside the open bathroom door Cordelia leaned over the curving reception counter, tied there by the short cord on their old-fashioned counter phone. "Dennis," she said, "I know you're there. You pretty much have to be, don't you? Listen—I know you worry when I don't come home, but I promise, everything's fine. Finer than fine. Really. So no disappearing act with my CD collection, okay?" She hesitated, then added cheerily, "Okay, bye!"

But Fred was standing in the bathroom doorway and saw the thoughtful way in which Cordelia hung up the phone. Slower than usual, and distracted. Fred cleared her throat slightly to remind Cordelia she was there and ventured, "Things just don't seem right this morning."

Cordelia turned to face her, leaning back against the counter and nursing a morning mix of hot chocolate and coffee. "Oh, I don't know," she said. "Life is good. Life is fine. Everything's perfectly under control. What could be—" She stopped herself and made a wryly thoughtful face. "Huh. That's *not* right, is it?"

In the background, Charles and Wesley seemed to be arguing; Fred couldn't imagine about what, since Charles had only recently returned to the hotel. He'd left only moments after they all woke, puzzled and uncertain and not sure why they weren't all stiff as a result of their various strange sleeping positions. He'd been a man on a mission. But now Charles was saying, "You don't gotta tell me, man—I *know* we were there. I was definitely there. And Cordelia's flashlight, it was there too. Dead batteries and all. But there's no sign of whatever it was that happened there. Those tunnels are as slick and clean as . . . never. I gotta say I never did see such a spiffy storm sewer."

"That doesn't make any sense," Wesley murmured, fingering the ragged holes in his shirt sleeves. "There's every evidence we went out last night. Our clothing . . . weapons strewn about the lobby—"

"*Us* strewn about the lobby," Charles reminded him.

"That too. And I was so certain we were in the storm sewers last night. There, where you found the flashlight."

"Not to mention my clothes have that not-so-fresh sewer aroma to them, if you know what I mean," Charles said. "Be nice if we knew where Angel got off to."

He didn't trust Angel, that's what he meant. Of all of them, Charles trusted Angel the least. Fred didn't understand it, not quite—but then, she knew she'd seen the worst of Angel, the very worst of him, when the fullness of his demon emerged in Pylea. Just the two of them, then. He'd overcome that, and she knew he could do just about anything.

Charles, Cordelia, and Wesley knew he could do just about anything too—and that he *would*. That seemed to be the problem.

Not to mention that incident they all didn't talk about but never forgot, the part where Angel had fired them all and gone off to wreak havoc on his own.

Fred sighed, and thought to sniff her shirt to check for sewery aroma, but remembered the whole dried snot thing and decided against it. She was headed for the stairs to go change when Cordelia said in the most puzzled voice, "Did I have a vision last night?"

"You asking or telling?" Charles looked over from the lobby entrance to Wesley's office; he still held Cordelia's big clunky camping flashlight.

Cordelia frowned. "I'm not sure. Something about soccer . . ."

"I'm afraid that's hardly specific enough to follow up on," Wesley said.

Charles gave a big grin, the one that made Fred's heart speed up a little. Okay, a lot. But she liked it. Enough so she almost missed his suggestion that they have a good rousing game of street soccer. Or courtyard soccer, right there behind the hotel.

"I'm in," she heard herself say, and a surprising rush of the giggles came upon her from the inside out. It was odd, odd, odd, and she should be taking note of it, writing down observations and puzzling over them and maybe taking a little blood sample and—

But she'd lost her notebook sometime during the night. And then again . . .

She just didn't care. She caught Charles's eye, giving him a secret smile that maybe wasn't so secret anymore. "I'll be right back," she said. "I want to get out of these clothes."

"Now there's an idea," Charles said, not so secretly smiling back at her. Fred blushed in a way she could only hope was prettily, and ran up the stairs.

As long as she was on her way up, she might as well stop in and see how Connor was doing, or if Lorne knew anything about Angel's whereabouts. It wasn't normal for him to be gone and out of touch, especially not since the baby's arrival.

She tapped on the ajar door of 312 and it swung open at her touch. Lorne sat next to the bassinet in the first of Angel's two rooms, the one with the kitchenette and lots of chairs and resource books and sketches piled about. A big, brightly colored package of infant-sized diapers seemed incongruously out of place beside the old-fashioned bassinet. It made Fred smile, so easily amused, and she didn't particularly notice the look on Lorne's face when she said, "We're going to play soccer in the courtyard. Do you want to?"

Lorne looked down at the neatly swaddled baby in his arms; Connor was beginning to gurgle and play with his milk instead of swallow it. "A little busy here, pumpkin pie."

"Oh well," she said, not particularly deterred. "Maybe later. You know, there was another reason I came up here. . . ."

"I don't suppose it might have been to check for Angel? Or are none of you the least bit concerned that our resident hunk went out to fight the good fight with you last night and that you came back without him?"

"Oh, I'm sure he's fine," Fred said, breezy and unconcerned as she plumped herself down on one of the chairs, close enough so she could reach out and finger Connor's blanket. "I mean, *we're* all fine and—" She stopped, suddenly realizing what he'd said. "We did? We went out to fight something? *I* went out to fight something?"

He frowned, bringing his nose and his chin closer together. "You most definitely did. And you know, I'm not altogether convinced that you won."

"But . . ." Fred hesitated, but it was long enough for a rush of bubbly euphoria to sweep in and remove all her concerns. She didn't know what Lorne's problem was, but for sure he was just being a big old worrywart. "That's silly," she said, and got up. "You can see for yourself that we're all fine. Finer than fine."

"Yeah, and it's that last part that worries me. When was the last time anyone around here said *that*?"

Fred shrugged; didn't know, didn't care. "Guess I'll see you later, then."

But when she left the room, her downward glance fell on a rusty smear. Hard to see against the old carpet with its old stains and its funky pattern, but it was there all the same, and it piqued her finer than fine curiosity. She crouched, rubbing her finger across it. "Hmm."

She hadn't closed the door behind her, and so Lorne was quick to place Connor in the bassinet and leave him there gurgling in surprise at the abrupt loss of adoration. "Dried blood," she said to him, a bit of wonder in her voice.

Lorne's reaction was much more grim. He quickly spotted another smear of it, and just as quickly realized the next door down the hall wasn't quite latched. While Fred hesitated, somewhat lost in the feeling of everything being fine so why follow through, Lorne strode ahead and pushed the door open.

"Oh, Angel," he said, in the same sadly remonstrating tone he might use on Connor's crayon wall-art several years from now.

"What?" Fred said lightly, supposing he was overreacting to whatever it was. This was Lorne, after all. Karaoke Drama Demon. She pushed her way beside him at the door, and . . .

Blinked.

Couldn't, at first, understand what she saw. All the blood, she got that. Not great big pools of it, but enough to grab the eye and keep it from putting together the shape and shadows of the rumpled thing on the bed. The rumpled thing that looked torn and battered and that was, when it turned its head ever so slightly to gaze at her from pain-filled, barely open eyes . . .

Angel.

Fred gave a little shriek and backed away. "Oh," she said. "*Oh.*"

"Right," Lorne said. "Everything's just fine."

CHAPTER FOUR

I'm getting good at this, Cordelia thought, carefully cutting up the length of Angel's badly ripped sweater sleeve. And then she paused a moment to wonder if that was a *good* thing.

Wes and Gunn stood behind her, near the doorway of the appropriated room. Fred sat cross-legged near the head of the double bed, occasionally reaching out to touch Angel's shoulder—but always biting her lip and withdrawing the hand before making contact.

It was hard to find a good spot, all right.

"It's all right," Angel told Fred, and even though he had that dazed look, his voice was gentle and comforting. The very thought that he saw the need to comfort anyone because of his own injuries struck Cordelia as alarming. Unusual. Something to worry about. Oddly enough, she . . .

Wasn't.

No, this time there were no smart remarks, no silly glee at being doctored. And while Cordelia thought this should also probably concern her, she was so pleased to be newly fearless—even if she didn't understand why she suddenly felt such freedom—that she was having a hard time focusing on the whole notion of concern.

Besides, he *was* a vampire. And he was here, safe in the hotel. Ergo, whatever injuries he'd taken wouldn't dust him.

What kind of way is that to think? She frowned; the others no doubt thought it was at what she saw as she worked. *How callous can you be, Cordelia Chase?* He was her friend and he was hurting. Hurting badly, to judge by the flinching and twitching. Shocky. Dazed and maybe a little confused. Even a vampire could lose enough blood to stop functioning until more came along.

Angel caught her eye as she cut efficiently through his sleeve and grumbled, "Favorite sweater."

Ah, good. A smart remark. A really lame smart remark, but it was an attempt.

"Not much left of it anyway," she said. "I could try to fix it for you but I think we both know how that would turn out."

"As long as you're talking," Wes said, straightening slightly and moving into the room. Like everyone else but Cordelia, he'd managed a change of clothing and now wore yet another in his interchangeable collection of button-down shirts. They'd all taken to stashing a few extra clothes in this or that hotel room as preparation against the inevitable gore of the trade. And since Cordelia had bluntly told Fred—whose clothes had the nastiest remnants of their mysterious evening—to change before she came back into this room, Cordelia alone remained blood-stained.

Well, and then there was Angel. When it came to stainage, this time around he had them all beat.

With obvious struggle to keep his train of thought, Wes finally finished his question. "We all seem to be having a difficult time recalling what transpired last night. Do you suppose you could fill us in?"

Angel hesitated, and, watching him, Cordelia hesitated too—because he didn't just say nothing, he intentionally didn't say *something*. She knew him well enough for that, could see it right past the pain in his eyes and the tremble in his limbs. Finally, ever so slightly, he shook his head. "Can't remember. I don't even know that we were"—he closed his eyes, letting a difficult moment pass— "together."

"Well then," Gunn said suddenly. "Don't need any more hands here that I can see. And as much as I'm down with the whole wincing in sympathy thing, we've got enough people here doing that." He eased toward the door, looking as restlessly vague as Cordelia felt. He said, "I'll be down-stairs."

"Hmm," Wesley said, a neutral but not quite convinced sound as he regarded Angel. "You're sure . . . ?"

"Don't pick on him, Wesley," Fred said, more sharply than Fred usually ever said anything. Cordelia raised an eyebrow; Fred's leftover hero worship was showing through, along with an edge Cordelia hadn't seen before. Then again, Fred hadn't ever met Angelus. That tended to tarnish the whole hero worship thing somewhat.

But not, said a truthful little voice in her head as she returned her attention to his sweater, *not entirely*.

Hmm. Where had that come from? Some hidden little part of her that had been freed by lack of fear . . .

"Ow!" Cordelia jerked her hand back from the scissors; she'd let the tips run into her hand and they'd sliced deeply into her palm below her thumb as the scissor blades closed. Nasty little wound, even looked like it could use a stitch. She held her hand up and scowled at it. "Well if that's not just what I need—"

But she cut her words just short, and Wesley moved closer even as Fred leaned in slightly.

The bleeding stopped before it started. And was the cut smaller? Just a little—no, definitely—

Healing.

"Well, I'll be a triple-headed Marfok demon," Wesley said, and couldn't keep his jaw from dropping just slightly.

"You—," Fred said, stared a moment at the hand, and took a breath to try again. "You're healing!"

"It would be more accurate to say she's . . . healed," Wesley corrected her, waiting an instant to finish the sentence so there was literally nothing more than a pink line on Cordelia's hand.

"Whoa," Cordelia said, hardly able to believe her eyes. She flexed her fingers. "That could *really* come in handy." But when she looked at Angel, he glanced away—as if he had something to say and decided not to say it. Or maybe just thinking the obvious—that *he* was the one who should be healing, while she ought to still need a quick stitch. Defensive at this notion, she said a belligerent, "What?"

Lorne came to lurk in the doorway, arms and demeanor both crossed. "Nice to see your concern," he said. "Giggle chatter tee hee, and here our boy Angel is bleeding to dust right in front of your eyes."

"Maybe it's part of the whole demon thing," Fred suggested to Cordelia, looking anxiously between them. As usual, not eager for strife between her friends.

"Oh, I get it." Cordelia finally pulled away the remnants of Angel's sleeve. "Like, I'm a demon, you're a demon, wouldn'tcha like to be a demon too?" But she stopped as she looked down, and swallowed hard. Three great gashes along the length of Angel's forearm had opened it nearly to the bone, a clean dissection in most places, exposing muscle.

Fred made a face, turning away to close her eyes.

"Ew," Cordelia finally said after a long, awkward moment. "We're going to need more water here. And more bandages. What the heck, let's just start ripping up sheets."

Wes slipped past Lorne's disapproving eye, wordlessly disappearing in search of supplies. Cordelia hoped he'd remember what he'd gone for; he was as foggy and distractable as the rest of them. Tentatively, she touched Angel's arm, considering that the bandages would at least hold it together for easier healing—and then admitted, "I don't get it."

"What's to get?" Lorne asked. "That maybe you and the rest of the Angel Sunshine Band have been taking someone for granted? Even with all this," he waved a hand at the mess in the room, and then at Angel, "you still figured he'd be up and running in no time?"

Angel shifted, winced, and gave the slightest of

finger-waves. "I'm here," he said. "Really. I may look dead, but I can hear you."

"Well," Cordelia said, paying Angel himself no attention at all as she thought about Lorne's words, considering all the times she'd seen Angel gravely wounded. If it were particularly bad, he'd lurch around for a while, and then there'd be a couple days of scarring. And then . . . "Well," she said again, "Yeah."

She looked at her own healed hand, and then she looked at Angel. He made an infinitesimal motion that another time would have turned into a shrug. "Still loving the being talked about." It was a voice that tried for casual but barely managed audible.

"Yeah, well, even when we wait till you're not around to talk about you, you hear it anyway," she said, keeping in mind all the times he'd been upstairs and still heard a discussion in the lobby. But she got serious for a moment, picking up the washcloth and small basin she'd initially thought would be enough to do the trick. Carefully, she sponged the arm clean. It was hard; she felt the blood rush to her face. She'd never been aware of hurting him before. It had always just faded so quickly. She said in a low voice, "Are you going to be all right?"

"Now she asks," Lorne said, orating to an invisible audience—or perhaps to Fred, who had a miserable, guilty look on her face. Cordelia could understand why, if Fred felt anything like she did.

Because in spite of the horrid nature of Angel's wounds, in spite of the terribly strained look on his face and the soft little groan that had just rumbled his chest, cheerful elation kept trying to grab Cordelia by the mood and carry her attention away—just as it had carried away Gunn.

"Yes," she said, with tart assertion that couldn't quite hide either guilt or distraction. "I'm asking."

And Angel hesitated again, but this time she could read past his pain and weakness to see his uncertainty. This time, he really didn't know.

"None of it makes any sense," she said, squeezing the washcloth out. It ran red until the whole basin was tinted pink.

A moment later, Wesley appeared in the door, laden with sheets—good to see he'd taken her so literally—and a huge cooking pot from the kitchen. He dumped the sheets, filled the pot in the bathroom tub, and returned. At which point he said rather breathlessly, "None of this makes any sense."

"You see?" Cordelia said. *Right again.*

"Angel should heal—even from this—and he hasn't even started. You, on the other hand, healed up like a pro. And there's evidence that all of us were wounded at some point during the night, which none of us remembers and none of us bears any signs of."

Fred mostly ignored this. She even mostly ignored

Cordelia, which Cordelia didn't appreciate. Instead she looked across to Lorne, and asked in a near-whisper, "Is this enough? Shouldn't we take him . . . somewhere? I mean . . . stitches?"

Cordelia snorted most ungenteely as she secured the end of a bandage with tape and carefully started wrapping Angel's arm, trying to keep the right edges together. He made a pained sound; she took a steeling breath and continued. *It's not right. I'm healing . . . he's not.* And still—*still*—she felt a trickle of elation at the thought of how easily and painlessly her cut had healed.

Lorne said, "Take him where? To where people are going to be checking for a heartbeat? Don't think so, Fredlilocks."

"Aren't there demon . . . doctors? People who deal with this sort of thing?" Fred persisted.

"All of whom would be glad to spread the word that our Angel here is now unexpectedly vulnerable," Lorne said implacably. Then his face brightened, which was pretty much a scary sight. "I do know this fellow in Peru. . . ."

"Mortician?" Fred said desperately. She got Angel's attention with that one, not to mention a tinge of alarm. "He could fake being dead, and those guys can do incredible things. Like plastic surgeons, almost."

"Fred," Angel said, not quite smiling through gritted teeth, "the problem there is that dead people don't move. And if he pokes at me, then I'm going to—ow! Dammit, Cordelia. . . ."

"I'm trying," she said, feeling herself flush again. Fred was right. This was way out of her league as official dispenser of Band-Aids.

Abruptly Wes said, "A little experimentation might be in order," just before he took up Cordelia's scissors and jabbed them into his arm, right through his shirt. Fred gave a little cry of dismay and Cordelia used bloody hands to snatch the scissors back.

"Are you crazy?" she snapped.

"Possibly," Wesley said, wincing slightly as he unbuttoned his cuff and started to roll back the sleeve. Too slowly and neatly for Cordelia's taste— now that he'd done it, she wanted to see, and she glanced back at her own hand just to be sure—

Yep. Still healed.

And then at Wesley's exposed arm—which, in the time he'd taken to roll back the sleeve, had healed completely.

"Wow," Fred said, subdued. "That's even faster than Cordelia."

Wesley said slowly, still looking at his arm, "So maybe Cordelia's assumption was wrong. Maybe the reason you healed had nothing to do with being a demon. Look at Angel—he's got plenty of demon in there and he isn't healing at all. And I, who am entirely human, healed faster than both of you."

"Hmph," Cordelia said, to herself as much as

anything. "Seems like if I'm gonna be part demon, there ought to be an upside." Although she already had the major upside—no more splitting headaches with the visions.

On the other hand, if she'd had a splitting headache hangover, she'd *know* whether or not she'd had a vision sometime during the night. These vague impressions of a soccer ball weren't doing anyone any good. Absently, she taped off the bandage for Angel's arm, and tried to decide what to tackle next. His side had been shredded, to judge by the condition of his shirt. He had a huge split knot on his forehead, and probably a concussion, especially considering the way his eyes dazed out now and then. No doubt some broken ribs among the bruises. What was she supposed to do about all that?

Three stories down, something in the lobby crashed into something else; glass broke. Gunn shouted up to them, most unconvincingly, "Not a problem!"

Wesley didn't even blink. "This needs research," he said. "Quite clearly, something has happened to all of us."

"But not necessarily the same thing, at least not to Angel," Fred pointed out. She'd finally settled a hand into Angel's, giving up on the shoulder-patting idea altogether. "We don't even know that we were with him last night."

"True," Wesley said, not happily. "I'll have to be flexible with my search parameters. But for now, this is our primary case—we need to know what's happened before we can know how to conduct ourselves in the field." He glanced over at Fred, as if assessing the importance of her role here and dismissing it. "Fred?"

Fred squinched her nose with reluctance, and her free hand played with her long, sloppy braid. "But—"

"We can do Angel the most good by understanding what's been done to us. Done to *him*," Wesley added, almost as an afterthought.

Fred sighed, but even Cordelia could see her eyes light at the research challenge. She gave Angel's hand a squeeze and said, "But I'll be back soon to see how you are. Maybe by then you'll feel better."

Carefully she eased off the bed; Wesley was already heading out the door. Cordelia looked after them; she couldn't help but think what life might be like if they could figure out what had happened, maybe even bottle it up or reproduce it at will. What would it be like to *always* be like Angel—to know what didn't kill them instantly wouldn't kill them at all? To know the little hurts and pains that constantly plagued them could be healed in moments?

No more hangnails, even . . .

"Go, why don't you," Lorne said suddenly. "You

want to. I'll take care of things here. I think I'm better suited for it right now."

Cordelia heard the disapproval in his voice, but it seemed far away, and the lure of being able to keep this little bubble of confidence was right up close. "All right," she said, adding a note of reluctance just because she thought she should, although fooling Lorne about that sort of thing was chancy at best. "I really need to go change, anyway."

"By all means," Lorne said, coolly.

"Go," said Angel, and his voice held a sandpaper edge of desperation that nearly stopped her, but when she looked back he nodded, and so she went.

"Never you mind them," Lorne said, stripping off his subdued taupe jacket to reveal an eggplant shirt so ripe it all but begged to be made into casserole. He rolled up his sleeves, picked up the scissors, and got to work in a matter-of-fact way. "They're not acting right. *None* of them are acting right. And you, my friend, know more than you're telling."

Angel closed his eyes. Lying wasn't his strong suit at the best of times; he generally just directly refused to discuss those things he didn't want to discuss. But he didn't have the strength to fight them on this, especially when his trust in the little greenish creature named Kluubp was far from complete. Lorne, however . . . He bit back a sudden groan at whatever Lorne was up to, aware too, that he was no good at this. Good at getting hurt . . . not good at staying hurt.

Lorne said firmly, "Never mind. I'm not sure I need to know right now. I'm not sure they need to know, *ever*."

"Exactly," Angel said, barely a whisper. And set himself to endure.

Some eternity later Lorne returned with the softest, finest cotton-silk shirt in his own collection, a big boxy thing that slipped easily over Angel's head and did absolutely nothing for his complexion—normally pale, now gray. Even grayer against the chartreuse of the shirt. Then together they somehow made it into Angel's room, where his own bed was a strange comfort for a vampire who'd had so many beds over his long life span.

Once he was settled, Lorne got him a glass of blood, and a nice mint to clear his mouth. He said, "I know someone who wants to visit," and brought Connor in, bolstered him with pillows, and left him where Angel could hold his tiny hand between two adult fingers. "I'll just be in the next room," he assured Angel. "Don't worry if he fusses, Uncle Lorne is here."

"Thank you," Angel told him, and closed his eyes, appearing to succumb, for the moment, to the fierce pounding in his head and body.

But that wasn't it. That wasn't it at all.

He had to hide the terror he knew showed in his eyes—that Lorne, out of all of them, would perceive in an instant. For the moment his two trembling fingers closed over Connor's hand, he understood the true ramifications of his situation. Never mind the pain, the personal fears that came swooshing back into his life after several hundred years of being, to put it mildly, a fast healer. Because he was still a marked man, and Connor was therefore just as marked.

Only now Angel didn't know if he'd be able to protect his son.

Wesley settled his headlamp more firmly at his forehead, aiming the light down.

"Are you sure this is the best way to go about it?" Fred asked, her voice a little tremulous in the darkness. She clung to Gunn's side, but he wasn't as solicitous as usual; his near-to-black eyes shone with the prospect of adventure, even in the dim artificial moonlight of the LED. It was all they had for now, at least until they ran to Costco for another giant helping of flashlight batteries.

"We need more information," Wesley said firmly. This time he wore a rain slicker, with respect to the state of their clothing from the night before. "Don't tell me you're afraid?"

"That doesn't seem to be much of a problem

right now," Fred said. "I was just thinking that if we hit the books, we might find something to help Angel."

"He'll be fine," Wesley said with words that sounded automatic.

"Why?" Fred asked, feeling a surge of irritation. That, too, was new to her. When you're busy watching your back, you don't have the energy to get irritated over causes. But now she felt a new confidence—a new boldness. "Because he always *is*? I'm not sure we can apply the usual standards in this case."

"This is important, Fred. More important than I can begin to articulate. We *must* understand this situation better—and to do that, we need to have a better idea of what happened last night."

"Speaking of the usual standards being not so usual anymore," Gunn said, hefting his mace like he was just aching to sink it into something, "I gotta ask—what're the chances that him being down like that will let the always-lurking Evil Angel come out to play?"

Wesley hesitated to look back at them, and then seemed to remember the headlamp and think better of it, pointedly keeping it directed from their faces. "That's a good question. To judge by Cordelia's slower healing response—and by the fact that Angel's healing is one of his demon traits—I'd say that Angelus is deeply wounded right now. But it's certainly something to follow up on. It could be that we need to have Angel confined until we know for sure."

"Oh, right," Fred said, incredulous that either man could be entertaining serious thoughts of Angel as a threat, "in case he falls out of bed and comes crawling after one of us?"

"Fred," Wesley said, his tone just a touch too patronizing for Fred's liking, "you don't know what he's like when—"

"Of course I do." She pulled away from Gunn slightly, keenly aware of the buoyant—and likely artificial—courage that made it possible. "I saw the real demon inside before any of you, and don't you forget it. And I saw him fight it too."

"Fred . . ." Gunn exchanged an impatient sort of look with Wesley, although Cordelia stayed out of it, looking distracted in her own right as she glanced around the tunnels, frowning. Gunn finished lamely, "It's not the same—and you know it."

"No, I don't—and neither do you." Wow. Amazing what a little extra self-confidence could do for a person.

"I know we were here somewhere," Cordelia said suddenly, frowning at the unnaturally spiffy storm tunnel around them. "But . . . this place looks like Mr. Clean just came through."

"It certainly doesn't appear that any significant activity has occurred here recently." Wesley scanned the area, his headlamp lighting section after gleaming section. "In fact, it looks just a little too scrubbed to be true, don't you think?"

"Don't make any difference," Gunn said in disgust. "All that means is that there's something going on here. Well, we already knew that, didn't we?"

"Let's keep looking," Wesley said, but his voice had lost that lift they'd shared over the past hours and taken on a frustrated tone.

Fred wondered if she was the only one doubting the wisdom of their search—the only one not really liking what she saw in themselves. The instant healing, sure that was nice and all . . . but some things weren't meant to be found. And sometimes when you found them, you got nothing but trouble.

CHAPTER FIVE

Connor slept deeply in his baby way, a small bubble forming at the corner of his rosebud mouth.

Angel slept not at all, just drifted with waves of pain. They started in his arm or his ribs, welling from the worst spots to spread over his entire body, finally sparking off the swirling ache in his head before fading away. He was most grateful he didn't actually have to breathe, even though—like most long-lived vampires—he had learned to fake it without thinking. Things never turned out well if someone noticed you weren't breathing.

Lorne puttered in his own room down the hall, humming something show-tuney between clients; he'd managed to set up quite a nice little service for private readings since Caritas had met its final demise at Connor's birth. Aside from a demon or two who refused to accept the honorary peace zone restrictions upon running into the Angel Investigation humans, it worked out well for everyone.

Every now and then he came and glanced into Angel's rooms, and a couple of times he came all the way to the double doors that closed off the bedroom, but neither he nor Angel said anything.

There wasn't much to say. Here he was at his most vulnerable hour since . . . since . . . well, maybe since *never*, and his closest friends were off hunting the goose that laid the golden egg.

Angel's biggest fear was that they'd find it.

What if it didn't work the second time? What if that beast just ripped them apart? He should have lied, should have told them it only worked once. At least to delay them until he understood better what was happening, and could protect them from themselves. Or the selves they became under the influence of the many-armed terror in the tunnels.

No wonder the underground was restless, if his own fate reflected that of other demons, especially the ones used to quick healing. He'd gotten off easy compared to what had probably happened to most of them—word would spread fast under those circumstances.

He heard the slightest of noises out in the other room, smelled warm blood. Lorne again.

Except when the point came when Lorne should have been within Angel's field of view . . . he simply wasn't.

Angel didn't move. Not quite. But he made ready to. Ready to snatch Connor out of harm's way and throw himself into it.

"Tsk," said a characteristic of a voice. "It's only me." And Kluubp came into view, finally—too short to be seen until he was nearly up to the bed. In the indirect daylight from the windows, he was very definitely green, and the wry humor in his expression much more notable. Not to mention a little twist around his lips that spoke of fretfulness. "Not only that, I bring gifts of food. You're not used to being in this condition, and I doubt very much you're taking the sustenance you need. Besides, you wouldn't want to swallow these on an empty stomach." He held out his hand, lifting it so Angel could see. Substantial-looking oblong white pills. "Extra-strength. The kind that Hollywood stars love so much. Bet you're ready for some of that, eh?"

"Eh," Angel agreed, for lack of anything else— and still struggling with the impulse to move Connor to safety. But Connor only gurgled slightly and slept on. And really, the impulse wasn't because of anything Kluubp had done . . . it was because of what Angel felt so incapable of doing.

Protecting his son.

He gave a mental sigh of relief when Kluubp leaned his staff against the wall and moved around to the other side of the bed . . . and thought from

Kluubp's expression that the little creature . . . demon? . . . had known exactly what he'd done. Except he didn't stay there; he took the dirty glass from the bedside, briskly moved back out into the kitchen area to rinse it, and returned with it full of fresh blood. Straw and all. "Here," he said. "Take one of these, drink this, and we'll talk."

Angel took the blood, gave it a wary sniff. "What's your interest here, Kluubp? Don't get me wrong, the blood is very nice and the painkillers have bought you a few extra moments here. But I've had some time to think, and it's occurred to me . . . you've gone to an awful lot of trouble to help me. There's always a price."

Mostly not true, at least the part about having a lot of time to think. When his head wasn't spinning, his thoughts had been full of Connor, not Kluubp. Until this moment, he hadn't truly expected to see his rescuer again.

Which didn't make his observation any less accurate.

"Well," Kluubp said, climbing into a chair beside the bed and looking less than dignified when his short legs stuck straight out, "quite obviously I want something from you."

Angel didn't blink. He gave a slight nod and said, "Straight talk. Okay then. I can respect that." And then he gestured with the glass at the painkillers and said, "Not that I don't appreciate it. But let's talk first."

"Fine," said Kluubp, and folded his hands in his lap to assume a lecture face. "The demon that harmed you last night is called a Giflatl. On your world, where they evolved, they're a menace. On our world, to which we transported every last one of them many, oh, *many* years ago, they're a necessary part of our life. I am one of their keepers—it's a prestigious position, I assure you. But one of them has escaped from our world to yours, and I need to recover it before it's too late."

Angel grunted. "Define 'too late.' I'm thinking . . . sometime last night."

"Too late," Kluubp said gently, his floppy ears flattening with displeased anticipation, "is when your friends find it again, figure out how to harvest the supernatural venom that harmed you and helped them, and try to use it to change your world. Not, I might add, for the good."

"No, of course not." Angel let his head rest back on the pillows. "That would be too easy, wouldn't it?"

Cordelia eyed Fred in the dim, barely reflected light of Wesley's headlamp, emboldened by the darkness; even if Fred looked straight at her, she wouldn't be able to tell Cordelia had her under scrutiny.

Cordelia thought that Fred wasn't really with the program.

How anyone could not be wildly enthusiastic

about following up on an incident that had left them pretty near invulnerable—*and oh, please may it last a long time*—Cordelia couldn't quite fathom. Especially not when they were in a business that left them sticking all their vulnerable selves out in front of pissed-off demons on a regular basis.

Then again, Cordelia often couldn't follow the way Fred thought. Only natural, after all of those years Fred had spent on the lam in Pylea. And she seemed to be the sensitive type, anyway.

Then Fred looked straight at her and Cordelia had the sudden impression that she'd discerned every thought, never mind the darkness. And she felt a moment of shame, suddenly touching on how much Angel meant to them all, how much he meant to *her*. . . .

In another moment she forgot it all, stopping short in the tunnel to watch the flash of a newly painless vision take over her mind's eye.

Mostly blurry, just a vignette, a close-up of a rather plain-looking young woman. Light brown— no, just plain mousy—hair cut in a chin length bob, short up the back. Unremarkable light brown eyes. Skin a little blotchy under her modest makeup.

And then she opened her mouth to sing, and her lackluster appearance transformed her into something shining and beautiful, and the pure soprano notes hung in Cordelia's mind like an internal music she never wanted to lose.

But halfway through the song, the young woman seemed to choke on something, and though she tried to recover, when she opened her mouth, no sound emerged. She made a visible effort to compose herself, but the panic rose on her face and—

And Cordelia blinked into the darkness. "The Powers That Be sent me a vision about someone with stage fright?"

"A vision?" Wesley said, looking at her a little more intensely than she liked. "Are you sure it didn't have something to do with our current situation?"

"Yeah, finding a way to keep us on the job without down time and pesky stitches seems like something they should be interested in," Gunn said. "Seeing as how we're out here doing their work and all."

"Hey," Cordelia said, letting her annoyance show. "I can't help what they send me. And I'm still getting used to this new connection." Not having the splitting migraines and all sorts of brain damage due to cerebral overload remained a refreshing relief, but even a good change meant adjustment. "Maybe if I could remember that soccer thing . . ."

"Right," Gunn snorted. "Soccer and singing. I can see where that fits right in. As opposed to hunting down this thing that while, true, hasn't done our memories much good, seems to have a whole lot to offer on the demon-hunting—"

A gravelly scream cut the air, rumbling through the tunnels, obscuring its own origin with reverberation.

Fred paled, visible even in the dim light of Wesley's headlamp. "Can't remember the last time I heard something that sounded so big sound so . . ."

"Pants-wetting scared?" Gunn suggested. "Don't worry. I'll watch your back."

"We'll *all* watch her back," Wesley said, but hastily added, "I mean, we'll watch one anothers' backs. This might be our chance. . . . I think it came from this direction." And off he went, although Cordelia couldn't help looking over her shoulder at the three-way intersection where they'd been standing, struggling with a feeling of familiarity.

And she couldn't help but think that the Powers didn't send her visions without meaning . . . except in the very next instant, she forgot the vision and turned her complete attention to finding their fountain of healing.

"It's probably already too late," Angel told Kluubp, settling back into pillows fluffed higher so their conversation wasn't so physically awkward. "They're out there hunting your Giflatl right now.

It won't be hard to find that intersection again—not with the mess that thing made of it." *Made a mess of me, too.*

The Giflatl keeper gave Angel a smug look that really didn't sit well on those big-eyed features. Features that kept reminding Angel of . . .

"They won't find that intersection," Kluubp said, interrupting Angel's thought and still mightily self-assured. "Their primary drive is to hide their den. Every Giflatl carries a certain number of scavenger demons on its body. By now that area is cleaner than it's ever been."

"Suddenly I feel grateful for the rats," Angel said.

"They weren't rats," Kluubp told him.

Scavenger demons. Nice.

"Do you understand, now? How the Giflatl survives in your world? It kills any encroaching demons without mercy, and its venom makes it well-equipped to do so. But the humans—who now run this world and who would organize to hunt it down with vengeance—it allows to survive. That same venom even interferes with human memories and moods, and heals wounds so quickly that by the time those people are in their right mind again, there's no trace of injury—or any memory of the encounter."

"So my friends are relatively safe to hunt this thing."

The keeper shrugged. "As long as they don't press it so hard that it accidentally kills one of them outright, yes."

Angel glanced over at Connor, still very much in touch with his fear at being there for his son . . . being able to protect him. To see him grow up—safe, and unmolested by any of the dangers of this world.

Especially those dangers that were after Angel himself.

"It must be like that for them all the time," he murmured. It was hard to keep in touch with what their daily demon-fighting existence must mean to his friends. But this last twenty-four hours . . . oh yeah, brought it all back. He looked straight at the keeper. "So they find the thing. Maybe they even find a way to subdue it, and harvest the venom. Is that really such a bad thing?"

"You can't even imagine," Kluubp said.

If they were back at the hotel, they'd be looking into news stories about concerts and rising new vocal stars. They should be. Fred knew it, and she'd seen it on Cordelia's face, too—back before they'd started off after their new quarry. But now Cordelia was as intent on the hunt as Gunn and Wesley.

Both men were thoroughly immersed in their search, following the weakening cries of the bass-voiced demon with the concentration of professional trackers.

The worst part was, even though she knew better, Fred couldn't have torn herself away from this search if she'd tried. She still felt brave and adventurous and excited, and she wanted more of it. She wanted to know she could *have* more of it.

So she should have spoken up, and Cordelia should have spoken up, and Gunn and Wesley shouldn't have needed anyone to speak up.

But no one said anything. They followed the sound of something dying, and hoped to profit from it before the day was over.

"You can't even imagine what the lure of the Giflatl venom does to humans. Normally decent humans at that." Kluubp shook his head most sadly. "Here, are you sure you don't want to take this?" He held the painkiller in his stumpy fingers. "By the time it takes effect this conversation will be over. And you're looking pale."

"Vampire. Always pale," Angel reminded him absently. "Not sure I trust you that far, keeper. Sounds to me like maybe you just want this Giflatl to yourself."

"Tsk," the keeper said, but then sighed. He replaced the pill on the bedside table. "It's true they play a crucial role in my home. Our sun has grown strong, and the Giflatl excretes a substance that

can be combined with various fibers to protect u
from its emissions. Are you sure you won't at leas
have the blood? You had some last night, after all
And since I want your help, I really don't have any
motive for doing you harm."

Maybe just a sip.

On any other day he would have heard Lorn
coming. On this one, he didn't notice Lorne's ap
proach until the demon had reached the oute
doorway, and hesitated there to take in the scen
with obviously growing alarm. Hard not to se
those red eyes getting wider. Angel hastily disen
gaged the straw from his mouth and tried not t
feel like a three-year-old home sick in bed. Besid
him, Connor stretched, sticking his feet in the ai
and waving his arms, adorable in his little footi
outfit.

"If I'd known we were having company, I'd hav
baked a cake," Lorne said, complete disapprova
radiating from his expression. "Or not, dependin
on the company."

"Relax," Angel said. "He's a friend."

"Right, and there's so much you could have don
about it if he wasn't." Lorne didn't have to say
"Why didn't you call me?" Not with a scowl lik
that. He swooped in to take Connor, hesitating
moment to tickle the sleepy baby and make a trul
frightening exaggerated smile before turning bac
to Angel.

"I didn't mean to alarm you," Kluubp said, his ears drooping even lower. "I . . . I *like* children."

"With our visitors that's not always a *good* thing," Lorne said, no forgiveness in his voice.

"Lorne," Angel said, setting the blood aside, struggling with the whole bandages-pillow-pain thing until Kluubp rescued him and took the glass, "this is Kluubp. Without his help, I'd still be passed out in a storm sewer. It's okay. Really." And he gave Kluubp a clandestine glare that meant, *it better be*.

"Right," said Lorne. "Yoda comes to visit and you don't call for me, even though Connor's right there beside you. This sounds okay to you?"

Angel gave Kluubp a surprised glance. "I knew you looked familiar—"

"Except for the ears," Lorne said, not noticing or else not caring that Kluubp had grown increasingly exasperated, to the point of emitting a small grinding sound from both sets of vocal cords.

"Upright ears are more expressive," Kluubp said suddenly, and sounded like he was quoting somebody. "Upright ears look more humorous, and will subliminally signal that the character isn't threatening."

"Ooh," said Lorne. "Someone carries a grudge." Then, abruptly and entirely serious, he said, "So what's going on here?"

"I'm not sure you want to know," Kluubp said.

"I'll let me be the one to decide that, short stuff," Lorne shot back at him. Connor made an unhappy sound and Lorne gave him a few gentle bounces in the crook of his arm, all the while glaring at Kluubp.

"Fine," Kluubp said, his ears canting back in a most stubborn way. "I'm not sure I want to tell you."

Angel felt his patience utterly and suddenly peter out. "Lorne," he said, "later. Okay?" Lorne gave him a look that meant protest was on its way, and Angel cut him short. *"Later,"* he said, managing just enough *I really mean it* to get the point across.

Lorne made a brief but clearly disapproving moue with dark red lips. "I get the picture, Angelcakes. Don't think we won't talk about this later. I hope it won't inconvenience you too much if Connor and I see to his bottle." And he turned on his well-dressed heel and stalked out to the kitchen area to busy himself with opening and closing the refrigerator and microwave, banging several pots and pans that had nothing to do with bottle preparation at all. Connor gurgled happily.

Angel suddenly realized he was watching with a wistful expression. A vulnerable expression. He schooled his face to something less revealing.

"Get used to it," Kluubp said. "Until this is over,

you'll either be lying to your friends . . . or you'll be part of the problem."

"Ew," said Fred, looking at the remains of the demon before them, her courage making way for an uneasy stomach. "Someone needed Visine."

"Too late now," Gunn observed. He toed a body part. Not an identifiable one.

Fred crouched down before the largest chunk of the dearly departed. One arm, the torso, even the head. "Kind of Conehead-y," she said. "But probably could have used blinking lessons." The elongated head before her bore a pair of the bulgiest, most bloodshot eyes she'd ever seen, stuck in wide-open-staring position.

"They're always like that," Wesley said absently, looking around the area, his headlamp lingering on various pieces of this and that. Fred found herself distinctly disinterested in what this or that might actually be. "Wardjon demon. Never does blink, actually. They've evolved other means of protection for their eyes. They also have a voting share of stock in several eye drop companies. Generally not a demon that starts trouble. Also generally bigger than this one."

"I think this one *was* bigger than this one," Cordelia observed. "Before . . . *whatever* . . . got hold of it."

Fred felt a flutter of trepidation—only a flutter,

but the closest thing to real fear since the previous night. "If it didn't start trouble, then whatever did this must not be the friendly type."

"Whatever nailed Angel wasn't exactly the friendly type, either," Gunn said, leaving the unidentifiable body part alone to crouch by Fred and ponder the Ping-Pong ball–sized eyes of the Wardjon. "So I'm thinking we're on the right trail."

But then they tore themselves away from the various locations of the Wardjon, they moved on to another entirely spiffily clean section of tunnel and turned to each other in mutual frustration.

"It would be too easy if this was easy," Gunn grumbled.

"Maybe it shouldn't be easy," Fred offered. But she wasn't surprised when they turned to her in disagreement, still looking like they were ready to charge off on a trail they'd just lost.

And they might have, if the air hadn't filled with a new sound. A hauntingly beautiful Charlotte Church sort of sound. Light, airy, floating so easily on the air so Fred thought if they were outside it would float right up to the heavens; only the tunnels kept it trapped here.

"Soccer and singing," she murmured, and Cordelia gave her a stricken look.

"Will you help me?" Kluubp said it simply, and after several moments of silence.

With a start, Angel realized he'd lost track of the conversation. He gave the slightest shake of his head. A careful movement. "I don't know," he said. "I can see how they would want to pursue something that keep them safe. Keep them from pain." He eyed the pill on the bedside table, realized that at some point he would take it. How different was it from wanting the Giflatl venom?

"Do you understand?" the keeper asked. "Truly, have you thought about this thing? As long as the Giflatl is here, demons will die. It doesn't matter whether they're evil or simply minding their own business in the wrong place at the wrong time, die they will. And in the end your friends will find the venom to be of little use—once it's in their systems, they're not capable of thinking clearly . . . and yet those moments in which they use the venom will be the ones in which they need the clearest minds."

"Afterward, then," Angel said, but he heard himself grasping at straws. From the other room, Lorne—humming in the equivalent of sticking his fingers in his ears—cast him a resentful look and took Connor, the adorable footies outfit, and the bottle down the hall and into his own room.

"So they can be under the influence afterward? While innocent beings continue to die? Humanity *has* managed to kill off the Giflatl's single natural predator—it's one of the reasons my people removed them from this realm entirely. We'd been importing them for many years before that happened."

"Afterward," Angel said, still stuck on the keeper's earlier words. "For how long afterward will the venom affect a human? How long will it affect me?"

"And then, who chooses?" Kluubp asked, continuing his soapboxing unabated. "Who is allowed to live or die or heal in agony? Does a burned human deserve to go through the many painful months of rehabilitation while a member of your agency heals from a broken arm in a day?"

"How long?" Angel repeated, trying for patience. Yoda, he recalled, had been a creature of few words. Definitely another area in which details had been changed.

But Kluubp was lost in his own thoughts. "True, your people are doing the population an unrecognized service, but does this entitle them? What about cancer patients? Should they die while one of yours avoids stitches? And can you imagine the hostilities that will break out when word of this gets out—and it *will* get out—what do you think initiated the trouble at Salem?"

"How long?" Angel gave up on patience and ground the words out with the same intensity that had chased Lorne off. His entire body twitched with the need to reach out and grab the little being

by his robe front, and even the twitching hurt. So many years of fast healing. . . . He didn't have the *patience* to be a patient.

Kluubp blinked. "Oh. Well. Point's made, I take it."

Angel just looked at him.

"Well then. Harrumph." The throat-clearing was impressively done, with two sets of vocal cords on the job. Kluubp smoothed his wispy hairs along his alligator-skin pate and said with scholarly importance:

"It depends."

"It depends," Angel repeated flatly. He twitched again; he thought in another moment he might just be annoyed enough to forget about all the parts of him that weren't functioning and give Kluubp a good shaking anyway.

Kluubp might have seen it in him. He cleared his throat again and spoke more hastily. "On how much of the venom they received in the first place. You, for instance—you clearly got a terrible dose. A non-undead creature probably wouldn't have survived. It's going to be days before your healing processes speed up, and possibly a week before you're functioning normally again. By vampire standards, that is."

Angel relaxed slightly. A week. He could deal with a week. As long as nothing went apocalyptic, started prophesizing, or got them the attention of Wolfram and Hart.

Or threatened Connor.

This time it was Angel who cleared his throat, shaking off those thoughts. "How about the others?"

"Same situation, really. Humans tend to process the venom more quickly, but it all depends on the initial exposure. Your people, I have to say, have had an intense dose. As a rule, humans do not approach a Giflatl on purpose, never mind with the fortitude and intent to engage in deliberate battle."

Angel gave him a one-eyed squint. "One day we'll have a talk on using fewer words to say more." But he let his mind go back to the moments of the fight—those few moments he saw clearly. Gunn had taken a serious blow, maybe more than one. Cordelia and Wesley had taken nasty wounds, but not as badly. And Fred . . . just the cheek. "Fred," he said, more to himself than to Kluubp.

"It doesn't matter," Kluubp said. "You can't tell any of them. Not even if you sense one of them might be sympathetic to our cause."

"Your cause," Angel said quickly, but couldn't put any heart into it. He'd heard all of Kluubp's fussy babbling, every word of it. And while arguments had risen immediately to mind, none had been worthy of giving voice.

"One way or the other, it will be *our cause*," Kluubp said, his avuncular tone giving way to something much more serious. "You may think you can avoid choosing sides, but you can't. And if you don't act to help me now, you'll soon enough be facing much more grave decisions."

They looked at one another in silence a moment. Then Kluubp hopped off the chair. "Will you help me, then?"

"Help you, I will," muttered Angel.

Kluubp prepared to leave, wearing a well-satisfied smile on a wide mouth below an incredibly pug nose. He left a small baggie on the bedside table; a glance revealed the contents to be more pain pills.

With impeccable timing, Lorne returned, easing Connor down into his crib. "There," he said. "You're fed, you're changed—not like daddy *changes*, of course. Time to cross your eyes at the crib toys for a few moments and then fall into a well-deserved sleep." He stood, then looked over at Angel, quite perceptive enough to realize the secret stuff was over. "Though if he doesn't settle, you may have to drag yourself over here and make vamp face for him. He seems a little gassy this afternoon."

"Afternoon already?" the keeper said. "I must be off. Appointments to keep, you know."

"Great," Lorne said. "From Yoda to the white rabbit. Don't be late and all that." Then he spotted the baggie of pills and in a few long strides swooped over to pick it up, examining the contents carefully. After a moment he gave a grudging nod. "Not a bad idea at that, Angelkins."

"It will make the time less onerous," Kluubp agreed, moving around to hesitate at the end of the bed. There he added all too wisely, "And it will have no negative ramifications on the rest of your world."

Angel briefly rolled his eyes, but no one seemed to notice. Lorne hefted the baggie of pills and frowned. "Hostess offerings of blood, prescription drugs without the inconvenience of a prescription . . . for someone with the look of an out-of-towner, you seem to get your hands on just what you need."

"Oh yes," Kluubp said, his expression transforming to delight. From inside his robe he pulled out a gold and black book, *Fodor's Guide to Los Angeles, Underground (Auto-Update Version)*. "Food, lodging, specialty needs—they're all in here. In fact, you're in here. But mostly as a warning. Stay away from, etc. You're a new listing for this edition. Current employees—two white women, one all-purpose and one with intellectual specialties; one black man, muscle and street smarts, one white man, extremely dangerous research specialist, and one white vampire with a soul. I knew right away who you were when I found you."

"Hold on there," Lorne said. "Just hold on. No mention of me there? In an auto-update version? Someone's not doing a very good job then, are they?"

"No, but there is a sad footnote noting the

demise of Caritas." Kluubp flipped through the book, finding the page. "A tragedy, really."

"Tell me about it," Lorne said dourly.

"Oh dear," said Kluubp. "I didn't mean to bring back a difficult past."

"We have enough *difficult* right here in the present." Angel hoisted himself up on one elbow, ignoring the repercussions of the movement. "Not that you and your people have made it any easier."

Kluubp raised nearly invisible eyebrows at him. "But you'll do as I ask."

Angel told him, "For now."

CHAPTER SIX

Fred sat cross-legged on the lobby chair by the split stairs, flipping slowly through one of Wesley's ancient resource books. *Hobart's Essential Grimoire.* Wesley had chosen demons and she'd been left with spells and rituals, which suited her fine. But she wasn't in the mood to tackle the research as Wesley had, with an intensity interspersed with moments of . . .

Well. Just plain silliness.

So Fred let herself be distracted, browsing through the musty, fragile old book as she used to do with encyclopedias as a child. It occurred to her that such a book as this should have a spell for preserving paper and binding and keeping itself from turning into this ancient, fragile thing, and she spent some time looking for one of those. She also spent time making faces at Connor and reaching out with a foot to wobble his bassinet in the way that made him laugh.

Charles walked into the lobby from the main entrance, and the briefly open door revealed falling darkness. He had a puzzled look on his face, a deep-in-thought look. Fred smiled to herself, ducking her head so it would remain to himself. He was in fact a lot more thoughtful than he considered himself in general, but she wasn't quite ready to let him know she'd noticed.

Not yet, anyway.

"Hey," he said. "Where's . . . ?"

"Wesley, office," Fred said. "Lorne, giving a private reading. Angel, not functioning. And Cordelia went to an open audition this afternoon. She said something about feeling the luck, though actually I'd always thought she's put that behind her. How about you?"

"Do I feel the luck?" Charles asked, glancing in Wesley's office through the idiosyncratic window-in-the-wall to see the top of Wesley's dark ash brown hair as he bent over his work. "Beats me. This day's gone every which way. Pretty much like yesterday. You seem pretty solid, though. And . . . ?" He gave Wesley another meaningful look.

"Depends on the moment," she said, deciding she liked it when he wore the sleeveless, hooded dark blue sweatshirt over red. It brought out his rich coloring.

"Be nice if we could figure out just what happened that night," Charles said. He didn't have to identify which night. Three nights earlier. The one none of them could quite remember but all of them had a sense of. *That* night.

"You mean, it would be nice if Fred and I could figure out just what happened," Wesley said from the office, not lifting his head from the current reference tomb.

"Not my gig," Charles said matter-of-factly. "You got any one-man demon slayage to send me out on, fire away."

"Cordelia hasn't called," Fred said. "She said something this morning about seeing a man throw his magazine across a park bench in frustration, but between whatever's happened to us and her new painless demon-vision, I don't think she quite knew what to make of it."

Noise from above and behind distracted her from whatever Charles might have replied, and seemed to distract Charles from whatever he might have replied, too. Fred twisted in the chair, barely able to glimpse the stairs and the awkward movement of the man descending them. "Angel!" she cried, both delighted and concerned.

"Hey, man, let me give you a hand—," Charles said, starting for the stairs, and even from her awkward viewpoint Fred could see the look that stopped him in his tracks. She put the book aside and stood up on the chair, improving her vantage considerably.

"Are you feeling better?" she asked. "Because you

know, you've been looking pretty puny. Pretty much like an orphaned kitten out in the rain, all sad and droopy and—"

Suddenly she realized that she, too, was getting The Look. The steady, dark-eyed, inescapable, just crossing over from brooding to threatening look. The one that was deeply aware of the shabby lack of concern from the highly distractible Angel Investigations gang over these past days. "Or not," she said brightly. "Are those pills helping? Did you start healing? 'Cause earlier today you didn't look like you could make it down these stairs without—"

Still The Look.

"Maybe I'll just do some research," she decided out loud, and dropped back into the chair, going cross-legged on the way down.

She heard Angel stumble slightly. She winced and scrunched up her shoulders in unhappy anticipation; Charles did the same—or his manly Gunn version of it, anyway.

But Angel didn't fall, and after a moment he made it to the short tier of steps below the platform that led from both stairways and the courtyard, where he sat—somewhat heavily, but clearly by choice. "Better," he said, once again within Fred's field of view. "Not how it should be. But improving. And damned tired of being in that bed." He spotted Connor and his entire demeanor changed, growing lighter in posture and somewhat goofy in expression. "Hey there, Connor," he said "Who's a good baby? Booblybooblyboobly . . ."

"Okay, now that *is* strange," Charles said. "Maybe you should still be in bed after all."

"Or not," Angel said. But he scrubbed his hands over his face and through his hair—with anyone else this would make a discernable difference to the hair style, but Angel's appeared unaffected—and sighed. "The painkillers do make me a little woozy," he admitted. "It's . . . not the same as when . . ." But he trailed off, as if trying to decide how to put it.

"When the horrible demon inside you instantly heals your undead body?" Fred offered brightly.

Angel brought out The Look again. And then he simply said, "Yeah. That."

"But you *are* better," she persisted. "Good enough to come downstairs. Or should I check those bandages?"

"No," Angel said, quickly enough. "They're fine I'm just . . ."

"Bored?" Fred guessed.

"No, I'm—"

"Ready for action," Charles said, decisive and understanding in an I-got-your-back way.

"Capable of finishing my own sentences!" Angel said. He stood, and Fred thought he might still look a little pale, but then again who could tell?

"Ready for some fresh air. Ready for some sunshine, too, but we'll count that out."

"You want to go out?" Fred said in some alarm, abandoning her disinterested pose to come to her knees in the chair, looking over at him.

"Sure," Charles said. "Maybe we can go help a granny cross the street or something."

"Don't get all dramatic," Angel said, totally missing the irony of the Brooding One accusing someone else of drama. "I was thinking a walk. With Connor."

Fred clapped her hands together before she thought not to. "That's a wonderful idea!" She left the *Hobart's* on the chair and went to scoop Connor from the bassinet. "It's a really nice evening."

"Me," said Angel. "I was thinking me. And Connor."

Charles snorted. "Not gonna happen. Not that we're worried about your sorry ass, but if something happens out there, someone's got to be around to bring Connor back."

"Me," said Angel, without hesitation. "And you."

"And me!" Fred said. When they both looked at her, she added, "Please?"

"Whatever," Angel said. "Let's *all* go."

From inside the office came Wesley's muffled voice. "Busy . . ."

"Whatever," Charles said. He hit the call button for the elevator and snatched the stroller out of its current hiding place, zipping it over to Fred as if it were a race car . . . complete with sound effects.

"Charles," Fred said, hesitating beside it, "Are you sure you're . . . you know, feeling well?"

"Couldn't be finer," he said. "And neither could you."

Fred lost a moment, blushing. Then she quickly bent over to place Connor in the stroller, fussily straightening his twisted romper. She finally straightened up, ready to go. "Do you want to push? 'Cause I'll push."

"Or me," said Charles, but Fred thought he still had a little too much of a race car expression in place.

"Me," she said.

"I'll push," Angel said firmly, and ended the discussion by coming over to do just that.

Charles got the baby-stroller combo up the stairs and out they went, through the courtyard and the open iron gates and onto the street.

"Let's just go to the end of the block," Fred said, thinking of the bus stop bench there and aiming them that way. It was a place for Angel to rest even if he wanted to pretend he didn't need it.

"That's not a walk," Charles said, keeping pace with her. "That's a practice walk."

"It's good enough," Fred said firmly, hoping Angel hadn't followed their exchange.

She shouldn't have worried. He turned to her with his somewhat goofy daddy face and said, "See? See how they're looking at him?" For of course everyone who glanced at the stroller gave a little smile, and with work out and dinnertime over, there were plenty of people glancing. "It shows. That he's special, I mean."

Fred didn't bother to mention that every baby drew those kinds of looks, even the ones not impossibly borne of two vampires. As Charles fell behind them, distracted by someone's call, she said, "Of course he's special."

He gave her a side glance. "You're patronizing me."

With a reluctant wincy face, she admitted, "A little."

"Fine," he said. "Just as long as this is where it stops."

Fred found she had nothing to say to this, and that cracked concrete squares had finally given way for the bench on the corner. "Here," she said, and they sat. "And look, with that little tree by the garbage can we could kind of pretend it's a park."

Angel gave a glance at the small tree, illuminated to a more sickly color than normal by the overhead streetlight. "Is that even alive?"

"Hmm," she said. "I did have a lot of time to develop my imagination on Pylea. So maybe not quite a park."

Angel gave a token nod and pushed Connor's stroller back and forth a few inches with his foot. "Charles?"

Fred looked over her shoulder, trying to see past the pedestrians between them and the club. "I think he ran into a friend. Or something. Isn't that him back by that . . . really colorful club entrance?"

Angel glanced back. "Looks like it."

She frowned. "That's not like him. To leave us like that . . . and . . . he just went *in*." She spent a moment of disbelief, knowing that Connor and even Angel shouldn't be out here with just her, although he *was* looking better. And then Fred said suddenly, in that unplanned way that happened to her sometimes and that she hated, "I think there's something going on that you're not telling us. And I'm not sure I want to know. I'm definitely not sure the others should know. At least not yet. Am I right? No, wait, don't tell me. You know, normally Charles is so sweet, but lately he's been so . . . distractable. Since, you know, that night." She made no attempt to define which night. They both knew. "And Wesley forgets what he's doing and goes out looking for trouble. Cordelia's gone to every open audition she could find and me, sometimes I've been so forthwith I hardly recognize myself. And here you are, still hurt. And mostly not telling us the whole truth about things. I bet you think we won't notice, because we're all being so odd. But we did. I mean, *I* did."

He waited for her to finish, apparently devoting his entire attention to Connor. And then he said, "Yes, no, yes, yes, not really."

Fred gave him a little scowl. "I'm not sure that's fair."

"No," he said, ceasing to rock the stroller back and forth. "It's not."

"Because you know something's going on. The others think they know what's going on, and I think what they think is going on *is*—but there's something else too."

He gave her a steady look, and his silence. She rolled her eyes a little and contemplated a short but intense pout.

Connor forestalled her. He wasn't moving any longer and he knew it. His face tightened up in that hard-concentrating baby face, the one that meant only one of two things. "I just changed you!" Fred told him, but it was the other thing.

Crying.

"There, there," Angel told him, not at all convincing. And no wonder—Connor crying was Connor on a mission, rarely soothed by anything less than Angel's vamp face.

Angel reached over to tickle Connor, his single hand spanning the baby's torso. And Fred, seeing the sweetness in it, started to smile—

Only to spring to her feet with an entirely different expression as a shabbily dressed woman rushed them, darting against traffic from the corner across the street. The woman shrieked, *"Shutupshutupshutup!"* with triumph on her face, as though she'd wanted to shriek this particular thing for a very long time.

"Angel!" Fred cried, which meant, "Run and take Connor with you!" except of course he couldn't, he'd just barely walked to this bench. But he sprang up and put himself between the stroller and the raging woman, right about the time Fred realized the woman wore bloodied, ripped clothes—but showed no sign of injury.

That looks familiar.

Homeless woman, possibly barely sane to begin with, spending time in the shadowed hiding places near sewers and storm drains. Vulnerable and un-aware of the new threat. And now . . . fast-healing and out of whatever mind she'd had.

Too familiar.

And coming this way fast, zeroing in on Connor's lusty cries. Fred glanced back at Angel's utter de-termination as he shielded the stroller, and threw herself in as the first line of defense, braced for im-pact and determined to avoid hurting the older, undernourished assailant.

The woman barreled into her and then through her, shrieking all the while; Fred found herself sprawled on cement, skinned hands, and elbows stinging, so stunned she barely recognized the sounds of struggle she heard—those of Angel, weakened, and his berserker assailant. She shook her head clear and scrambled back to her feet, climbing right on top of the bench where just a moment ago she'd been in peaceful discussion.

And she felt a hint of the confidence and assertion that had newly been hers after her own mysterious healing, and she didn't wait to understand it; she went with it.

Angel struggled to keep the woman away from the stroller, pushing back at her—the woman, for all her intensity, had no idea how to fight; she went in with a straightforward girly slapping-reaching-grabbing approach and hadn't yet tried so much as a good solid punch or kick.

And still, she drove Angel back, so the stroller inched toward the curb and Angel's unsteady knees buckled closer to the ground.

Fred leapt up on top of the bench and grabbed the woman at every flailing grabbing spot she could find—hair, tattered clothes, flying arms—shouting, "Git off! Git offa him! Gitgitgit!" and in the next moment there she was on her back end on cement sidewalk, reskinning her hands and elbows and barely aware of the small crowd they'd gathered.

Frantic, Fred looked around for a weapon. Garbage can—bolted down. Bench itself—bolted down. Stroller—occupied. Loudly occupied. Her own body—not substantial enough. But as she climbed to her feet she caught an eye-level glimpse of a briefcase, an old, solid, survives-the-baggage-compartment type of briefcase. And she snatched it away from its owner without heeding the protesting cries, jumping up on the bench to draw the briefcase back for her best baseball-bat swing—

But almost toppled over backward as the incensed man tried to reclaim the briefcase. They engaged in a struggle; from here Fred had a perfect view of his complex comb-over, and how few hairs were truly involved. She also had a perfect view of Angel going to his knees beside the stroller, knuckles white and clenched on the push bar and clearly at the very end of his strength in spite of the intense determination on his face. And yet no one else seemed inclined to step in to help, as if Angel had managed to frighten away everyone but the woman who counted.

Face to face they came, directly over the stroller. Connor wailed on. The woman shrieked on. And Angel, entirely out of options, flashed the face at her.

Connor stopped crying.

The woman stopped in midshriek to stare.

Fred drew back on the briefcase, bit down on the owner's clutching hands, snapped, "You're bald! Get over it!" as the man snatched his hands back with a cry of disbelief. She walloped the distracted crazy woman across the shoulders with the briefcase. The woman staggered, and Fred threw the case back at its owner and jumped off the bench to grab the woman, jerk her around to face the corner from which she'd come, and shout, "It's that way! It's that way!"

With a gleam in her eye the woman reprised her cry all the way across the street. *"Shutupshutup-shutup!"* and then onward into the darkness, to battlegrounds unknown. Those bystanders watching the encounter suddenly realized they might be called upon to help clean up after it and offer aid, and they melted quickly away.

Fred dropped to her knees beside Angel. "Are you all right? You're bleeding! Can you stand?"

"I'm all right," he said, though clearly not; his brow, right where the ugly vamp bumps would emerge, remained slightly furrowed. "She never touched Connor, that's the important thing. The blood . . . old stuff. I shouldn't have come out here. Not with Connor." Connor gurgled slightly, and Angel reached in the stroller to offer the baby a finger. Connor obligingly engaged his grab reflex, capturing the finger.

Fred gave a little snort. "As if you could predict that crazy old woman—"

He interrupted her with a barely perceptible shake of his head. "That's the point. We can't predict. *Especially* we can't predict. And right now . . . it looks like until we get this situation taken care of, we can't count on anyone to act normally."

"I don't think she ever acts *normally*," Fred said. "But I get your point. It's not just us anymore."

His face got that faraway look, the pensive look. The one that meant he was thinking about something, and not about to share. She almost asked him anyway, and decided against it. Later, when she had a better chance of getting something. Instead, she looked at her palms, ruefully turning them this way and that to catch the lamplight. "I guess whatever's going on . . . it's not going on with me anymore."

"No," he agreed, gently disengaging his finger. "I don't think it has been. Whatever did happen that night . . . less of it happened to you."

"And a lot more of it happened to you," she said.

"We don't even know that it was the same thing," he said, just a little too quickly.

"Let's not do that," she suggested to him, helping him to his feet and grunting with the effort of it. Solid boy, their vampire. They started back down the street. Slowly. "Let's not get into lying and such to each other right now. I think we need to concentrate on getting you and Connor back to the hotel. I just wish Charles hadn't—"

"Yo, G!" Charles called, half a block away. He closed the gap in moments, jaunty in expression and step.

Angel waited until he closed step with them, and a moment longer. And then he stopped short, turning on Charles with an expression that Fred thought might possibly be worse than facing vampface. "I'm not your G. And if you ever skip out on Connor like that again—"

"What?" Charles said, gone from whimsical to deadly serious—to worse, with a glint in his eye. One that said he could whip Angel's ass if he wanted to, right here and now . . . and that he wanted to. "What, you gonna take me down? I'm not finding that a really scary thought right now. Did Fred mention you're leaking blood again? Maybe you need to remember which of us is the one who—"

"Charles!" Fred said, somewhat in desperation. "Look!" She thrust out her hands; the blood glinted wet and black in the artificial light. "It doesn't last, Charles."

Charles shrugged, still looking at Angel with that gleam. "What of it? I still got mine. For now. Now is long enough."

"But right *now*," she said, "we need your help getting back to the hotel. Please, Charles?"

He moved a little bit closer than she expected. "For you," he said, and met her eyes for a long moment. When the moment was over she found herself starving for air and realized she'd stopped breathing. *It was only the effect of whatever happened to us,* she told herself. But she found herself wishing it hadn't been. And realizing that it was one more in a list of problems that the side-effects of the fast healing caused.

She couldn't be sure of him—or of Cordelia, or Wesley—one way or the other. Had Charles meant the intensity behind a look that had literally made her forget to breathe? She couldn't be sure.

Had he meant to leave them alone out here?

She doubted he'd even given it an instant's thought.

Cordelia felt great.

Sure, she'd hit a few auditions for which she hadn't been especially suited. Cat litter . . . she thought she'd been very cat-lovable, actually, but the cat star would have nothing to do with her. She suspected that when it came to demon cooties, there was no fooling a cat. Though really, the thing didn't have to puff up to twice its size and take giant slices out of its handler. Cordelia, trooper of aspiring actress that she was, had continued her reading right over the shrieks, for what little good it had done her.

Didn't matter. Maybe once she would have been desperate for even a cat litter commercial. Now, though . . .

Now she opened the Hyperion's lobby door and breezed through with confidence. She'd try again tomorrow, and the next day, and soon enough someone would recognize her talent.

Unless, of course, she was so distracted by de-demonizing L.A. that she didn't have the time, and her acting career stayed on hold until she was old enough that breaking in became an impossibility. Face it, she was already pushing those years, being post-teens and everything, and if she didn't find post-teens and everything, and if she didn't find work soon . . .

She stopped in her tracks, letting her black carries-everything satchel thump to the floor. "Brrr!" she said to the empty lobby. "Not much liking *that* thought."

"How's that?" Wesley's voice came faintly—from his office, no doubt, and from the sound of it he had his nose in a book.

"Nothing," Cordelia said, confirming that the rest of the lobby was abandoned. "No point in going there. Healed a paper cut this morning . . . you?"

"Stubbed my toe," he said, still sounding distracted. "Badly. All better."

"So it's still happening." Cordelia reclaimed the satchel and took it behind the reception counter, stowing it beneath the desk perpendicular to the back wall. Her desk, really, although sometimes someone else absently sat there. She went to the opening between the reception area and Wesley's office and leaned there. "Whatever 'it' is. Any luck on that front? And where is everyone?"

"Out for a walk," Wesley said, finally glancing up. More than glancing up; closing the book and shoving it aside to take up residence at the edge of the large pile on the desk. Another nudge and the stack would tumble on to the floor. Cordelia raised her eyes at the implication—the intensity of work Wesley had been doing.

Some of us go to auditions. Others . . . turn into research maniacs. She'd take the auditions, thank you.

He followed her gaze, and gave an annoyed shake of his head. "Nothing in there," he said. "I have a hard time believing that an effect so profound has gone entirely unnoted."

"Maybe it's a brand-new thing. Maybe we're the first. If so, maybe we should be making our own notes." Cordelia invited herself in and threw herself down in the firmly padded chair against the wall. Something crinkled beneath her; she frowned.

Wesley didn't appear to notice. He slapped his hand down on a hardcover journal. "Already done," he said. "I've started a separate set of notes just for this."

"You must be expecting to make a lot of them," she observed, twisting aside to grope around in the chair cushion.

"I certainly hope so," he said. "My next chore is to start a healing experiment—I think possibly that effect is slowing down, and there have been moments today . . ." He trailed off, and something in his face made Cordelia think of the moments when her own trepidations had come flooding back. But he took a breath and looked at her with determination lighting his gray eyes. "Think what this could mean for us! For *everyone*, when it comes to that." Though he hesitated, and—thorough as usual—added, 'Assuming we could create some sort of steady supply."

"And if not, what . . . finders keepers?" She found the corner of something deep in the cushion, carefully grasped and withdrew it.

"When you say it like that, it doesn't sound terribly noble," Wesley admitted. "But our *cause* here s noble . . ."

"The mission," Cordelia agreed. She regarded her prize, a crumpled and torn piece of paper, and attempted to flatten it over her thigh. "Definitely a noble mission."

"What have you there?"

Cordelia regarded the results of her efforts. Lined paper, covered with block printing worthy of a second-grader. "You tell me," she said, rising to hand it across the desk even as she quoted it. "'Remember: Angel hurt. We lost him. Charles is still not a woman.' Sure, that makes sense."

Wesley stared at the page, flipping it over as though he might find the explanation written on the back.

"It's not a grocery store puzzle book," Cordelia said dryly. "We'll have to figure this one out on our own. If you think it's worth it. Me, I've got a list of auditions to prepare for."

"Worth it?" He frowned at the paper. "Most certainly. We have to assume one of us wrote this . . . it

rather looks like Fred's handwriting, or what he
handwriting might look like if she were eight. W
already know we've each got a memory loss of tha
night . . . what if we *knew* it? What if we wrot
notes to ourselves?"

"Note," Cordelia said. "Unless you want me t
check under the cushions of all the chairs." I
wasn't an actual offer.

"It might not be a bad idea." He tapped the
paper with a decisive finger. "He lied."

Cordelia gave him a blank look. "What?"

"Angel." Wesley tossed the paper onto the desl
where it fetched up against the stack of books. "H
said he couldn't remember. He said we might no
even have been together."

"*We* couldn't remember, why should he?"
Cordelia said, thinking she sounded reasonable
and even more so when she added, "I didn't mea
what I said about checking chair cushions. Skanky.

"Think, Cordelia! If he *was* with us, then clearl
he's been affected in an entirely different way. W
already know that whatever slight demon has man
fested within you, it caused you to heal slower tha
we do. Angel isn't healing at all . . . there's no reaso
to suppose his memory was affected as ours wa
And at the same time, if we wrote one reminde
note to ourselves—as little sense as it makes—w
probably wrote more. So where are they?"

"Not checking the cushions," she repeated, ju

in case there was any question. "That's like examining someone else's belly-button lint, don't you think?" Just not into it today. She'd rather think about auditions.

He just looked at her.

She didn't back down. "And don't you think you're being just a little bit paranoid? Just a little bit someone's-out-to-get-me?"

"No," Wesley said, in the tone of a patient elder. "I think *Angel* is being less than reliable, and that in fact it translates to being out to get *us*. How else would you interpret an attempt to obstruct our investigation into these healing powers?"

Cordelia thought perhaps she was still at an audition, and had been sucked into reading a ludicrous script. "Which is the obstructing part?" she asked. "The part where he can't remember but you think he does, even though he's clearly been head-smacked out of his wits? Or the part where the possibly non-existent notes don't actually exist?"

He gave her a hurt look. "I thought you were in on this with me. Fred's been less enthusiastic from the start and Charles seems bent on proving he never left his streets, but you . . . I thought you understood what we have to gain."

"Oh, I do," Cordelia said, pushing herself up out of the chair. "A career, that's what. I haven't felt this jazzed in—"

"It won't do you any good if it doesn't last. If I

don't find a way to *make* it last."

Always with the Mr. Gloom. "I'll help," she said. "As long as it doesn't interfere with my career."

"You don't *have* a—"

"And as long as it doesn't involve searching belly lint chair cracks."

"Is there anything you *can* do?" he asked, sparing no sarcasm.

Cordelia froze, struck by that instant of vision-here-it-comes. "You had to ask." *Young people . . . skateboarding. Having a good time, their bright, baggy clothing flashing through her thoughts and leaving ghostly trailing images of color.* "Skateboarders," she said out loud, and waited for something big and nasty to leap in among them, creating havoc and inflicting terrible things.

No such thing happened. In fact, nothing happened at all. One of the 'boarders fell, the flashiest one of them all. He fell hard, and for no particular reason that Cordelia could see. For an instant, her inner eye tripped over something familiar-looking, a lumpy-oatmeal type rock and a really big one at that. And then the vision went into choppy mode, and she thought she saw the 'boarder falling about a zillion times, but possibly just once and stuck on instant replay.

"Anything helpful?" Wes was asking, still standing behind the desk, looking unperturbed by anything but his research predicaments. As far as she could tell, he hadn't moved a muscle to catch her in case she fell. Hmmph. As much as she appreciated the lack of falling to the floor in agony, it *had* been kind of nice when the guys sprang to the ready, determined to keep her from hitting the floor.

So she said, "No," a little sardonically when she finally said it, leaving Wesley with eyebrows askew. "Skateboarders. I don't get it. Soccer, singing, skateboarding . . ."

"They all start with the letter *S*," he offered.

Cordelia gave him a look and walked back to the reception area. "If this were *Sesame Street*, that might even be useful."

Silence from Wesley. Cordelia rummaged on her desk for the next day's list of audition opportunities. A slight noise from the lobby caught her attention. She walked out to stand in the middle of the patterned tile, one eyebrow raised at the entrance.

One of the lobby doors opened slightly, then closed again.

"Someone's working up the nerve," she said.

"Let me know if they succeed," Wesley muttered, making notes in the special incident journal.

From outside, muttered whispers; a discreet argument of sorts. And then finally the door opened again, all the way this time, and a harried middle-aged woman came in, trailing a young woman behind her.

A young, plain-faced woman with mousy brown hair who opened her mouth . . . and no sound came out.

CHAPTER SEVEN

Definitely healing.

Just not fast enough.

Angel let Fred push the stroller back to the Hyperion, although it occurred to him that the stability of the sturdy little vehicle might come in handy; the encounter with the crazy woman had exhausted him. Gunn was oblivious, and even Fred seemed to think that Angel on his feet meant Angel all better, the fresh blood notwithstanding.

Gunn trailed them, alert and looking for trouble. More like the Gunn who had slowly started to mesh with the gang more than a year earlier instead of the man who had softened enough of his hard edges to work as part of the team.

Angel himself walked carefully beside the stroller, wiggling his fingers at Connor and sneaking in illicit flashes of fang-face when he thought no one was looking. They dawdled briefly in the courtyard so Fred could hoist Connor up in her arms and Gunn folded the stroller and tucked it under his arm, looking entirely capable and even a little disappointed that they'd made it back without so much as a hint of trouble.

Except they did have trouble. The Giflatl was proving itself to be exactly the menace about which Kluubp had given warning, and they hadn't even gotten to the part where people understood enough to obsess about the apparent fountain of health.

Except for the gang, of course. They knew; they wanted.

Angel knew, and he couldn't tell them.

This wasn't going to end well no matter what.

They trudged up the stairs to take the balcony entrance at the split stairs, and Angel opened the glass-paned doors to lead the way back inside and—

Visitors.

Good. It'll give them all something to think about other than the Giflatl effect.

He eased casually down the short riser into the lobby, doing his best to hide the toll the short walk—and scuffle—had exacted from him. Behind him, Fred murmured, "I'll take Connor upstairs," and peeled off to do just that.

"Angel," Wesley said. The visitors had dragged him out of the office, then, and away from his obsessive research; all for the good.

Cordelia turned, that way she had of twisting around without actually moving her feet and he wondered if she knew how it accentuated her curves? *Of course she knows. Aspiring actress. Probably practiced it.* "Angel!" she said, somewhat more welcoming than Wesley. "This is Mrs. Waterman and her daughter Lisa." After a pause, she added, *"Clients,"* just in case he didn't get it. And to the clients, in case they hadn't gotten it even though Wes and Cordelia had twice addressed him by name, "This is Angel. And Gunn. And Fred went upstairs, I'm sure she'll be down in a moment. So you see, we'll have the full manpower of Angel Investigations working on your case."

From the look on Wesley's face, Angel wasn't so sure of that. On the surface Wesley merely appeared patient, but his body language gave away his eagerness to return to the office—the angle of his torso as he sat on a chair arm, the way one foot was already headed in that direction. Gunn had already outdone him, muttering something about his mission and "later" and heading back out of the hotel.

Cordelia came over to Angel, taking his arm and turning him away for a few confidential murmurs. "The girl was in one of my visions. The singer. It didn't make any sense at the time—okay, it still doesn't make sense—but somehow she's lost her voice. The doctors can't find any physical reason for it. Is that blood on your shirt?"

"Hard to tell on black, isn't it?" he said. "And you thought I wear dark colors just to be broody."

"I thought you wore them because they perfectly compliment that Black Irish coloring," she said. "Or else that you had so little color sense you were afraid to try anything else."

He gave her a searching look. *Almost sounds like the real Cordy. Not Giflatl Cordy, but*—he almost thought, *my Cordy,* but stopped himself. Out loud he said, "Have they given us anywhere to start?"

"Not really," she admitted. "Just made sense of my vision, more or less."

From her seat by Wesley's office, Mrs. Waterman said, "She has a college scholarship, a voice scholarship. Please . . . we don't know where else to turn."

That's what they all said. *And by the time they get here, it's usually true.*

He turned to the mother-daughter duo, both seated on the edge of the gray roundchair across the lobby—the mother hopeful, the daughter dull and defeated, barely bothering to look around herself. "Actually," Angel said, "we're already working on your case."

"How—?" For an instant, Mrs. Waterman held hope, but it changed to puzzlement. Like her daughter, she was no beauty, but she had a poise about her, a self-presentation, that went beyond physical attributes.

The strain, however, had begun to show.

He knew the feeling. Cold blood trickled down his side and into the waistband of his black jeans; hot pain traced the source.

"We've been running down some unusual activity in the area," Angel said, stretching the truth as far as it could possibly be stretched. "By coming in, you've given us a lot more to work with. Cordelia will take down the particulars of your situation, and we'll combine that with what we already know."

Cordelia raised an eyebrow at him. "Not your secretary," she said, moving her lips without much sound behind them. Nope, not "his" Cordy after all—the Giflatl effect was still in play.

He looked back at her and muttered through a forced smile that was entirely for the Watermans' benefit, "About to fall over."

In a mixture of suspicion and concern, Mrs. Waterman said, "Are you *bleeding*?"

Angel looked around the lobby to see who she might be talking about and found her gaze settled on him. "Who?" he said, sliding into his can't-lie-worth-beans voice and ignoring Cordelia's wince. "Me? No, of course not."

A drop of dark blood splatted to the tile at his feet. He didn't look down.

"Your shirt," she said.

He looked down. "Oh. That. Just . . . spilled something." *Right, my blood.* "I, um, stopped a mugging outside. And there was coffee."

"Just quit while you're behind," Cordelia muttered, swooping back into the center of the lobby to take the attention from him. She grabbed a notepad and said brightly, "Happens all the time. All part of the service Angel Investigations provides the city. Now, let's get some details while Angel *changes his shirt*." She cast a final glance his way, just to make sure he'd gotten the message.

He'd gotten it, all right. Get out of there, go upstairs, collapse. He took a few steps back, put a surreptitious hand on the stair rail.

Mrs. Waterman had a strange, puzzled expression—but it had nothing to do with him. She groped around in the tightly fitting cushions of the roundchair, where the seat snugged up against the central pedestal that made up the back support. After a moment she came up with a large index card.

Angel winced, forgetting to hide it. Didn't matter—both Cordelia and Wesley's attention was riveted on the index card.

Apparently Kluubp had missed some cleanup.

Angel could only hope there hadn't been more than one.

The stairs beckoned. And now that Angel had shown some signs of mildly accelerated healing, the others no longer offered much help with the whole bandaging routine, or even evinced much concern. Back to taking him for granted—although until this past week, he'd had no idea just how much taking-for-granted was going on around here. Even Fred, the least affected of all of them, was still easily distracted by the intensity of Wesley's research. But then, that was pretty much Fred under any circumstances, from university to cave.

Tired. Sit a moment, then go upstairs. No one is going to notice one way or the other.

That much was the truth. Angel sat.

Cordelia scribbled notes with the Watermans, casually appropriating the index card, passing it smoothly off to Wesley as he returned to his office.

Too smoothly. Something was up, there. Otherwise she wouldn't have bothered to give it to Wesley at all, or at the least suggested in her Princess of Pylea voice that he toss it out for her.

Movement caught the corner of Angel's eye; he got a glimpse of a small figure scurrying around the corner at the top of the stairs. A distinctly Kluubp-like figure. A moment of surreptitious watchfulness rewarded him with Kluubp's reappearance. The keeper made sure no one else could see him and then pointed upward.

Up? Angel said with his eyebrows, thinking of his room on the third floor. Kluubp gestured more emphatically. *Up, UP?* Angel asked, giving his eyebrows as much loft as possible and mouthing, *the roof?*

Kluubp gave him a quick thumbs-up—damn, did that guidebook cover everything?—and withdrew.

And of course Cordelia had just ushered the mother-daughter clients out the door and turned to him just in time to catch his fading but still exaggerated expression.

He did the only thing he could think of. He faked a sneeze.

"Uh-huh," she said, and went behind the counter to fire up the computer, new interview notes in hand.

At the moment he didn't care whether she'd been fooled or not; at the moment he was frozen in a seizure of pain from ribs to bruises to the renewed ache in his poor smacked around head. "Not meant for this," he muttered out loud. "Definitely not meant for this." But he hadn't meant for them to hear, and they didn't. He'd just sit here quietly a few more moments, thinking fondly of the quiet sanctuary of his room, and then he'd make his way up to the roof. Maybe it was time to get more answers from the keeper. Maybe, given a few moments, he might even work up enough menace so the little being would do more than simply laugh.

"Voice-stealing demons," Wesley said. "Nothing in the obvious references. Did they leave a retainer check?"

Cordelia leaned out from her desk slightly and waved the check where Wesley could see it from his office.

"Excellent," he said, but it seemed to be approval of habit rather than true interest.

"Don't forget," Cordelia said, tucking the check carefully away, "I saw her in a vision—and I've seen others in similar visions. No one else was singing, though. The singing part might not be the key."

"What I don't understand," Wesley said, his voice becoming more thoughtful, and even a little lower—no human sitting across the lobby on the riser leading to the split stairs and the courtyard would have been able to hear him at all. "What I don't understand is what the demon gains."

"What do you mean?" Cordelia, drawn by his lower tones, left her desk to hang by the opening between reception desk area and Wesley's office.

"Those humans it encounters, it gives the ability to heal. Pretty altruistic behavior, especially for a demon wreaking the kind of havoc we saw."

"That Wardjon was pretty messed up," she admitted. "Not that this has anything to do with—"

Hang in there, Cordy. There's more going on in L.A. than an escaped Giflatl, and you know it. Stick with the vision.

But Wesley talked right over her attempt to bring the conversation back to the Watermans and the visions. "And on top of that, add a period of amnesia or near amnesia—"

"*Near* amnesia. We all know something happened.

We all have a vague idea where it went down."

"Even so. Near amnesia, followed by a period of what I can only call . . . well-being." Wesley's voice gave him away; he was frowning at whatever sparse notes he'd gathered.

"Confidence," Cordelia agreed, for all intents entirely distracted from her own research, and even the retainer check. "Or maybe . . . an absence of fear."

"Yes," Wesley said slowly, and Angel got the impression Wesley was searching his mind for fears, old and familiar fears.

And not finding them.

Or if finding them, not responding to them.

To judge from Cordelia's face, she was doing the same. There for a moment she'd been with the mission, tuned into her visions . . . driven to help the people in them—driven so much, in fact, that she'd recently almost sacrificed herself to keep them.

But not today. Today, aside from those few brief moments, she was as obsessed with the Giflatl effect as any of the others—if not in solving it, in taking advantage of it.

She seemed to sense his scrutiny; she looked over her shoulder at him. "You're not bleeding on the carpet, are you?"

No. He could feel the blood, as cool as the rest of his body, trickle down to gather at the waistband of his black jeans. But he said, "I thought it might add to the decor. All part of the Angel Investigations service."

But his allusion to her earlier casual dismissal of his reopened wounds was lost on her. She frowned. "Maybe you should go upstairs."

"Now *that*," he said, carefully pulling himself to his feet, "is exactly what I had in mind." And he made his slow way to the elevator. If he'd simply been going up to his room he'd have used the stairs in spite of his condition; the elevator was slow and klunky and regardless of the forged papers provided by Lilah Morgan in her attempt to undercut her Wolfram and Hart colleague Gavin Parks, it hadn't been inspected for far too many years. But the roof?

Yeah, he'd take the elevator.

Cordelia didn't notice.

Getting soft, Angel, he told himself, feeling the wince of her not-caring. And he wasn't referring to his physical condition.

On the roof, Kluubp looked pleased with himself, and turned to greet Angel with a smile that in truth looked a little creepy on that wizened almost-Yoda face. "You made it. Excellent. In a few days you should feel almost as your old self. Your, ahem, very old self."

"Been doing more reading?" Angel asked him, in no mood for joviality.

"More like asking around." Kluubp gestured at the overturned milkcrate that seemed to be the only excuse for a chair on the old roof. "Please. I can't have you swaying while we talk. I'll worry, and then I'll forget to say something important."

Angel didn't argue. He sat.

Kluubp gave a conspicuous sniff, then gestured to the re-opened wound on Angel's side. "Tsk. Your friends don't seem to be taking very good care of you."

"They're distracted," Angel said, feeling the odd urge to defend the gang . . . even though Kluubp was only echoing Angel's earlier thoughts. "They're not used to . . . this."

"All the more reason for their alarm, I should think." Kluubp quit looking out at the cityscape and came over to crouch by Angel, looking perfectly comfortable in that hunkered position. "But they're not. I hope you've had a chance to see how I spoke the truth . . . that the presence of the Giflatl venom not only alters the behavior of good people, but incites far too much interest."

Angel didn't answer directly. There'd be some sort of plea for help attached to this meeting, he was sure of it. Looking out over the lights of the city himself, he said, "Wesley's working pretty hard at it. And Fred, too, at times. I've never seen them stumped yet."

"Oh, they'll have no luck with this one." Kluubp

sounded much more confident than Angel felt. He fluttered his fingers together in a self-satisfied gesture, and his ears twitched happily. Angel tipped his head down slightly, looking up at Kluubp from beneath his brow; it was enough to convey his skepticism, and the keeper gave a little chuckle in response. "Angel, my friend—may I call you friend?—rest assured we've been dealing with this situation for a very long time. We began scouring this dimension of references to the Giflatl before humans even had a written language." He paused, then added thoughtfully, "Practically before they had a spoken language, if you must know."

"There are other references that reach back that far," Angel said. "And there are humans who have learned to decipher those languages. The elder languages. Wesley . . . man, he's a pain in the ass sometimes but I gotta give him this much—if he can't translate those things directly, he'll track down the references until he gets it done."

"Yes," Kluubp said. "And my investigation indicates the young woman, Fred—I'm still sorting out your naming system, but I have to admit this particular one has me stumped—in any event, Fred has a remarkable ability to follow up on the faintest hint of a clue."

He gave Angel a serene smile. "All the same, they'll find nothing."

Angel considered the keeper's words a moment.

Then—moving carefully—he scrubbed his hands over his face, a weary gesture. "They'll be back to normal soon?"

"Very soon," Kluubp agreed.

"Yeah, well once they are I think you might find you're underestimating them." For as intense as Wesley was, he wasn't yet able to concentrate fully on any one line of inquiry; he kept switching from book to book—and he had very little back-up from either Cordelia, who was entirely focused on turning her new confidence into a career, or Fred, who was too baffled by everyone's behavior to put herself in the middle of it for very long. Gunn's defection this evening had hurt her, he thought. It had definitely hurt Angel, albeit in a much more tangible fashion. "And you've got something else to consider. I can't keep the truth from them forever."

At this, Kluubp's confidence fell away, leaving his wizened face a little startled and forlorn enough that no doubt this expression alone often got him what he wanted. "I thought you understood . . . that you'd seen enough so you *could* understand . . . revealing the existence of the Giflatl—and the effects of its venom—will cause nothing but trouble."

Angel gave a short shake of his head. "That's not it. Look—I can tell them the truth, or I can tell them I *won't* tell them the truth. But I can't keep things from them entirely. I'm no good at it."

"I think you've done quite well so far," Kluubp said, a little stiffly.

Angel snorted softly. "I've been unconscious most of the time. That's changing. They've been under the influence most of the time. That's changing too. When they start thinking straight, they're also going to start thinking things through—they'll know something's up. Fred already does." He hesitated, hunting a way to help Kluubp understand the very thing he couldn't possibly—not truly. "Here's the thing. You know I have a soul, right?"

"Oh, indeed." Kluubp made a resonant trilling noise that might have been a stand-in for a giggle. "And without it, your worser half rules. Angelus. I found plenty of reading material on Angelus."

Great. Unauthorized biographies. "Then you understand what my friends live with, and the risk they accept."

Kluubp nodded as if this was a given. "Yes, yes, that circumstances might return Angelus to the fore. Even so much as a loss of control on your part."

"Then you should understand how important it is to them that they can trust me."

Kluubp waved his arms before him in an emphatically negative gesture. "You can't tell them!"

"I'm not talking about telling them. I'm talking about telling them I'm not telling them."

This time, Kluubp took a moment to work it through. When he did, his ears drooped; the corners of his wide mouth turned down in distinct displeasure. "Such a confession would confirm to them that there's something worth hunting. A secret to find."

"I'm telling you, they already know that. And soon enough they'll figure out that I'm keeping something from them. I have to come clean with them before then."

A stubborn look crept onto the keeper's face; he looked like a thwarted old uncle, and quite peeved about it. Angel leaned forward slightly, ignoring the pain it caused him . . . which was not, in fact, as much as he'd expected. "Just in case you have the mistaken impression this is something you have a say in, let me be perfectly clear: You don't."

The keeper emitted a double-voiced noise Angel had no doubt was a rude one in his own culture. Angel sighed, pretty much the same way his long-departed father used to sigh over a particular recalcitrant great-uncle. A great-uncle lucky enough to have died of natural causes before Angelus got anywhere near him. With the most even tone he could muster, Angel said, "How close are you to tracking this thing down?"

Kluubp's gaze suddenly moved off to the side, where he could be looking at nothing but a roof vent. "It has been covering more territory than usual; these creatures usually stake their denning turf and stay there. But it seems to have been disoriented by the journey here; it hasn't yet settled down. My usual tracking methods won't work until it does—unless, of course, I should happen to get lucky. Things would go much faster if you were helping."

"Why did you come alone in the first place?" Angel asked. He put his fingers to his side under his shirt; the bandages remained sticky-damp, but there was no new flow. And he thought . . . he *hoped* . . . he felt the particular twitchy tingle of healing flesh.

Kluubp made that rude noise again. "I'm well-trained to move between worlds; I know how to hide and how to find the resources that let me accomplish my tasks. There are not many of us . . . and frankly, don't you think it might just attract some attention if a great number of my people suddenly showed up in the area?"

Okay, that's a point. "If you're right, I'll be back in action within a few days. Come back then. We'll see how your Giflatl hunt is going." He climbed to his feet, wearied but not quite as pained as he'd come to expect. The grate of bone no longer accompanied his movement; the ribs were starting to knit. But at the doorway of the roof he turned, looking back at Kluubp. "We could tell my friends right now and you'd have the help you need," he said, holding Kluubp's gaze across the darkness. "You underestimate them. Once the venom is out of their systems, they can handle this."

"No," Kluubp said, but he said it sadly. "They could not. And in your soul you know it, or you would have told them what you know regardless of my pleas."

Damn. That hit home as hard as one of the Gi-flatl blows.

"The *HMS Bounty*," Lorne repeated to the gang assembled around him, having received very little response the first time he said it.

"Sounds like a boat," Charles responded, and none too cheerfully. Like the others in the lobby, the day had dawned to prove them all entirely vulnerable to cuts, toe-stubs, bruises, and by deduction, the more grisly attention of any random demon out there.

"A ship," Fred said, more or less automatically. She'd been back in the toe-stubbing business for days, hoping and waiting for the others to come around. Now that things were back to normal—and Cordelia was off in the bathroom running cold water over the coffee pot burn that more or less proved it—none of them were any too cheerful.

Except Angel, who although not quite back to normal, had accelerated his healing well enough to be pretty darn close.

Everything as it should be.

Except now Wesley was more determined than ever to find the explanation behind what had happened to them, and Charles was more determined than ever to track it down in the tunnels where they'd first found it, and Cordelia couldn't seem to decide whether to follow her vision, help Wesley, or continue hunting some way to apologize to Angel.

She hadn't yet, but Fred thought she would. Among the three who were the most affected by whatever experience they'd had, Cordelia seemed to be the one who realized how badly they'd treated Angel.

Except she, like Fred, was also honing in on the certainty that Angel was keeping something from them.

"It's neither boat or ship," Lorne said. "It's a bar, and from what I hear they can use your help."

"A bar?" Fred repeated.

Lorne made a big hand-waving gesture, as if he were erasing air. "Not a bar exactly. I mean, yes, but with food. 'Food and Grog.'"

"*Grog,*" Charles said, hanging near the pillar at the end of the curving reception desk. "That sounds like trouble right there."

Fred ducked her head to smile. Charles had been subdued since the healing and random silliness had worn off; she wasn't sure if he was embarrassed or disappointed.

"What?" he said, having seen her in spite of the ducking. Or perhaps because of it.

"Nothing," she murmured. *Just nice to see you being you again.*

"The grog is fine, if you go in for that sort of thing," Lorne said, letting slip just a little bit of bar-owner's superiority syndrome. Or former bar-owner. Holtz had pretty much put an end to that . . . one complete renovation and repair too many for Caritas. "But their lighting scheme—which is to say, dim—has attracted some clientele from the wrong side of the grave, if you get my drift."

"Hmm." Wesley actually looked up from the notes he was doodling. *Doodling* being the operative word as far as Fred could see. For all his efforts, he'd made very little progress this past week. A quick upside-down reading—she didn't think he realized how easily she did that—revealed this to be a short list of references he intended to acquire. He asked, "Paying customer?"

No doubt the new references would not come cheaply.

Lorne gave Wesley a look of great skepticism and said, "Are you channeling Cordy, or am I in the wrong Angel Investigations?"

"Hey!" Cordelia said from within the bathroom, but without much heat. "I'm not *that* far away, and I'm not even running water anymore."

Wesley drew back defensively, closing his

notebook on the counter. "It's a reasonable question. We are a legitimate business, after all. We have . . . expenses."

Cordelia came out of the bathroom altogether, a wet washcloth wrapped around her fingers. "Good luck," she said. "That line never works for me."

"Yes, yes," Lorne interrupted impatiently. "I'm sure you'll be paid. If you approach them right, that is." But his initial confidence almost instantly faded to waffling. "Although . . . I heard about it from a friend of a friend, if you know what I mean—it's not exactly the kind of place where I'd be welcome. Gordon—that's the owner—knows something's not quite right, but I'm not exactly sure he'd be receptive to the idea of vampires. So you'll have a hard time getting him to pay for getting rid of said vampires. If you catch *that* drift."

"Just do it," Cordelia said suddenly. "We need to. We need to get back in the swing of things, and taking down a few unsuspecting vampires sounds like just the thing. Especially now that we've got Angel back on the job."

Angel sat on the top of the gray roundchair, using the center pedestal as the seat, and the seat as a prop for his feet. He gave Cordelia a glance that looked more sour than enthusiastic. "So you noticed I was out of commission after all."

"Well, sure," Cordelia said. "What with all the blood and all the bandaging and . . ."

And nothing. She trailed off, as if suddenly realizing no one had given him much TLC beyond that first day at all. No one human, anyway. Fred had tried, she really had, but she just hadn't been able to concentrate, and by the time she could, Angel was having none of it.

It would be a while, she thought, before he resumed his silly gleeful practice of taking Cordelia's nursing for relatively minor wounds.

Minor for Angel, anyway.

Tension hung between them, until Fred couldn't stand it and said brightly, "That's it, then? Should we go?"

"You up for it?" Charles said, looking at Fred specifically.

"Oh, no," Fred said. "I mean, basically I'm still just a big coward. But I can take a crossbow, and cover your backs."

Wesley tucked the notebook under his arm and gave a short nod. "It's settled, then. We'll go. I think Cordelia's right—it's a good opportunity to get back into the swing of things. If we can find a way to get paid for our efforts, all the better."

They took the GTO to an area of restaurants and hotels that Angel remembered as once being among the classiest. No longer. Not quite a slum . . . but definitely doddering, as neighborhoods went. Wesley, checking a Thomas Guide, would have taken them directly to the bar itself, but Angel pulled into the parking lot of the adjoining Gaylord Apartments.

"Oh, like a little walk is going to hurt you," Cordelia said when Wesley gestured mutely at the map.

Angel looked over at him and said, "This was my turf a long time before it became your turf. Take a giant leap of faith, Wes."

Just as mutely, Wesley dropped the map on the seat between them. Gunn hadn't even waited; he was on his way out of the convertible, not bothering with the door.

Angel bothered with the door. He checked his wrists for the stake rachets and checked the inside pocket of his thigh-length leather coat for the spares. A glance back told him Fred had her crossbow—it looked bigger than she did, but she handled it well for all of that—and a great big cross jammed into her waistband. Cordelia—holy water, cross, stake. Mostly defensive, but getting more confident even if she did need that precision practice. And Gunn— never subtle, he had his favorite ax and plenty of stakes. Wesley kept a machete down low by his side—purely a defensive weapon for this job—and his jacket pocket bulged with stakes.

An inconspicuous group if Angel had ever seen one.

He gave a barely discernible shake of his head

and started off for the apartments. As he led the way into the lobby, Wesley gently cleared his throat. Angel murmured, "Trust, Wesley."

The lobby opened before them, spacious and in some ways familiar.

"It used to be a hotel!" Fred said, glancing from the elevators in the back to the ever-present reception desk, currently in use as a convenient work surface next to the bank of mailboxes.

"Bingo," Angel said, then looked back at them. "I can say that, right? I mean, without tarnishing my tough-guy image."

"No problem here," Cordelia told him. "But about the bar . . . ?"

Angel gestured at the shadowed spot beside the elevators, where a padded brown leather door quietly resided. "Hotel. Bar. Symbiotic relationship." He shrugged his shoulders, loosening them . . . testing for the remnants of stiff and sore and finding them, but not so much as to hinder him. "It's tight quarters in there. I'll bring them out here we were have some room to play. You might see about calling the elevator down and blocking it open so no one walks into the middle of it all."

"You knew," Gunn said suddenly. "All that business with Lorne about food and grog and what the bar was all about, and you knew the whole time."

"Didn't know about their pest problem," Angel said. "I know the bar. I even know Gordon. Jack

Webb used to hang out here, and Mickey Mantle . . ."

"You *knew*," Wesley repeated.

Angel shrugged again, this time purely just to shrug. "You didn't ask. Be ready—this won't take long." And he pushed through the padded leather door. The richly appointed door showed signs of wear, but still spoke of the luxury and care with which these establishments had once presented themselves. Once inside the bar itself, he spent a moment reorienting himself, sorting out memories from what he now saw.

Pretty much the same. Gothically dark amber lighting scheme over a dark walnut and leather decor with brass appointments—the odd porthole, an authentic ship's lantern, the bar rail. Except . . .

Right away he spotted the table squatters in a dim corner, sucking down foamy dark beer and eyeing the other customers with a discreet but distinctly predatory eye.

Not to mention the way their very presence raised his hackles.

He took a step toward them.

Or he meant to.

Almost instantly, he froze. He froze with *fear*. In disbelief, he tried to shake it off—literally tried to shake it off, a body memory of shaking snow off his shoulders.

Fear.

Fear of pain.

How long had it been, since he'd had that fear of pain? Since childhood? Certainly not as a young man, when he'd been convinced he'd live forever . . . and when Darla had given him the opportunity to turn conviction into actuality.

Still, even Liam had had his coping mechanisms, his approach to the world . . . some way of dealing with the bar fights and bruised ribs and split lips and hangovers, and knowing he'd wake up the next day with no more care than the day before. As much as he tried to avoid those memories, the young, callow creature he'd been, Angel stood in the shadows of the apartment entrance and hunted them, hunting the solution to this all-encompassing, crippling fear that washed through him in waves. *Connor, growing up without his father. Angel himself caught up in agony, living through it not for the moments, but for the long haul.*

The hesitation bought him nothing. Nothing but a sharp disgust when he realized that nothing of Liam's experience would help the man he'd become. They were too different of nature . . . carousing young man versus crusader. Liam had had no drive to atone; Liam hadn't even understood the concept. Liam had accepted no responsibility.

But Angel . . .

Angel had responsibility. He had a mission. He had a *son*.

And he had no idea how to cope with the fear that left him powerless in the shadows with a mind that expected to stride forward with confidence somehow stuck in a body that wouldn't even move.

CHAPTER EIGHT

Quit thinking.

Just move. A couple hundred years of instinct must be good for something.

So he did. Ignoring the startled, wary looks of the few customers he passed, Angel made his way from the secluded entrance to the equally secluded corner table, wincing internally at the blare of the loud jukebox. Free jukebox . . . it never stopped playing. Discreet conversation . . . not gonna happen.

They looked up as he approached the table. Three men and two women—and pretty spiff as vamps went; not left behind in their own time period, but more or less blending with the times except for one woman who seemed stuck in the eighties. Otherwise . . . drinking beer, leaving tips, smiling in the right places and not laughing too loudly at their own jokes. But they were hungry, and they had a predatory glint in their eyes that any vampire would recognize. Even one with a soul.

The women nudged each other as he approached. Subtlety . . . but not subtlety enough. They were here on the hunt, all right—and sleek and well-enough fed that they'd found the *HMS Bounty* to be bountiful indeed.

He smiled at them, a making-moves kind of smile, and when he was close enough so no one else in the room could see, he flashed a vamp-face.

The women smiled back. They might have suspected, but here with the noise and the humanity—and the beer—they hadn't been sure. Now they were.

The guy on the outside seat of the table didn't smile. He scowled. Especially after the women smiled, he scowled. Angel met his glowering expression and tilted his head toward the back corner in a *let's talk* suggestion. The guy was happy enough to get him away from the women—one of them lowered her eyes to look up at Angel through thick mascara'd lashes and the other giggled—and rose from the table, a buff surfer-dude type who did all his boarding at night these days. He willingly followed Angel back to the alcove that held the door, still within plain sight of his friends—who did not disguise their interest or their sharp scrutiny.

Surfer Dude didn't wait for introductions. As

soon as Angel turned to face him—not that he'd ever fully turned his back on the vamp—Surfer Dude leaned in close and said, "This is our turf."

"Exactly," Angel said, quite congenially. Inside he still flinched at remembered pain and still thought, *Connor needs his father,* outside he was the picture of quiet unconcern. "But that's the problem."

The other gave him a suspicious look in response. "It's not *our* problem. It might be yours, but . . . oh, gosh, I don't give a damn about that, do I?"

"No, no, it's your problem all right," Angel said. "You've got me all wrong. I'm not looking to move in on your turf. Your turf is sullied, because you took too much of a good thing and forgot to be inconspicuous. That makes things hard on the rest of us, you know? Conspicuous vampires on the social scene? That's never good."

"Soooo . . . what?" the blond vampire asked. "You're here because you want us to abandon prime feeding ground, is that it?"

"Actually, I just want you to die," Angel told him. While the vamp's face worked to register scornful disbelief, Angel pivoted around him just enough to hide him in the shadow—if not from his friends—and flicked his wrist to shoot a stake into position just as he thrust his arm forward.

Vampire dust.

A nearby patron sneezed, blinked hard, and

then scowled in bafflement at the sudden appearance of grit in his food.

Angel looked over to the table of vampires, saw astonishment quickly turning to outrage, and raised a hand to wiggle his fingers in whimsical farewell just before he exited through the Gaylord's door.

A bristle of weapons greeted him on the other side. He held his hands up in a quick no-threat gesture. "It's me!"

They backed off, expressions varying from puzzled to accusing to Cordelia—who, of course, could hardly be defined in ordinary terms but of all them, seemed content to wait for events to become more obvious. Fred waited across from the elevators, crossbow ready and trembling.

Frightened.

Oh god I know the feeling.

The door from the bar slammed open and irate vampires stormed through, ready to avenge their friend—just as an apartment resident of the old-and-cranky variety opened the fire stairs door beyond the elevator, saw the elevator blocked, and said, "What's going on here—"

Fred's crossbow twanged, impaling one of the vampires to the wall through his arm not far from the door; the old and cranky man grew suddenly spry and wise and disappeared back into the stairwell without another word. The vampire himself gave a bellow of pain, jerked the crossbow bolt free, and flung it to the floor, glowering at Fred.

"Aw, Fred," Gunn said, "I told you that just makes 'em mad."

"*Already* mad," one of the women said, eyeing Gunn. "But about to make it better."

"Oh please," Cordelia said, shifting her grip on the stake she held. "Big hair, electric blue eye shadow, pink lips—there's *no* making it better."

Quippage, Angel thought. Just like normal. Just like none of the pain, the healing, the not-healing, the whole Giflatl effect . . . like it had never happened. Except for Angel, who stood momentarily frozen, his mind entirely blank of quippage.

Only one thing to do for it.

He headed for the vamp who'd targeted Fred, zero to sixty in no seconds flat, and on the way he grabbed the big-haired vamp by the arm, spinning her around in a warp-speed do-si-do. She bounced off the wall and into the path of Cordelia's stake, and by then Angel had moved on to her boyfriend, a quick forehead slam to leave the vamp dazed and within the reach of Gunn's ax. The second woman leapt at him with a feral snarl, and he went down before her, a deliberate retreat while taking her with him. He rolled back on his shoulders, curling his legs between them and then shooting them out straight to propel her back against the wall and within Wesley's easy reach. Turning the motion into a kick-up flip to his feet, he walked without haste to intercept the wounded vamp who menaced Fred, kicked his knees out from behind, and staked the vamp as he fell backward, arms flailing wildly—and then suddenly just a screen of dust in motion.

The Gaylord Lobby—and the *HMS Bounty*—were newly vamp-free zones.

Not counting Angel, of course.

"Wow," Gunn said flatly. "I guess we're done here."

"Unless someone brought a dust buster," Cordelia said, looking around at the suddenly gritty lobby. "You know, if that had lasted a little longer, I'm pretty sure I could have come up with two, maybe three more smart remarks."

"I have to admit I thought we'd get a bigger fight out of them than that," Wesley said, pocketing his stake.

The door to the stairs popped back open, revealing the cranky old man in his newly armed format—he carried a miniature fire extinguisher, and brandished it with some fervor. "Back off!" he cried. "I've called the cops!"

"Well, then," Wesley said without alarm, as they stood quietly in the lobby, no weapons in sight. Even Fred's crossbow had found its way behind a potted palm. "Perhaps we'd best flee while we can."

The old man gave them a look of disbelief. "You can't fool me," he declared. "You were up to something. Fighting and bellowing and . . ." He gave Fred a most suspicious look, she who looked the least likely of them all to be involved in fighting and bellowing. She gave him a small apologetic shrug.

"You can go about your business," Angel muttered in tones that wouldn't carry to the old man. "Move along. Move along."

The old man gave their apparent innocence a baleful look and retreated into his stairwell. Angel blinked at him and began to wonder about the whole Yoda thing. And could it be catching?

"Well, that's that," Wesley said, emitting enough satisfaction to use up the entire gang's quota. "I guess we're 'back in the swing,' as they say."

"As *I* said," Cordelia pointed out, leading the way for the lobby door. Not hanging around, although Angel was pretty sure the old man had been bluffing about the cops.

"That *was* pretty tight," Gunn said, pausing just long enough to nod to himself in a silent but quite evident *yeah* of confirmation. "And Fred—wicked with that crossbow!" He held the door open for her.

"I almost missed him," Fred said, puzzled at such praise as the door closed behind her.

And Angel still stood in the lobby. Feeling the echoes of his startling, unfamiliar fear, and knowing he had to overcome them or he'd be no good to anyone—never mind to his own son. The fear would drive him to overcompensate—as he'd done this evening. Or cause him to hesitate.

But mostly he stood in the lobby staring after Wesley, Cordelia, Gunn, and Fred, feeling a new and less personal fear. *They didn't take it seriously.* Not their own peril—always a factor in a fight with unknown vamps—or their limited role in this engagement. *They truly don't realize I carried that fight. Maybe they never realized.*

They'd certainly taken him for granted the night he was injured—that he was okay somewhere. They'd lost him, but weren't concerned about it. And when they found him, they still weren't concerned about it.

The venom did that to them. It changed them.

But here and now, they'd had no venom in their systems. And they'd taken him for granted so thoroughly that they took his part in the fight as theirs, strutting away all tough and successful and unscathed.

The question was, had they been this way before? Or were they still struggling with the aftermath of the Giflatl encounter? Or . . . both?

And would he have noticed at all if Kluubp hadn't been whispering in his ear?

"You know," Wesley said from his office, a disembodied voice to those in the reception area, "maybe I've been going at this all wrong."

Only Cordelia, seated at her desk, could see him,

and only the edge of him and his desk at that. She looked up from the personals ads—they found a surprising number of demony clues in the personals—and said, "Wait, did I really just hear him say that, or was it only in my head?"

"You're the one with the visions," Gunn said, running a whetstone along the edge of his favorite ax—not that it had taken any dings from the action of the night before, but they didn't have anything else going, and even Cordelia saw the value of keeping the weapons as sharp as possible. The easier to cut something's head off. "It's *always* in your head."

She made a face at him, *ha-ha,* and returned her attention to the personals. *Hmm, "old-time religion," that could mean something a lot less pious than implied.*

Wesley continued as though none of them had said anything. "I've been hunting references to the healing and mood changes, but it seems fairly evident to me at this point that I won't find them. What if I were to search for other things we've experienced? The rash of grisly demon deaths, the way all trace of those battles disappear shortly after the events . . ."

Gunn checked the edge of his ax. "Hmm . . . English could have something there."

Fred turned away from the big bookshelf between the bathroom and the weapons cabinet.

"That's good," she agreed, book in hand. Cordelia gave up on the personals and looked back up to listen to the conversation. Fred added, "Besides, you've got to think outside the lines when the lines aren't taking you anywhere, right?"

"So that's what you're doing?" Gunn asked.

"Me?" Fred gave him a startled look. "Oh, no . . . I'm looking for something to read to Connor."

"You're kidding," Cordelia said flatly. "From *that* bookshelf?"

"Sure," Fred said, and her enthusiasm built. "There's nothing like the droning voice of a professor to put you to sleep, hadn't you noticed? Not that I ever had that problem because, well, you know, I just developed my own work when I was in those classes. But look at this—*A History of Watcher Rules of Order.* Don't you think it's perfect?"

"She may have something there," Gunn said, but Cordelia quit paying attention because *here we go again,* not only a vision but another one of the mysterious ones, the ones that made no sense, gave them no direction, and just plain kept happening.

"Cordy?" Fred asked, her voice going back to its habitual uncertainty.

Cordelia held up a hand, hostage to her mind's eye. "Another strange one," she said. "I can't see any demons . . . there's just these two women, walking downtown somewhere, not a great neighborhood but not so bad. And one of them . . ." *is lip-reading*.

Two friends enjoy the morning L.A. sunshine, walking for coffee during their break. They chatter to each other, but one is always careful to face the other. They turn the corner; conversation briefly stops while they re-orient so the deaf woman is not squinting into the sun as she watches her friend's lips move. They have to navigate sidewalk construction in the process, stepping around large lumps of concrete and debris, after which the hearing woman does not hesitate to pick up the conversation again.

The look on her friend's face stops her immediately. Furrowed brow, blank expression. The friend repeats what she's said, making sure to look directly at the other. Then repeats it again, changing the phrasing in case that particular combination of words is a problem.

The deaf woman gives a slight shake of her head; panic crosses her face. "I can't understand you," she says.

Her friend is soothing; she'll just write it out. Sometimes they have to do that.

"No! You don't get it." The deaf woman's voice rises, her words shaped by many hours of hard practice but still not quite right. People glance their way. "I *can't understand* you—not any of it! I can't see what you're saying! I can't do it anymore!"

Tears stream down her face.

Tears ran down Cordelia's face. She emerged from the vision with the strange conviction that she wouldn't hear her own voice as she said, "This has got to stop!"

"But I thought you chose to have the visions," Fred said. "They aren't hurting you again, are they?"

"Yes!" Cordelia snapped at her, which was hardly fair. She herself should have been more assertive about following up on these visions, but things had been so . . . *strange* lately. "Watching these people lose bits and pieces of themselves when I can't do a thing to stop it? Yes, that hurts!"

Gunn put his ax away, glancing at Wesley's office. Fred, too, looked in that direction, but also at Cordelia. She said, "It's not exactly like we've done a lot to try to figure out whatever's happening."

"What's to do?" Cordelia tossed aside the personal ads and stood, commencing to pace in the small space, then abruptly going for the coffee. "Sure, a girl comes in, can't sing anymore and I saw it happen. But what's it *mean*? And where are we even supposed to start?"

"We've made headway on less," Angel said, suddenly in the conversation. When he'd arrived Cordelia didn't know, except that he was pretty thoroughly mussed. He stood beneath the arch that led to the first floor rooms and the basement, looking grim and dissatisfied.

"And what's that supposed to mean?" she said, a sharper tone than she generally took with Angel, especially when he had that mussed look that meant fighting had happened—even if she had no idea exactly what fighting. She winced inwardly at her own sharpness, because she knew it gave her away in an instant.

So did he. "You know what it means," he said, his voice that remarkably even giving-away-nothing and carrying all the more impact for it. "It means you have to actually try before you can fail."

At this Wesley emerged from the office, taking in Angel's condition; whatever clearly confrontational thing he'd been about to say only made it as far as his lips.

"You should have seen the other guy?" Angel offered.

"Is there a case we should know about?" Wesley asked. Still confrontational after all, in his quiet but intense Wesley way. Cordelia tensed a little. They *all* tensed a little.

Odd thing was, she wasn't sure any of them knew why.

Angel shook his head. "Side-effect of something we're already working on," he said. "Didn't amount to anything."

"Ah," Wesley said. He didn't sound like he

believed it, but also like he didn't care enough to push it . . . because he was back to whatever he'd intended to say in the first place. "Speaking of things we're working on . . . I've been meaning to talk to you about that night a week or so ago."

They all knew which night he meant.

"We haven't really spoken of it directly before," Wesley said. "Preoccupied, I guess."

"That's a fair assessment," Angel said. His tone might have sounded even to anyone else, but Cordelia heard the short quality of it. He crossed the lobby and opened the weapons cabinet, matter-of-factly replacing a handful of antique African throwing knives and removing his jacket to roll up his sleeves and unbuckle the stake rachets.

They were empty.

"The thing is," Wesley said, "for whatever reason, none of us can remember what happened that night. We were hoping . . . you could tell us."

Angel cocked his head slightly, raising one eyebrow ever so slightly. The trouble look. "Do you happen to remember what shape I was in when you finally noticed me?"

"Yeah," Fred said, speaking up with astonishment that reflected her discovery and not much awareness of the tension between Wesley and Angel. "You looked *terrible*. I thought you were dead! Except of course you weren't dust. But I didn't think of that just at first."

Wesley waited for her to realize Angel hadn't been addressing her, which only took a moment; abashed, she put a hand to her mouth and said, "I'm going to sit down over here if anyone needs me. Not that you might, but just in case, you know—," and once more stopped herself. She sat down on the spot, still in front of the bookshelf.

And Wesley said, "My memory's spotty, I'm afraid. But I recall enough."

"I had a concussion," Angel pointed out, apparently just in case Wesley did not, in fact, recall enough. "You asked me once before about that night and I told you I couldn't tell you anything. That hasn't changed."

"Can't," Wesley said softly. And then he straightened, taking a deep breath. "I'm afraid I'm not sure I believe that. I'm afraid . . . I think you might be keeping things from us."

"Can't," said Angel. "Won't. It's the same in the end."

"Doesn't seem right," Gunn said. He leaned against the reception desk, arms crossed, eyes half-lidded. "You know what happened to us after that night. We healed, just like you do. Just like you *normally* do. I almost get the feeling you don't want us to have that."

"I think," Angel said, with that low and danger-ous voice and that low and dangerous brow that al-ways reminded Cordelia, quite suddenly, that he could be where he wanted, when he wanted. "I think," he said, "that you're all acting strangely and that while I trust the people I know, I'm not sure I know you right now."

Fred made a little sound in her throat. It might have been a gulp; it might have been a breathy, *"Oh dear."*

"KLUUUBP-CHOO!"

Cordelia jumped. Big. With one hand to her pounding chest, she pinned her severest glare on the perpetrator of the sneeze. As far as she could tell, everyone else in the lobby was doing the same—except for Angel, of course, who wouldn't have been taken unaware and now calmly closed the weapons cabinet.

Lorne looked down at them all from the balcony, wincing at his reception. "Maybe now's not a good time," he said. "I'll just come back later. When the air waves aren't set to *fry,* for instance." And he eased on down the hall a few steps, then turned and made a hastier escape.

Angel headed for the stairs. If the conversation hadn't been over, it was certainly over now. Cordelia glanced at Wesley. He'd pushed pretty hard, and he hadn't gotten much for it; the frustration of it showed on his face.

She couldn't blame him.

There was nothing more obstreperously evasive than Angel when Angel wasn't talking. The trick was . . . knowing what he wasn't talking about. *Not always what you think it is.*

From the floor, Fred said tentatively, "I was going to read to—"

"Later," Angel said, not even looking over his shoulder as he mounted the stairs.

"But . . . I—"

"Later."

And that, thought Cordelia, was that. Another afternoon of not discovering the reason behind her visions, not getting any closer to learning what had happened to them That Night, and certainly not having the faintest idea how to recapture the healing effect.

Definitely not having a clue what was up with Angel.

"Could you have been any more subtle than that?" Angel said, hearing the exasperation in his own voice, knowing it showed in the way he threw his arms up. "Kluubp-choo? I mean . . . is there even the slightest bit of subtlety in that?"

Lorne seemed not the least affected by Angel's reaction as he led the way to the room beyond Angel's. "Now, Angelcakes, they didn't suspect a thing. It's not like they know there's a Yoda-clone named Kluubp wandering freely in and out of the hotel, is there?" His voice held a hint of accusation as he gestured at the door. "I thought best not to put him in your room, since the others are here. And clearly the roof is out."

Until sunset, at least.

"Yeah," Angel said, grudgingly approving. "Though it's not like I can't have visitors now and then, you know."

"Right, right," Lorne said. "Because it happens so often."

"I could hurt you," Angel said, suggestion in his voice.

Lorne chose not to acknowledge this with more than a wave of his hand. He opened the door himself and invited himself in. "Judging from what I just saw down there, I think it's time I knew more about whatever's going on here."

Losing my menacing touch, Angel thought. *Have to work on that.* Out loud he said, "There's only one problem with that—"

And Kluubp finished, "You can't tell anyone." He sat propped against the headboard, his short legs folded beneath the robe and his fingers intertwined over his belly in the most imaginable Wise Master pose possible. Except for the half-eaten bag of Doritos beside him and the orange seasoning dust on his fingers, he might even have pulled it off.

"Oh please," Lorne said. "What's my avocation? I read minds. If I couldn't keep secrets, I'd be dead by now."

"You read minds?" Angel said, suddenly uneasy. He closed the door behind them. "I thought you could only get . . . you know, the gist of it . . . the whole nebulous future thing."

Lorne shrugged, adjusting the fall of his jacket. "Define it how you want to. The point being, I'm not going to squeal on you and your stature-challenged friend here."

"He's not my friend," Angel said, giving Kluubp a hard look. "In fact, the only thing I can say for sure about him is that he's causing trouble between me and the people I *do* consider to be my friends."

"If you thought they could handle it, you would have told them by now," Kluubp said, a little too confidently to be diplomatic.

And dammit, he was right.

"So you're here to . . . what? Rub my nose in that? That my friends are human and they get hurt and they don't like it? That they're afraid of what might happen to them when they go out to fight dark things in dark places? Because I'm pretty much on their side when it comes to that."

"No, I find all that irrelevant right now," Kluubp said.

"Good, because it's getting tiresome." Angel crossed his arms and leaned back against the door. "Just what *is* relevant? Because I haven't spent enough quality time with my son today, and I'm really getting tired of these sneaky little conversations."

"I need your help," Kluubp said, simply enough. His ears gave away his anxiety, shifting forward.

"Don't tell me," Lorne said. "He's your only hope."

Kluubp gave Lorne a sour look. "If you must put it that way." He belched discreetly, a bare hiccup covered with his hand, and briefly eyed the Doritos bag. "In truth, in spite of my intense need for secrecy, I suppose I could hunt out another demon with the strength to help—but not many of them have souls, feel personal responsibility, or have set themselves up as champions for the Powers That Be."

It was Angel's turn to look annoyed. "Was that in your guide, too?"

"No," Kluubp said, quite prim. "It is on the streets. Now, do you care to listen to my dilemma?"

Angel gave him a mildly sarcastic by-all-means gesture, and wondered if the ache in his recently broken ribs was real, or merely inspired by the moment.

"I found the Giflatl," Kluubp said, more concisely than was characteristic. Truly tense.

Truly needing help.

"Good," Angel said, not feeling so helpful. Caught up, instead, in what this had done to the Hyperion family and in his own personal challenges. *Getting over this . . . fear, running around looking for trouble to do it.* "Take it back to your home, where it can provide your people with the sun screen you need. With my blessing. Was that it?"

"The beast has grown strong here in its native environment, with prey so thick on the ground," Kluubp said, pretty much ignoring the comment. At Angel's surprise, he added dryly, "Surely you knew it wasn't merely strewing body parts around the sewers for the scavengers. No predator can be so wasteful of its energy."

"No, right," Angel said quickly. "I mean, I knew that."

"In any event, I . . . can no longer vanquish it with the—hmmm, let's call it a *net*—I brought for that purpose."

"So you need muscle."

"Yes. As much as I regret the need, the Giflatl must be killed."

Angel gave him a long stare, under which Kluubp seemed not the least bit uncomfortable. Finally he said flatly, "You and me. Alone. Kill the creature that nearly shredded me into many tiny little pieces and then defeated my four friends and romped off without-out a scratch."

"Do you think your friends will help us, if they know what the Giflatl is?"

Angel didn't hesitate. "No."

"And are you willing to lie to them outright about its nature, to lure them into the fight?"

"No."

Kluubp shrugged, as if that said it all.

I suppose it pretty much does.

Perhaps not quite all. Kluubp added, "By the way, it's about to spawn. If we don't do this soon, there'll be a whole colony of them to deal with."

Can it get any better?

"Let me see if I have this straight," Lorne said. "Seeing as I'm so good at reading between the lines. You"—he pointed at Kluubp—"are trying to rid the area of the very creature who not so long ago turned our resident warrior into mysteriously non-healing mincemeat, and you want *him*—remembering the mincemeat part here—to help. Meanwhile, our human pals downstairs have been frantic and uncharacteristically obsessed for same said creature, rightly convinced that it holds the key to their rapid healing. Plus, of course, its apparent ability to churn out endless quantities of snot."

"Most humans wouldn't have remembered any part of the encounter," Kluubp said crossly. It's only because your friends have such vast experience with demonkind in the first place, not to mention their extensive battle experience."

"I'll take that as a yes," Lorne said. He looked like he'd be more comfortable with a drink in his hand—for prop as opposed to the actual liquid—but he persevered, and he had that look in his red eyes that Angel had grown to respect. The one that every once in a while made it clear Lorne was not, deep down, entirely defined by the pussycat persona he showed to the world. "But you know, munchkin, you never did actually say it. You took my words, but you didn't say it. Angel *isn't* your only hope, is he?"

Ah? Nice catch, Lorne.

Kluubp looked back at Lorne with a sudden bloom of grumpiness. *Or maybe it's just gas,* Angel thought, startling himself. Having a baby on hand . . . talk about unexpected side-effects of thought.

"He's my *best* hope," Kluubp said, unfolding his legs beneath the robe in such a manner that Angel suddenly wondered just how many joints he had. He stood in the middle of the bed, and was still shorter than either Lorne or Angel.

"But you have something else you can try," Lorne said, still implacable. "So before you put Angel in this position, try it."

"It's noisy." Kluubp's ears flattened so thoroughly as to change the shape of his head into a giant ovoid. An ovoid with prissy, annoyed features. "It could attract attention."

"If it's successful, what will it matter?" Lorne asked. He took a step closer to the keeper and looked down. "Do it."

"Huh," Angel said. "So this is what it's like to have someone stick up for you."

"Don't get too comfortable with it," Lorne

suggested as an aside without breaking his stare-down with Kluubp. "I'm sure something will come along any moment to make it but a distant memory."

Angel said to Kluubp, "Try your second best thing. If that doesn't work, then we'll talk. Until then . . . I have other things to do."

Kluubp did look away from Lorne then, and straight to Angel. "You will not find your courage on the streets," he said. "You will only find it where you lost it." He walked to the edge of the bed, hopped to the floor with little loss of dignity or hesitation in stride, and left the room.

Lorne glanced at Angel. "Don't let it bother you," he said, shaking his head. "He's obviously taking that Yoda thing far too seriously."

"It's not bothering me," Angel said.

But it was.

CHAPTER NINE

"Yes!" Wesley muttered to himself within the office, audible in both the reception area where Cordelia paged through demon resources, and within the lobby where Fred did the same. For the first time they both worked on the demon from Cordelia's visions.

"I've got it!" Charles burst into the lobby from the courtyard entrance and bounded down the stairs with his usual manly display of physical authority. Definitely audible in the office, reception area, and lobby . . . and probably several floors up.

Fred glanced over at Cordelia and exchanged the slightest of shrugs. Cordelia said, "Work it out, boys—who wants to go first?"

"The scavengers—"

"The clean tunnels!"

"I'm not sure it matters who goes first," Fred took the pencil that had been between her teeth and stuck it behind her ear as she set aside *Specialism in Demons and Other Elder Life Forms (Enhanced Version, Employment Records Through the Centuries)*. She'd started off looking under parasitism and found it too limited to demons who literally attached themselves to a host, and had gone on to perusing the index with the theory that if you didn't know what you were looking *for*, sometimes it was good to see what you had to look *at*. So far, nothing, but it was an extensive index and she'd only been at it for an hour. She looked at Charles and smiled slightly. *Man of action.* "Given that you're both talking about the same thing as far as I can tell."

Wesley appeared in the office doorway, glasses in place and book in hand. "I've found a symbiotic scavenger, very ratlike. Only a hint of a reference, but it does exist—and now that I've got a start, I know what to focus on. If those scavengers have anything to do with our experience and whatever demon caused it, I should be able to track it through them."

"Never mind the book way," Charles said. "Grab yourself some weapons."

Wesley pulled off his glasses, hesitating before he folded them. "What did you have in mind?"

"You know, I *am* finally getting somewhere with the visions," Cordelia pointed out. "Okay, maybe only 'somewhere' as defined by eliminating possibilities, but at least I'm working on it. Don't you think I ought to stay working on it? You know, before the Powers brighten my day with another vision of someone's life being ruined? Besides, we took money."

Charles assumed his most stubborn expression, stiff through the shoulders. "Look, if I'm right about this, then we can tackle whatever it is that you're after without any worries of coming out of it all scathed."

"I'm not sure it'll be that simple," Wesley said, and this time he did fold his glasses. "But . . . I'm all ears."

"This part *is* simple," Charles said. "We should have seen it before. Or not seen it. You remember that spot we're so sure we hit the night all the strangeness happened . . . the one that was all Mr. Clean the next time we went there."

"Of course," Fred said. "We all do." And then thought maybe she'd spoken out of turn considering the wacky nature of their memories during the past week and more, but no one spoke up to correct her.

"Well, what if we *were* there, and it was a mess? So maybe something came along and cleaned it up, just like the other clean spots we found. Some kind of demony carrion beetle."

"You've been watching *CSI*," Fred said, impressed.

But Wesley didn't hear her; he almost spoke right over her. "Of course. So if the carrion demons come along where the other has been, then we can map its presence by locating the clean spots. We don't need to know what it is at all to find it again, and once we find it we can discern what it is."

"Exactly my point," Charles said. Then he frowned a little and added, "Though I don't think I would have said 'discerned,' exactly."

"So . . ." Fred cast a glance at her interrupted research. "You want us to go look for clean spots."

"Lorne's watching the baby, isn't he?" Wesley said, glancing up at the stairs as though child care issues were the only possible obstacles. He ducked back into his office, returning an instant later with the headlamp.

"He is," Fred confirmed, and thought she should say something about Cordelia's visions and the need to follow through on them. But not even remembered courage from the week before allowed her to speak up, not when Wesley and Charles both had such intent expressions.

Even as she hesitated, Cordelia turned the computer monitor off. "I'm not getting anywhere here. Maybe a break will clear my head." She glanced around the lobby. "Where's Angel?"

It was true, Fred thought—if Angel had been in the hotel, he'd have heard the conversation and he'd be nearby—ready to join them or talk them out of it, although in this case she wasn't sure which. She said quietly, "I think I'll stay here. Lorne said something about going out later on, and it's not fair to just assume he'll be here."

Wes gave her a nod, but his focus remained on Cordelia's question. "We don't need Angel, Cordelia."

"He's off bar-hopping, isn't he?" Charles said. "He's been strange lately, anyway."

"We've *all* been strange lately," Cordelia said, as blunt as usual.

"No matter," Wesley said shortly. "We'll do fine on our own." And he led the way out of the lobby.

The vampire leaping at Angel had a knife.

He held it low and dirty—*really* dirty, encrusted with dried gore—and he held it badly, in a fencer's grip.

It didn't matter. *If there's a knife in the fight, you're going to get cut.*

Not so long ago, that wouldn't have fazed him. Meet the guy head on, take the cuts, disarm him, and take care of him. Now, even though he knew he'd heal . . . even though he'd done this any number of times in the past few days, tracking down bar-stalking vamps, meeting them head on, taking care of them . . . now he still felt that moment's fear. *What if.*

Angel as a human had never dealt with these

moments of facing demons. Gunn did it all the time. Wesley did it. Cordelia was learning, and Fred picked up that crossbow even when she shook in doing it.

None of them has a son. Particularly not a son who was a constant target simply because of his lineage.

Angel waited till the vamp—a particularly crusty fellow, the vampire version of a short-lived, barely sane street person—charged in close, a no-nonsense, no-frills thrust at Angel's neck. With his mind full of Connor and responsibility and fear, Angel's explosive response came from centuries of conflict and battle. He slapped one hand inside the vamp's elbow and snatched the vamp's wrist with the other. The elbow bent, reversing the knife's path without losing any of the momentum; Angel held the elbow, pivoting in to control the angle of the knife. The vamp impaled himself, losing his grip on the knife in the process. Angel yanked it out and threw it aside.

The vamp looked down at his bloody abdomen and made a whining noise, a noise that said, *That's not fair.* He looked up just in time to see the stake coming.

Only when the dust sifted to the ground did Angel realize where he was. The back door of the bar, a new lock but the same door, still bearing the gouges where Kate Lockley had shot her way through to chase the possessed bartender, Angel beside her. She hadn't realized then what he was, or even what she'd truly been fighting. Just a cop, doing her job.

D'oblique, that was the name of the place.

Coincidence to be here?

He wasn't sure. Early evening prowl, looking for street predators of the fanged kind . . . he'd seen the raggedy vamp going after a street person so layered in rags he didn't even know if the victim had been man or woman. That person was long gone, now, leaving Angel here with his victory and his memories.

Kate Lockley. Eventually she'd figured out his nature. . . . But not until she'd lost too much to deal with it. He never saw Kate anymore. He didn't even know if she'd ever gotten her life back together.

Doyle. Doyle had been here, Irish street gambler in full brogue, on a mission to reconnect Angel to humanity, and to guide the baby steps of Angel's quest for redemption. Visions, half-Bracken demon ancestry, street smarts . . . Doyle had been the perfect guide. Until he'd died, leaving Cordelia with the visions and Angel not nearly redeemed enough.

There was no redemption, Angel knew that now. There was no making up for what he'd been or what he'd done. There was only the mission. The one Doyle died for, the one that had driven him away from Buffy not once but twice. The one that had grabbed up an unwitting Kate and shaken her like a rat, leaving her too wounded to carry on. The one that had almost killed Cordelia with visions her human body had been unable to withstand, and to which Cordelia had clung so grimly that she was now partly—in a still undefined way—demon.

Yet compared to Connor, all of that was nothing.

Not that it changed anything. Angel would deal with the fear. He'd put himself on the line until it no longer threatened to cripple him in every confrontation. For in spite of what he'd told the others, he knew the fear was a weakness that Angelus—now healed and healthy—would find a way to exploit. Sooner or later, he'd find the right moment . . . and he'd take it.

And in the meantime, the last thing on Angel's list of things to do was confronting the Giflatl again.

And in the meantime . . .

He just hoped he could say the same of his friends.

"Think of the good we could do!" Wesley made a notation on his hand-made diagram of known sewers and tunnels, the light from his headlamp bobbing against the page. "If we can track down the creature we engaged that night and get samples of whatever substance affected our healing rate . . . we might even be able to synthesize it. Who knows what ailments it might cure!"

"Demon-induced ailments," Gunn said. He crouched in the middle of the sewer, machete resting across his thighs as he gazed down the length of one astonishingly clean concrete pipe. "That's a very good start as far as I'm concerned."

"This place wasn't this clean when they first poured the concrete," Cordelia said, disbelieving. "This must be fresh. If it weren't, the nastiness would already be oozing through to take its natural place in the sewer scheme of things."

"I agree. We may not be far from our target at all."

"It's the third clean spot we've come across. I don't suppose your keenly analytical mind has found any pattern to the locations?"

"Mmm." Wes considered the diagram, shook his head—and stopped himself, as the light painted dizzying trails across the paper and the ground alike. "Not yet."

Cordelia said suddenly, "What about the goofy juice?"

"How's that?" Wesley looked over at her, remembering just in time to avert his head and use a peripheral gaze.

"You know what she means," Gunn said. "The my-aren't-we-stupid that came along with whatever happened to us. A whole night's memory, gone, and days of suddenly turning into too much of a good thing. Never thought I'd say that about myself, mind you, but there it was. I left Fred and Connor alone on the street because I was too full of myself to know better. That's one memory I wish I *didn't* have."

"And I went to auditions for *everything*," Cordelia said. "Even cat litter! Definitely not in my right mind for that one. And you—! Your nose buried in a book all the time, so totally obsessing on researching this creature that—"

She broke off suddenly; Wesley raised an eyebrow at her, hard to see with the lamp headband but she knew it was there. Undeterred she said, "No, wait. That's pretty much just normal for you, isn't it?"

"That might well be," Wesley said, "but rarely at quite that level of fervency. Your point is well made—there was obviously something about the encounter that left us unable to function normally for days. However, we don't know it had anything to do with the factor that allowed us to heal. And even if it does, that doesn't mean it will be impossible to alter that facet of the process."

"Angel wasn't affected like that," Cordelia mused, moving to the limits of the clean section.

Wesley finished making his notations and followed her, still looking at the paper. "We've already determined that whatever did happen, it affects demons and humans differently. As for Angel . . ." he looked up and straight at her, tipping his head-lamp up to bounce off the upper curve of the tun-nel. "He's as much as said he knows something he's not telling us. And I'm beginning to think Lorne knows too. There's been one too many significant glances between them lately."

Gunn brought up the rear, machete back down by his side. "Definitely back in yucky sewer terri-tory," he said. "And I'll bet Angel wouldn't be so secretive if it was *him* who got healed, instead of the other way around. He takes that whole thing for granted. He takes *us* for granted."

Cordelia didn't like the direction this particular conversation seemed determined to take. "We came out here to map tunnels, not engage in girly locker-room gossip—and when it comes to girly locker-room gossip, I should know. Was I not the queen at Sunnydale High?"

"Hey," Gunn said sharply. "Watch your mouth. Girly locker-room gossip, my manly—"

Wesley made a hasty interruption. "I see your point," he told Cordelia. "But it doesn't change my suspicions."

Cordelia had hit the point of exasperation. "Well, maybe he's got his own fears, you know?"

Gunn pushed on past them, leading the way into the next section of tunnel—a thoroughly filthy sec-tion. "I know he's your friend and all, and you don't want to hear this . . . but listen to the man, Cordy. Angel's not being straight with us. He's playing the demon interests instead of the human interests."

It stung Cordelia to hear it said so baldly. "He wouldn't!"

"No," Wesley agreed. "He wouldn't. Not like that. But he's playing *something*. Of that I'm certain."

With that, she couldn't argue.

Another tunnel, another clean spot. Well, clean-*ish*. Already returning to its natural state of ick. "Probably a day old or so," Wesley said, marking his diagram. "I do believe . . ."

Cordelia never heard the remainder of his sentence. She found herself looking at lizards. Not demon lizards, but real ones—not that she knew which kind, because, *ew*, but they were behind glass-fronted cages; and then she saw *tropical birds fluttering in the background, pet toys and collars lining the walls, cat play trees and even some kittens, their mouths open but no audible sound. No mewing, no shrieking birds, just weird silence in a pet shop . . .*

Until she heard a haunting, beautiful sound—a lyrical humming, not as part of the scene but in an overlay.

"Our voiceless girl has something to do with a pet shop?" she blurted, abruptly seeing the dim, slick sewer again, not to mention smelling its smell.

"You've had a vision," Wesley said. He was watching her, so was Gunn.

Cordelia suddenly felt like one of those lizards, being watched behind glass. With a crabbiness not behooving the new pain-free version of Vision Girl, she said, "With deductive reasoning like that, we'll have this solved in no time. *Yes*, I had a vision. It was a pet store. Wait, I even saw the name—" In the background, backward on the front glass. "Pet Scrape."

"That's what *I'd* name a pet store," Gunn agreed, sarcasm so dry as to be barely evident.

"Give me a break. It's backward. And we need a phone book—for the first time we've got a chance of being there. Maybe we can figure out what's going on . . . help that girl." *And all those other people I've been seeing.*

"Pet*scape*," Gunn said suddenly. "Skip the yellow pages—I know where that is. They have those cute rabbits, you know, the little ones with the droopy ears and the soft—"

Cordelia raised an eyebrow at him.

"—whatever," he said, hastily. "Hey, you wanna waste time giving me the eye, or do you want to go catch this whatever it is doing whatever it does? 'Cause it's this way." He nodded at the direction in which they'd come, and started off that way.

Cordelia reached for her cell phone, deep in the pocket of the sporty raincoat she'd learned to wear on sewer duty. "I'll call—"

"We don't need him," Wesley said, making no attempt to hide the abrupt nature of the interruption. He'd been like since That Night: Driven. Impatient. And especially impatient with the one person he blamed for impeding his work. "Supposing he somehow actually has his own cell phone turned on, he's no doubt in the middle of whatever it is he's been doing. And none of your visions has shown either a vicious demon or violence, so I think we can handle things just fine on our own. It's not like we didn't manage on our own when he pushed us out of his life the last time."

"This isn't like that at all!" Cordelia said. And it wasn't. Then, he'd fired them. Flat-out fired them. Driven them away for their own safety, though not a reason he'd shared with them at the time. Now . . . now was different. "Besides, if I remember right, *managing on our own* meant you getting shot."

"I haven't forgotten," Wesley said tightly.

But Cordelia left the phone in her pocket and followed Gunn through the sewers.

A darkened apartment building in a nasty part of town. A car full of people pulling up to the curb.

Young men disembarking first to assist wobbly young women to their feet. One of them said woozily, "Did you . . . something in my drink?"

Not what Angel had been hunting, but monsters nonetheless. He crouched on a sagging second floor balcony of the equally dingy apartments across the street, poised for the effortless jump to the street below.

Someone beat him to it.

One of the young men gave a startled shout into the shadows; the next moment he flew through the air to slam against the side of the car. The girl he'd been escorting sank quietly to the ground, not protesting even when someone—some*thing*—picked her up and lurched back for the shadows.

The second young man hesitated, glancing between his dazed buddy, the girl against his shoulder, and the figures in retreat. He settled for yelling, "Hey!" in an offended tone of voice.

"The word "pathetic" mean anything to you?" Angel asked, having made the distance from the balcony to the other side of the street in that turn of the head. He popped the guy on the chin with carefully measured strength, easing the girl to the cracked and crumbling sidewalk even as her "escort" folded. Into the shadows he went, not nearly so dense to him as to human eyes, and in an instant caught up with the interloper vampire. The smell of blood was fresh and strong, and for a moment Angel thought he was too late . . .

But the smell of blood wasn't *hot*.

"Hey, cut me a break," the injured vampire whined. "I didn't mean to step out on your turf. I'm desperate, man. I need blood. Just give me this one girl and I won't be back, I swear."

"Also pathetic," Angel said. But he was close enough to see what he'd smelled, that the vampire was slashed and bleeding . . . that there was enough blood present to indicate he'd *been* bleeding—and not healing.

The Giflatl was getting around. Whatever Kluubp had tried, he'd failed. And that meant the keeper would be back, asking the impossible of Angel. To risk himself when Connor depended so greatly on him. To betray his friends—more than he already had.

He appropriated the girl and propped her up against the red bricks of the building. Stake in hand, he looked at the lurching vamp's hopeful expression and muttered, "This is going to hurt you a lot more than it hurts me."

This time.

Fred eased down the hall, the thick copy of the watcher book tucked under her arm. *I'm so not sure about this*. A few feet from Angel's door, she hesitated. *Notsure, notsure, notsure,* a little monotonal inner hum. Then she turned herself around and went into blatant tip-toe mode.

Lorne's voice filtered through the door. "Come on in, charmbug," he said. "You might as well. I know you're there."

Fred stopped in her tracks, her embarrassment quickly replaced by a swelling indignation. "How'd you—," she said to the door. "That's not fair!"

The door opened to Lorne at his most charming—shockingly blue-on-blue patterned smoking jacket with wide silk cuffs and lapels over bright pink slacks and scuffed up fuzzy slip-ons. He beheld her with a wry resignation. "I'll say it's not fair," he told her. "The baby's asleep, I'm watching a reality show that seems to be entirely based on buns of steel, and you come along emoting your 'notsure' at me?" He rubbed his temple with one finger, making a pained face. "And don't tell me you're all twisted up over which fascinating chapter to read to Connor."

Fred glanced down at the book in surprise. "No," she said, as frankly honest as was her wont. "The book is only an excuse. I really came up to talk to you."

Lorne rolled his eyes in what could only have been the world's loudest silent *duh*, and opened the door wider. "But not out in the hallway, bedbug. Or am I wrong? That if you'd wanted to talk to me where the others would know, you wouldn't have waited for them to leave?"

"Not wrong," Fred mumbled. "And I *am* going to read to Connor."

"Of course you are. Would you like something to drink?" He plucked a short, stout glass from its coaster atop a stack of books and waved it in her direction. "It was a very good year for potatoes."

"No, thanks." Fred perched on the edge of a leather-covered chair in the public area of Angel's two rooms, glancing in at the crib in the bedroom. Connor slept. "You really don't mind this?" she asked.

"Mind that you've come up to talk to me? I'm not sure yet. Mind that everyone around here is behaving as if they're one lick short of the Tootsie Roll center of a Tootsie Pop? I'll get back to you on that one."

Fred gave a quiet shake of her head, and then looked over at Connor. "Mind that you seem to get stuck with the baby-sitting all the time. Half the time no one even asks, do they?"

"As a matter of fact, no. 'Taken for granted' is my middle name. Except for one thing." He leaned back in the chair, regarding her with scrutiny until she wanted to slink right off her seat and out the door. "Angel and I have an agreement. I figure . . . when you're a big broody guy in a truly smokin' leather duster, and when your job is rushing off to save the world at a moment's notice, you've got to have a built-in child-care system. Someone you can trust to be there. And since I *am* staying here, my own humble domicile having once more been devastated by the forces of evil, or at the least the forces of stupidity, that would be me. I have my own little moments, but only when I know for certain that one of you is here to watch the little guy. You know . . . here in a *reliable* way." He stepped up the intensity of his scrutinizing expression . . . right over the line into accusing. "I can't say as I've been moved to ask any of you lately."

Fred sat quietly for a moment, then heaved a big sigh. "I can see why," she said, but didn't add anything to it.

After a moment of that silence, Lorne swirled the ice cubes in his drink and said, "So what can I do for you, ladybug?"

"Bugs," Fred muttered. "I suppose that's better than pastries. But I'm not sure."

Lorne affected to be confused by the comment, but she knew better. He had so many dessert names for Angel that the rest of them had quietly begun to keep track—spotting a new one meant not chipping in for the next pizza.

Fred said, "I could sing for you, I suppose—"

"Except that would mean *me* doing all the work. Not so inclined, cupcake."

He'd done the dessert thing on purpose, she was sure. But she wasn't to be deterred at this point, so she said in a rush, "I think you and Angel know something the rest of us don't know, or at least have hints about something the rest of us don't know, and I think it's causing trouble between us, but that would be okay if it was one of those truly important secrets, like if human ears hear it they burst into flame, but I did want to ask, at least to find out for sure if it's a noble secret or just a selfish secret or if it's a demons versus humans secret which wouldn't be good at all—"

Lorne gestured her to a sudden stop. "And you wanted me to read that? Cruelty, thy name is Fred!"

Fred gave an abashed shrug. "I thought maybe you could read it simpler than I could say it. . . ."

"And no doubt you were right. Still. You might as well stop right there, because I'm not going to be Lorne-in-the-middle, the understanding empathy demon who makes things all right with everyone's feelings. If you people have a problem with something, talk it out amongst yourselves."

"You *do* know," Fred said with some satisfaction. "And not because you're the understanding empathy demon. Just because you *know*."

"I don't know anything," Lorne said. "Because quite truthfully, the more I hear, the less I actually know. There's only one thing I can tell you that might do any good, and while you might listen, right now there are other people frequenting this hotel that probably won't." But of course he hesitated, eyeing her.

Fred felt like she was being measured for something. Finally she said, "There's no telling when the others will get back, you know."

"And that's part of the problem, isn't it?" he responded. "Everyone off doing their own little obsessive thing . . ."

"Lo-orne . . ." Fred gave him her most beseeching look.

"I'll tell you this," he said, and looked straight at her over the drink in his hand, "Angel's doing what's best for all of you and not necessarily what's best for him. But then . . . that's not news, is it?"

"No," Fred agreed softly. "That's pretty much the way it is, when you stop to think about it." And she went in to read to Connor.

Crammed into its hiding place, the lumpy little demon watches the humans leave. Just plain silly humans, they are. Nothing worth taking from that bunch. The demon is not here for them; it is here to keep an eye on the larger one. The one that has killed so many, and is still killing.

A sudden shout comes from the direction of the large demon's lair. Not a human left behind; a strange double-throated voice this demon hasn't heard before. With all its meager courage, it emerges from its security and eases down the tunnels. Is being double-throated an advantage in any way? With two throats, would the recently acquired voice talent be doubled? A tempting thought.

But the voice rises from agitation to near-panic, and a sudden wash of intense blue light wooshes through the tunnels like cerulean flame. The lumpy demon does a hasty and awkward backpedal, its little arms pumping as it wobbles around to run turns to flee. The light washes harmlessly over it, but whatever the double-throated creature meant to do has failed; the angry roar of the big killer demon washes through the tunnels on the heels of the light. Healthy, angry, and undeterred.

Wisely, the lumpy little demon flees.

"Was I right?" Gunn said, gesturing at the Petscape door.

"This looks like the place," Cordy agreed, checking out the brightly lit plate-glass window of the downscale petshop. The fully exposed interior showed her most of the things from her vision, as well as tanks full of multi-legged creatures and rodent-faced things with which she wasn't keen on getting up close and personal.

"No, I mean the bunnies," Gunn said, gesturing at the window display of Mini Lops. Then he straightened slightly, giving them both a narrow-eyed look. "Just being observant."

"Right," Cordelia said, not bothering to sound convinced as she reached for the door. "Let's go see what we've got. Oh, and Wesley? Dorky headlamp?"

Wesley jerked the lamp from his head, unaware that it had left an impression on his forehead. Cordelia fought the impulse to rub it out with a finger and let herself into the pet shop.

A cheerful jingle of bells announced their entrance. Cordelia moved cautiously within the shop, but thought that knocking something off the closely spaced shelves was an inevitability. Her suspicions were quickly confirmed as one of the guys muttered, "Whoops," and she pretended she hadn't heard it as she smiled at the woman behind the sales counter. The woman, a large person with long stringy hair and an overworked expression, seemed to realize they had little potential as customers. She smiled back but said in a smoker's husky voice, "We close in a few minutes."

"Whoops!" Definitely Wesley this time, and Cordelia turned to find him hastily picking up a spill of fish food boxes.

"Yes," she muttered, "any demons in the area are on the run for sure."

"Just—," he said, and couldn't seem to find quite the right words as he finished repairing the damage and stood. He finally settled for, "Keep an eye out."

"Uh-huh." Cordelia walked the long narrow aisle, looking for something—anything—that might look specifically visiony. It was all familiar, but only vaguely so. None of the sharp, startling awareness that came when she saw real life exactly repeating a vision. Here were the tropical birds, there were the snakes, over there were a bunch of lizards, including one with a head that looked familiar—although she couldn't have said why, and she didn't think it had anything to do with the vision. She caught Wesley's eye; he joined her by the rows of glass-fronted cages. Gunn continued to prowl the part of the store suspiciously close to the rabbits.

"Ah," Wesley said. "A chameleon. I don't know which species." He lowered his voice. "Was it in your vision?"

She shook her head. "No, it just looked . . ."

"They *are* odd-looking," he said, assuming the wrong thing. "The way their eyes move . . . and of course their ability to match their color to their environment is fascinating."

She would have corrected him—never an opportunity to pass up—but she heard the faintest of glorious sounds, only snatches between the chatter of the finches in the corner but a few effortless notes Cordelia recognized in an instant. The singing girl's voice—apparently out wandering around without her. She grabbed Wesley's arm, getting his instant attention but absolutely no understanding. "Don't you hear it? The singing?"

"Yes, but I thought—" He glanced at the shop-keeper.

Cordelia moved in close, dropping her voice into the discreet but insistent range. "Two-packs-a-day there couldn't do more than croak those notes if she even tried. Say, if her mouth were *open*. That's the voice I heard in my vision of the girl. You know, the one who doesn't have that voice at all, not any-more? We are definitely in the right place."

"Still with no idea what we're looking for."

"No, but—" Cordelia stopped short, for that mo-ment suddenly caught up in the realness of the vi-sion, the intense déjà vu warning that told her their time was running out. And when she blinked and came back to the pet shop, she found herself looking at the lizard cage. "Wasn't that thing green-ish a moment ago?"

"Yes," Wesley said, somewhat impatiently and without looking, "but as I said, they change."

She crossed her arms, nodding at the cage.

This time, he looked. The chameleon blinked back at him with its independently swiveling eyes and no apparent awareness of the fact that it was now pure white. "That does seem a little extreme," he admitted.

Gunn eased up the aisle and looked over Wesley's

shoulder. "Damn," he said, somewhat admiring. "That's one white lizard."

The shopkeeper's head came up. "We don't have any white lizards," she said. "No one has any white lizards—unless it's an albino, of course." She heaved herself off her stool and came out from behind the counter, much more adept than any of them had been at avoiding the precarious merchandise. They moved out of the way for her, and she stopped a little short in her astonishment, quickly turning an accusing look on them. "What'd you do to him?"

"Do to him?" Cordelia repeated blankly. "From here? With what?" *Good question. Something stole a voice. Something seems to be able to steal just about anything, including color.*

"Maybe he's ill?" Wesley suggested, with the tone of someone who knows it's not true but wishes it were.

Gunn suddenly caught on. "You mean this used to be a lizard of color?"

"A lizard of many colors, actually," Wesley said. "A very useful skill."

The woman narrowed her eyes at them, as if still convinced that they had somehow affected the little creature, although the chameleon itself looked content enough on its branch, white or not. "I think it's time for you to leave now," she said, and looked as if she might grab the nearest object— and for menacing purposes.

"Just going," Wesley agreed, ushering Cordelia toward the door.

Normally she would have protested, but now . . .

A very useful skill. So was everything else that she'd seen in her visions. Athletic ability and expertise, lipreading . . . okay, she wasn't so sure about the singing, but it was pretty, and who wouldn't covet a voice like that?

But then she stumbled, going past a rack of basted, elongated dog treats. "Ew!" she said. "Do you know what that *is*?"

"Yes, but the dogs don't and the bulls are already dead so they don't miss it," Wesley said quickly, righting her and helping her right on out the door. The moment Gunn emerged behind them, the door closed with some force and the lock tumbled audibly into place.

"Damn," said Gunn. "Gonna have to find a new place."

"Right under our noses," Wesley said, glancing back into the shop.

"Don't I know it," Cordelia said. "We finally followed a vision and we *still* couldn't do anything about what happened. We don't even really know what happened!"

"We know more than we did," Wesley said with some assurance.

"We know that if the thing we're after steals color, I don't want to get anywhere near it." Gunn led the way back toward the hotel, and glanced back to make sure they were listening. "I'm not kidding about this, people."

Cordelia tripped over something, and turned back to frown. Nothing. She'd tripped over nothing. *Then why do my toes still sting?* But . . . nothing.

Or something she hadn't been able to see. Something camouflaged.

"Did you know," Wesley said, his tone casual enough both to alert Gunn and distract Cordelia from her painful toes, "that 'Gunn' is a Scottish name meaning 'white'?"

Gunn recoiled. "Now you're just being mean."

"It's true," Wesley assured him.

Scowling, Gunn took a few backward steps as he spoke, only long enough to say, "Man, I do not even *want* to know you right now." He reversed track, walking away from them and then cutting off across the street. "We're through for the night anyway. Later."

"Were we?" Wesley said. "I had the feeling we were just getting started."

"Never mind," Cordelia said. "Unlike some of us, he actually knows how to answer his cell phone. If something comes up, we can reach him. Right now, I'm more about me."

Wesley gave her a querying glance as they turned the corner, momentarily directly bathed by the light of a streetlamp.

She said, "My feet hurt, I smell like the sewers *and* that pet shop, and I just let some mystery demon do its mystery thing right under my nose. I need heavily flavored coffee, and I need it now."

"I suppose it would behoove me to write up my notes about our sewer travels," he said.

"That's not about me," Cordelia said by way of correction. "But if it gets us back to the hotel . . . I'll take it."

The hotel. Where Fred had stayed—and, with luck, maybe even had found a lead to the mystery demon. Cordelia felt a furtive flush of guilt. *But I'm doing my part. I've been doing my part. It's not my fault if the visions aren't enough. And where's Angel, anyway?*

Doing his part.

But doing it for whom or *what*, she didn't know.

CHAPTER TEN

"I know you're there." Angel spoke into the darkness. After a moment of silence he sat on one of the small curving benches in the Hyperion courtyard. The darkened lobby loomed behind him; he hadn't been in the mood to turn on lights, even though he knew the first thing the gang would do upon return would be to run around flicking switches. Fred hadn't been in evidence since his return, though he'd heard enough to know she was in her room.

After another moment of silence he said, "I can smell the Doritos."

Kluubp moved out from deepest shadow to merely night shadows and admitted, "I've developed a fondness for them." And then, "I just wanted to make sure none of the others were here. I've sensed your growing doubt about our secrets."

Angel jerked a thumb back at the lobby, careful

not to trigger the wrist stake rachet he still wore. "I'm the only one who sees in the dark. You'd know if they were around." If not by the illumination, then by the collisions and painful exclamations.

"Just being cautious," Kluubp said, somewhat defensively. "My situation here is tenuous enough. You'd think the Wisest would have sent—"

"Excuse me?" Angel said, tilting his head down and his eyebrows up. "Did you say the Wiseass? Because I'm pretty sure I heard—"

"Wise-*est*," Kluubp said, tacking on a glare as he climbed up on the next bench over. "You'll have to pardon me if I don't think you're taking this situation seriously."

"And you'll have to pardon me if I don't appreciate what your *Wisest* have done for us so far." Angel pinned the keeper with a return glare, an expression he'd kept to himself for a while. Hard to emote that sullen, brooding fury when every drop of energy goes to battling a brand new crop of fears. "I'm guessing they run things on your side of the portal. That when it comes down to it, they're responsible for the Giflatl's escape. They're responsible for a certain period of unnecessary, lengthy, and excruciating pain on my part. Not that I'm a stranger to pain, you understand, but I really draw the line at *unnecessary* pain. Unnecessary, and did I mention excruciating?"

"I saw," Kluubp said quietly, alluding to that

night he'd possibly saved Angel's life—from the scavengers if not another underground predator.

It didn't appease Angel in the least. "And now my friends—my current family—don't trust me anymore. And I don't trust them—not to make the right decisions, anyway. And why is that? Because of you and your Giflatl. So tell me again how I'm not taking this situation seriously?"

Kluubp said nothing. He swung his stubby legs back and forth above the ground, a sinuous movement beneath his hanging robe that only confirmed Angel's earlier impression of extra joints. After a moment he cleared his throat, a double-voiced rasp, but nothing more.

It didn't matter. Angel didn't really need to hear the words. "It's because I won't be your puppet, that's why."

Kluubp gave him a pained look. *"Please."*

"You thought I'd be grateful. Then you thought you'd found some kind of biddable champion. That I'd help you with the Giflatl just because you said it was the right thing to do. Appeal to my noble instinct, feed my ego, pat me on the ass, and send me off to battle."

"I didn't think it would be so hard to convince you to help," Kluubp admitted, somewhat crossly.

"That's because you don't know my world. Not just this world"— he gestured around the courtyard, and the city beyond that—"but *my* world.

That I have a son to protect, and that means being here to do it. That I care about my friends, and I care about what happens when there are lies between us. And it matters to me that they risk themselves every time they step out on a mission for the Powers That Be."

"From what I can tell of this city," Kluubp said, drawing himself up into a haughty posture, "they risk themselves every time they leave the hotel for any purpose."

Ha-ha. Angel gave him The Look, but didn't bother to say it out loud. What he said was, "I know why you're here. Whatever you tried, it failed."

Kluubp gave a martyr's sigh. "Yes."

Angel didn't like the sound of it. "You made things *worse*?"

"In a way," Kluubp said. "I tried to send the creature back without capturing it first. Not an optimal solution considering the ramifications in my world, but it was all you left me with. It didn't work; the Giflatl has grown too strong. Too much in the way of good eating, as I said."

"And . . . ?"

Kluubp sighed again, a nasal, doubled sound. "I did manage to send back some of the scavengers."

Angel hesitated, and Kluubp didn't wait for him to fill out the conversational gaps. "It means things will be messy down there. And it means your human friends will be able to track the Giflatl more easily." He made a *tsk* sound. "It's exactly what we didn't want. Exactly."

"Don't work yourself into a hissy fit," Angel said. "I'll help."

"If you don't, then you can expect all sorts of trouble," Kluubp warned. He tapped his fingers against the bench, an impatient sound. "Your friends will track down the Giflatl, and take all sorts of chances to gather the venom. They'll try to capture the Giflatl, of course—or worse yet, one of its spawn. Did I mention it was preparing to spawn?"

"You mentioned it."

"And then they'll test their new magic potion, trying to find the means to use it without losing every bit of common sense along the way. They won't, by the way. Can't be done."

"So you've said."

Kluubp climbed up on the bench and paced its length. "And then the word will get out, and people will come to this place, and if seeing the Giflatl doesn't change their worldview, then the eventual scuffles and riots certainly will."

"Did you miss the part where I said I'd help?"

Kluubp stopped his pacing. "No, not at all. I'd just worked myself up to a good rant and I was looking forward to it. I saw no reason to deprive myself."

"Reconsider," Angel said, cocking his head slightly as familiar tones of familiar voices filtered through the street noise and reached his awareness. Not happy tones. "We won't be alone much longer."

Kluubp stiffened. "Your friends?" he said, but didn't wait for Angel's response. He jumped off the bench, bouncing slightly on landing. "Meet me beneath your hotel. At the ten of your A.M."

"Noon," Angel said, with the slightest shake of his head. "If they see me leaving here before then, they'll *know* something's up." Besides, Connor expected to get his elevenses from his old man. "And just so we're clear . . ." He leaned over, elbows resting on his thighs, the confidential look of a confessor on his face as Kluubp blinked to find him so close. "I'm not doing this for you and your damn Wisests. I'm helping you so we can end this, and so the wedge you're driving between me and my friends will disappear."

As if it could be so easy.

And Kluubp, perhaps feeling the same, forebore to respond directly. He said, "Noon, then. Bring weapons," and scooted back into the darkest shadows.

Angel didn't bother to follow Kluubp's progress. He sat and glared at the empty fountain for a while, and then he looked up in time to greet Cordelia, Gunn, and Wesley, as Gunn led the way through the half-open iron gates leading into the courtyard from the street. He had obviously put aside the chip on his shoulder and decided to play nice with the others.

". . . big fat waste of time," Cordelia was saying. "I should have stayed here. Even going through the demon database one demon at a time would have done more good than standing around a pet shop watching a lizard turn white."

"That's not entirely true," Wesley countered. His headlamp dangled from one hand, a pencil resided behind one ear, and he waved a folded piece of paper in the air as though it meant something. "We made progress with the mapping. That's not insignificant."

"No," Cordelia admitted, "it's not. But it would be nice to do something about this current batch of visions. I can't remember ever having so many about the same thing. We never *needed* that many before."

"We're distracted. We've got reason." Gunn leaned his machete up against the courtyard wall and, in the first indication that anyone even knew Angel was there, looked his way and asked, "Did I hear you call someone a wise ass just now?"

"No," Angel said, truthfully enough. Behind him, beyond the double glass doors that led to the stairway entrance of the Hyperion, he heard bare feet on carpet. Light tread, moving fast down the stairs. Fred. An instant later she burst through the doors, not having bothered to turn on any lights.

"You're back!" she said. "Is everyone all right? Or should I ask . . . is anyone *more* than all right?"

"Just normal old us," Gunn said.

"Well I didn't mean that you were otherwise *normal*," she said immediately, and then tripped over those words too. "That is, otherwise normal in a boring way. Just normal in a good way."

Gunn grinned at her. "Of course that's what you meant," he said. Except he then turned on Angel and added, "Though I have to tell you, some of us are still pretty close to convinced that others of us are deliberately making every effort to keep us that way. Normal. Easy to hurt. Easy to control. That way."

"Mortal," Wesley countered, shoving his paper away in his shirt pocket. "Unthreatening. Less special than thou. You know, I can well imagine that a certain number of years as a vampire with a soul—the only vampire with a soul that we know of—could leave a person accustomed to being special. Accustomed to taking humans for granted in a certain way."

Angel regarded him in silence, considering the recent behavior of his friends . . . and the resentment in their expressions now. Yes, they'd become obsessed. Yes, they wanted the Giflatl venom and they wanted it badly. Yes, they suspected him.

He thought they had good reason for all of it.

"I'm not sure this conversation is headed in a good direction," Fred said, uneasy and hesitating at the top of the stairs instead of joining them. She looked like she might just leave altogether.

"I think I'm with you." Cordelia pushed past both men and headed for Fred. "I'm putting away my sharp toys and then I'm going home. I think we all need some distance from this thing . . . and maybe from each other."

Wesley said, "I don't think that's going to help."

"Neither do I." An entirely unfamiliar voice hampered by the characteristic lisp of someone with fangs intruded on their conversation. "In fact, there's nothing for it—you're too miserably angst-ridden to live. I'll just have to kill you all. Besides, your friend there staked my buddy not too long ago and I'm annoyed."

Angel found him right away, perched lithely on top of the tall entrance gates; the others didn't spot him until he leaped down to join them.

"You know, that's just not fair," Cordelia said, scowling mightily at the linebacker-sized vamp. Clean and well fed and strong; a survivor vamp, not just an uncontrolled predator taking his strength for granted. "He should have to be invited. Who makes these rules, anyway?"

"Public place," Angel said.

"Well, duh! But it's *our* public place." She put her

hands on the pockets of her pink zip-up sweatshirt, then back over her hips—uneasily checking for weapons and coming up only with the sharp toy she'd mentioned earlier, a small token of a knife. Gunn reached casually for the machete; the vamp gave him an evil grin, and Gunn hesitated, poised. . . .

Staring each other down . . .

Both leaping at once: Gunn went for the weapon, and the vamp went for Gunn, and they tangled heavily near the gate, the machete just out of Gunn's reach. Gunn struggled to free himself, wrestling the large vamp with only one thing in mind—reaching that machete. Wesley threw himself on the vamp's back, only to end up squashed under both Gunn and the vamp as they rolled over together with Gunn on top, arms and legs flailing as he fought to free himself.

Angel sat where he was.

"Angel!" Cordelia said, poised for action but clearly not certain just what action was best, not with the men tangled up like a ball of living yarn and her pointy things limited to a little knife that would only annoy the vamp.

Angel didn't move; he watched without expression, with no sign that he was ready to leap the instant he felt any of them were truly in danger. So far, the vamp was only playing.

Gunn grunted with effort, broke free, and lunged for the machete—only to fall just short as the vamp latched onto Gunn's leg, jerked back, and then got the leverage to fling him away. With only Wesley clinging to him, the vamp made it up to his knees in no time, grinning fiercely as he sent Wesley bashing against the gate.

"*Angel,*" Cordelia shouted, succeeding nicely in gaining the vamp's attention.

"Taken for granted?" he said. "I wonder what that feels like."

Cordelia took a desperate hammer grip on the knifelet and crouched, fists raised in what he recognized as one of their practice routine positions. She muttered, "Precision . . . ," to herself and snapped off a punch using the hand with the knife as the vamp—assertive, casual, and still grinning— came within range. A nice move, but of course not fast enough. The vamp caught her by the wrist, disarmed her with enough force to make her cry out in pain, and then tossed her across the courtyard.

"Just a warm-up," he said modestly, and followed her for seconds.

Cordelia darted a quick glance at Angel. "I get the point!" She scrambled backward along the wall. "Now get off your brooding ass and give *him* the point!"

"This isn't brooding," he informed her, getting to his feet. "If I were brooding, I'd just go inside now."

The vampire caught the meaning behind that, and hesitated in his pursuit of Cordelia to target and assess Angel.

Still that moment of fear. The body memory of the pain, slashing at his courage. Reminding him of the consequences of failure.

Angel *moved.* Not leaving the memories behind, but bringing them right along with him—just as he'd done the past several days of trying to hunt through to the other side of fear where he normally lived. The intruder charged to meet him, but at the last moment swapped brute force for a more wily approach. They exchanged a flurry of swift blows, punch and block and duck, until Angel took a hard hit. He staggered back, shook it off, and let his fangs show through.

"About time," said the other vampire, and leaped at Angel to start in all over again. Cordelia darted out of the battlefield, running to Wesley and Gunn. Both men were in that dazed state where standing up seemed tempting and staying down seemed wise, although Gunn's hand had finally closed over his machete hilt.

"You should have left my buddy alone," the vamp said, jamming an elbow into Angel's shoulder just below the collarbone, angled up. The audible crack of bone brought a flash of searing pain.

Angel snarled soundlessly, tucked his hand in his waistband to keep the arm out of the way, and unchambered a roundhouse kick that took the vamp in the upper thigh hard enough to take the leg out from under him—not broken, but not fully functional anymore. "Your *buddy*," he said, staggering back with balance compromised by his useless arm, "should have stuck to rats."

"Those tunnels aren't safe anymore," the vamp said, lurching to his feet. "We'll all be up here, soon. Not just our kind, either. The others. The ones who won't blend in. L.A.'s in for a real party." He grinned, blood dripping from a cut on his face; it almost looked like an invitation.

Behind him, Wesley had made it to his feet; Cordelia still crouched by Gunn, who was getting back enough focus to let fury settle into his eyes.

Angel gave a single shake of his head. "There won't be a party while I'm around. And even if there was, you wouldn't be around to make it." He launched a high kick, nothing fancy, just speed and accuracy, and sent the vampire staggering backward, arms windmilling—heading straight for Wesley, Cordelia, and Gunn.

Pricelessly astonished, Wesley froze for an instant. Then he snatched the drooping pencil from behind his ear and braced it in front of himself just in time to skewer the incoming vampire.

"Awright," Gunn said, still sounding dazed but climbing to his feet. "That's what I call a pencil pusher."

But Wesley and Cordelia exchanged less satisfied looks, and Angel left them there. He turned on his heel and strode past Fred, who only then reappeared on the stairs, literally dripping weapons from the cabinet. "Fight's over," he told her shortly.

Fred looked out over the courtyard, and then back at Angel, a glance he met right before he swept on in the hotel. Behind him she muttered, "Ohhh, I don't know about *that*."

Late morning after a nearly sleepless night. Not for Connor, who'd had a happy, burp-free sleep interrupted by a single feeding and a quick diaper change, but for Angel, who now held him for his late morning feeding. With Connor in the crook of his arm and the bottle in place, Angel paced slowly before his balcony doors, the ones usually covered with heavy curtains.

Not today. The direct sunlight had passed them by on the way up toward noon, and now he had the curtains open, pacing before the glass doors watching L.A. like a predator watches its prey.

Except he wasn't the predator. He was the champion. And he was about to put his child down and go out into the thick of it again. Worse than the thick of it . . . against the one foe who could rip him apart and leave him that way.

His collarbone ached as a reminder of how

accustomed he was to healing even in the midst of battle. It hadn't been a bad break and he hadn't taken any other serious injuries; it had healed quickly. An ache through the next day . . . small price to pay for victory.

He shifted Connor slightly and interrupted the serious nature of his thoughts long enough to make goobly baby noises and tease Connor's lips with the bottle nipple. But Connor wasn't to be had; he gurgled sleepily in a declaration of fullness.

Angel put the bottle aside and brought Connor to his towel-covered shoulder for burping, gently patting his back. "Don't miss the towel," he said. "Daddy has to go fight the bad guy, and the bad guy will not be impressed if there's baby puke on Daddy's back."

No doubt the Giflatl wouldn't actually care one way or the other as long as it killed Angel.

Wesley picked at his finger, holding it close to the light at the end of the lobby reception desk and squinting. He'd been working on a splinter for some time, while Cordelia paged through the demon database, and Fred sat on the floor by the bookshelf and flipped through something old and musty. Gunn arrived with stray rabbit fur on his jacket to announce that the chameleon was still pasty white and settled down to some Game Boy, waiting for Wesley and the morning's foray into the tunnels.

Cordelia gave a final sigh in a whole series of exasperated sighs, pushed herself away from her desk, and marched into the bathroom. She rummaged in the medicine cabinet and returned to the lobby holding tweezers before her like a weapon. "You're driving me crazy," she said. "Didn't they teach you this in Watcher school? Considering all the stakes you must have handled, I can't imagine why not."

"Not manly," Gunn said, not looking up from the game. "You're supposed to dig splinters out with your teeth." He gave Wesley an almost-innocent glance. "Or didn't you know?"

"It didn't come up," Wesley said, wincing in anticipation as Cordelia took his hand without so much as a by-your-leave and gave it a quick assessment.

"So it's only the rogue demon hunters who get splinters," Cordelia muttered. She saw her prey, squeezed Wesley's finger mightily at the base of the splinter, and attacked with the tweezers.

"Pencils weren't made for that particular use, after all," Wesley said. "And this need not have gone that far in the first place, if Angel hadn't hesitated so long."

Gunn looked up this time, and this time his expression was entirely too serious. "I don't get that," he said. "It's almost like he's not on our side anymore."

"I have to say I feel the same—ow!"

Cordelia smiled sweetly at him. "Sorry," she

said, with so little sincerity that not even Wesley could mistake her. "Let's not get carried away, you two. There's something going on with Angel, but you know . . . there's something going on with us, too. And he was making a point."

"I understand that," Wesley said, watching her with a wary eye as he spoke—no doubt in case being quiet fast became a good idea. But Cordelia had her eye on the splinter this time, and was going in for the grab. "I'm just not sure I agree with his point. Or the way he made it."

"Same here," Gunn said, and put the game aside. He looked at Fred, who was conspicuously quiet aside from the sound of turning pages, and he hesitated, like he might have been ready to say more but changed his mind. "We *are* going out, aren't we?"

"*Yes!*" Cordelia said in victory, withdrawing the splinter with a steady hand. And then she realized what Gunn had said and added, "I mean, yes. Now we can. I've put in a whole morning on Vision Demon and didn't get anywhere. I'm ready for a break."

"Good," Gunn said, and bounced up from his seat on the gray roundchair. "Let's go find us some clean spots down below. Now where's that good luck machete of mine?"

"You called *that* good luck?" Fred said, finally piqued into looking up from her book. "That whole being bashed-against-a-wall thing?"

"Yes," Gunn said, retrieving the weapon and hefting it with satisfaction. "I'm still alive, right?"

"I suppose so," Fred said, and smiled into her book as though she didn't want anyone else to see it. While Cordelia wrapped up the computer work, not bothering to sit as she bent over the mouse and keyboard, and Wesley—still sucking on his finger—went into the office after his maps and headlamp, Fred sat quietly with her book and was the first to lift her head to the stairs, noticing what Cordelia heard just an instant later.

Angel, coming down in the middle of the day. To judge by the voices, Lorne was at his side.

"And—*oh*," Angel said, looking at Lorne instead of the stairs as they descended together. "He only took half a bottle this morning. The rest of it's in the fridge, so if he gets fussy . . ."

"Right," Lorne said. "Because I've only been taking care of him since you brought him here, which is—oh, yes, since the day he was born. Angel, cupcake, if I haven't figured out the drill by now, you might as well take me out back and shoot me."

There was a moment's silence between the two as Angel hesitated a few steps from the landing where the stairs joined in front of the courtyard balcony to look at Lorne. Lorne raised a thoughtful eyebrow, shook his head. "Nah," he said. "I take that part back. But I still know the drill."

"It won't hurt you to hear it again," Angel said. "I

just want to make sure he's all right while I'm gone—" He stopped, turning to look as though just then realizing theirs was the only conversation, and it had drawn the attention of everyone in the lobby. He looked back at them a moment and said, "No. Really. We're just talking about Connor's bottle. There's no hidden code here, if that's what you're looking for."

"Might be useful," Gunn allowed. "Maybe then we could figure out what's up with you."

"The usual," Angel said without hesitating. "Vampire with a soul, tortured by past deeds, expert brooder, protective of son. You?"

"Just trying to figure out whose side you're on," Gunn said, wearing his implacable face as he let the machete swing slightly at his side.

Angel gave an exasperated shake of his head. "Are we still talking about that? I'm on my side, okay? It's just that my side happens to include your side, and my son's side, and this whole city's side. I do what I can for all of them."

"Must be awful crowded in there," Gunn said softly. "You sure there's room for us?"

Cordelia groaned ever so slightly, resting her elbows on the reception counter and putting her face in her hands, but not covering her eyes. Not quite.

Angel did just what she expected—turned to face Gunn more fully, drawn to rather than deterred by the quiet challenge. "I'm sorry if you're having a hard time with me right now—well, no." He cocked his head slightly, considering. "I'm not. We've wasted enough time talking at each other over what happened that night, and it's really not all that difficult. You've been living with the dangers of this work for years—or else you're Fred and you've been living in an alternate dimension and running for your life. It wears on you. It sometimes takes you damn near down to the ground. And then you had a night where it *didn't*, where you came back and healed like a vampire—"

"Only without paying the price of actually being demonically evil," Fred interposed.

"Except it wore off, and now suddenly the dangers are twice the burden, and it doesn't seem like you can continue unless you can get that protection back." Cordelia felt his words hit an unexpectedly deep spot. A vulnerable spot. She desperately wanted him to shut up . . . but knew he wouldn't. And he didn't. "News flash: You *can* continue, and you're going to have to. There are no easy answers. There never were, there never will be."

He came down the last short tier of steps, and Cordelia saw immediately that he'd gone into full stalking mode—a predator's lithe intent, the balanced readiness for anything. Head still in her hands, she muttered, "This is not good. This is never good."

But no one heeded her and she didn't blame them. They watched Angel, who strode through the lobby and out the back hallway, leaving them to deal with the wake of his intensity.

And the fact that he hadn't yet told them anything they didn't already know.

This is wrong, Fred thought at her book, blindly turning to the next page. *All this arguing and resentment and taking sides and—* "That's it!" she said, finally seeing the page at which she was staring. "The demon!"

"The one we fought?" Wesley stood just outside the office, his quiet vantage point to the discussion— if one could call it that—between Charles and Angel.

"The one from Cordelia's visions," Fred corrected him gently, but it was still a correction, an unspoken reminder that he, too, should have been helping to solve this particular problem. But not a loud unspoken reminder, because for all Fred knew they'd each been acting out of character, including herself.

She, too, remembered what it was like to heal so quickly the short days after their encounter with whatever creature had gotten snot all over her.

But Cordelia lifted her head from her hands, her face changing from what Fred thought was a glimpse of despair to determination. "Really?" she said. "What is it?"

Fred held the book up so Cordelia could see the woodcut illustration of the dumpy little demon—but not for long, because the book was as big and heavy as it was musty.

Long enough for Cordelia's expression to fall. "That? That little thing? That overcooked oatmeal lump?"

Fred consulted the book. "It's a—" She stopped, making a few experimental hacking noises deep in her throat, and then shook her head. "Sorry, I'm just not made for pronouncing all those Germanic consonants all stuck together like that. It's got a subtitle, though. It's called a 'glomming demon.'"

"Glomming demon," Cordelia said, trying it on for size. "What's its deal?"

The text wandered on in a self-important way, and Fred struggled to make something concise of it, aware that she wasn't especially known for being concise herself. "It looks like this thing doesn't have much chance out in the demony worlds, being puny and lumpy and not terribly strong, so it has this survival skill . . . it sees someone doing something useful, and it . . . well, it *takes* it."

"Singing?" Cordelia said, skepticism in place.

Fred shrugged. "Apparently sometimes it just takes whatever strikes its fancy, too. It's a simple-minded thing."

Charles, sounding entirely disgruntled from the encounter with Angel, said, "So let me get this straight. We're looking for a lumpy, singing, lip-reading, color-changing demon."

"Can't be too many of those around," Cordelia said, rolling her eyes ever so slightly. And then her eyes widened, and she took on a perfectly blank stare. Fred grabbed her pen and notebook and prepared to scribble. "It's by a gym," Cordelia said. "Bart's Gym. And it . . . ohh, a boxer." Suddenly she was seeing again, and she looked over at Fred and her pen, still poised for writing. "That's it," she said. "Bart's Gym. Sounds classy."

"It's enough," Charles said shortly. "Looks like tunnel-mapping will have to wait."

"Let's not be hasty," Wesley said, holding up a hand. "We can at least go through the tunnels on the way. Who's to say we won't be successful—and from there, we can go on to handle this glomming demon."

"My vision didn't come with a countdown clock," Cordelia informed him. "We'd be taking the chance we won't get there in time."

"In time for what?" Charles snorted. "So we can whup ass on over-boiled cereal demon?"

"It has the kicking and running skills of a soccer player," Wesley reminded him. "And who knows what else? Given that this particular demon seems to be stealing survival-optional skills, it may well have a complete offensive skillset already. But even if it doesn't, what better creature on which to test our own skills while we're under the influence of the thing we've been tracking?"

"It's true we know from experience that we don't necessarily think straight right after we encounter the whatever it is," Fred said, unable to avoid Wesley's logic. "It *would* be better to try it with an opponent we're not really worried about. Or to make sure some of us aren't affected."

"We don't know that we'll have that sort of control," Wesley said. "We need to assume we'll all be affected, and go from there." He hesitated a moment, going distant, and then said suddenly, "Right. We need index cards, and a marker. Fred?"

"Well, sure, but I don't—oh, you want me to make notes for us? So we don't forget things like we did before?"

"Starting with what we intend to do once we leave the whatever-it-is. Bart's Gym, and the glomming demon."

Fred shrugged, digging out her marker from inside the spiral binder of the notebook; Cordelia tossed her a pack of index cards.

"Okay then, people," Charles said, sounding glad to be on solid footing again. "Lock and load!"

Within moments, they were ready to go. And if any of them had any doubts, they didn't say anything.

And neither did Fred.

CHAPTER ELEVEN

Angel walked the underground with grim intent, loaded with weapons and headed first to meet the keeper and then for the Giflatl lair. He'd seen enough—his friends twisting around their needs, the city already cringing from the Giflatl-caused chaos in the demon layers of society. And the Giflatl about to spawn . . . things could only get worse. *Would* only get worse.

Unless someone did something about it.

He hesitated at the tunnel junction Kluubp had described to him—not the lair itself, but not far from it. The walls looked as if someone had loaded up a shotgun shell with demon parts and fired the results in thick random patterns. And the ceilings. And of course, the floor. He'd come through areas once cleaned and now slowly returning to their natural state, evidence enough of the scavengers at work. And now this . . . evidence enough that

Kluubp had told the truth about his attempts to remove the Giflatl.

He heard Kluubp coming long before he saw the keeper. Standing alone in the tunnel, darkly atmospheric shadows looming all around from the sparse maintenance lighting in this area, he closed his eyes and tipped his head back slightly and said, "I feel a disturbance in the Force."

Kluubp didn't rise to the bait. He said merely, "You came!" And he said it without any of his chatty fussiness, any of his overconfident pushiness. He said it with pure relief. Convincing relief.

So Angel opened his eyes and looked down the tunnel at the short dark figure of the keeper, and he said, "Yes. And just what is it you want me to do, exactly?"

Kluubp's ears perked forward in a most spaniel-like way. "Weaken it. Weaken it so I can use the netting procedure on it."

"Right," Angel said. "Last time I encountered this thing, it was like throwing myself in front of a tractor. And you want me to try to weaken it?"

Kluubp drew himself up to a profound posture and struck a reedier note than usual with his double throat. "Do or do not. There is no try."

Yoda-isms. "All right, I deserved that."

Kluubp relaxed, deflating somewhat, and grumbled, "It was one of my best lines. *Used* to be. Now everyone thinks *I* stole it. Come, the Giflatl isn't far. In fact, if we don't keep our voices down, it'll come out of its lair after us. We're well within striking territory."

Angel gave an obvious glance at the walls. "You don't say."

"*Tsk,*" Kluubp responded, although at what in particular Angel wasn't sure. He turned to lead Angel into the darkness, and in that moment of silence, Angel heard that they weren't alone.

Voices.

Human voices.

Familiar ones.

"My friends are coming," he said, stowing an incriminating crossbow and halberd behind a set of pipes. The sword at his side was inconspicuous enough—plenty of reason to be cautious in these carrion-ridden tunnels. "Looks like we're too late after all."

"We are *not,*" Kluubp said with a ferocity that took Angel by surprise. "I will never step aside to let your friends court disaster, just as I will never let them make public what they find. Do not underestimate me, Angel. As I have recruited you as the best help in tackling the Giflatl, I have recruited others during my time in L.A. I have the resources to follow up on my words."

Suddenly Kluubp's drooping ears and teddy-bear expression didn't seem so benign any longer. Angel gave him a disbelieving stare. "You're not afraid they'll create havoc for this world with the discovery of the Giflatl effect. You're afraid it'll create havoc for *your* world."

"That's right," Kluubp said, not the slightest bit abashed. "Should even the merest hint of the Giflatl's existence make it into print—or powers forbid, onto the output spewing entity you call the Internet—then my people and my way of life will never be safe again." He gave Angel what might have been a pitying look. "Nothing I said was untrue. I simply gave you the reasons most inclined to convince you to act. Those reasons are all just as valid now as they were when I cited them in the first place."

Angel said nothing. He'd seen for himself the truth behind those words.

"Now," Kluubp said firmly, twitching his robes away from a bit of nastiness near his foot, "get your friends away from here. I don't care how. Lead them off! We'll meet up shortly. I'll expect you." He stalked off into the darkness.

Angel stared after him a long moment, then threw his arms up in a helpless, exaggerated gesture, knowing there was no one to see.

Not yet, anyway. But the voices grew louder, perfectly audible to him even though they were little more than murmurs between companions on a hunting expedition. He put himself in shadow, and waited, then watched, as they approached. Theirs wasn't a smooth stalking approach . . . more like fumbling and discussing every step of the way.

"I just don't understand," Wesley said finally. "The clean areas are already reverting to their native filth, which I suppose makes sense, but . . . there aren't any new clean areas."

Fred snorted in her surprisingly unladylike way. "On the other hand, there sure is plenty of fresh looking . . . *yuck* . . . around here."

Wesley consulted the paper in his hand; it gave back a strong reflection from his headlamp, a bright spot in the gloom. "It's almost as if the cleaners went away, but whatever drew them in the first place was still active."

"It is, isn't it?" Angel said, but he kept his voice low. If they followed suit—and it was almost an instinctive thing in these sewers, the whispering—they might escape the Giflatl's attention.

They all looked sharply in his direction; Wesley's lamp, turned to its bright setting, shone directly in his eyes. Angel squinted, tipping his head to hunt relief. No doubt he was spotlighted like a vaudeville act.

"Angel," Fred said finally. "What're you—"

"On my way somewhere," he said shortly. "What're you?"

"Cordy got a vision," Gunn said. Wesley grunted as though perhaps someone had just elbowed him, and the light in Angel's eyes abruptly shifted away. "We're headed that way."

"Through the sewers?" Angel said, eyeing Wesley's paper. A map of some sort. And Fred . . . clutched in her hands were index cards and a marker, and he had a sudden image of all the notes he and Kluubp had found on the sleeping beauties in the lobby after the first Giflatl encounter. Not only that, but they each had cards already taped to their chests. They were prepared for a second encounter, all right.

"Well, no," Wesley said, moving a little closer and bringing the others with him. He had the tone of someone about to be blurtingly forthright, and an expression of pure determination. "Actually, we're down here looking for the creature we encountered that night." No one had to define *that night* anymore. They all knew. "The day after it happened, we discovered the sewer so clean of debris that we took it to be associated with the . . . whatever. We've been mapping the tunnels for activity on that basis, and though the situation with the cleaners seems to have changed, I still very much think we've closed in on the . . . whatever." He hesitated, looking at Angel; they both knew what was coming next. "And I have to say, I don't think it's any coincidence that here you are."

Angel gave the slightest of shrugs. "Not thinking there's much I could say to change your mind about that."

"You might try denying it," Gunn said bluntly.

"Might think I shouldn't have to." Even if it was true. If they trusted him to do what was right, it wouldn't matter where he was. "So you're taking the long way through the sewers with the hope that . . . what? You'll rediscover whatever hit you that night and pick up a dose of invincibility along the way?"

Gunn said, "Something like that."

Wesley cleared his throat. "Not precisely invincible. But you've got the gist of it. Perhaps you'd like to come along? Join us?"

Angel thought of Kluubp, and of the veiled threats he'd made. *I've got a choice here*, he told the keeper in his head. *Take 'em away from here and bail out on you for a while, or let them into your business.* He said, "Let's go, then. Where to?"

"Still hoping to find the whatever, actually," Wesley said, tucking his map away.

Cordelia made an impatient noise. "Look, I'm all for it, but the clock has been ticking. I think we'd better get to Bart's Gym."

"There's just one problem," Wesley said. "I'm not leaving without Angel." He looked directly at Angel, this time leaving his headlamp angled toward the ceiling. "I don't know why you're here, but I don't like the options I'm considering. I think it's in our best interest if you agree to come with us."

"Hello? What part of 'let's go, then,' means I haven't already agreed to do that?"

A low snarl rolled through the sewer. On the heels

of it, Angel heard a short, double-throated curse; he knew the others wouldn't. It was too low . . . and they were too keyed to the noise of the Giflatl.

"We can't leave now," Wesley told Cordelia. "We're almost there . . . this opportunity is greater than any one man's ability to box, I'm afraid."

Cordelia hesitated. "The Powers don't dial down the middle on a whim, Wesley."

"They obviously feel this glomming demon is important," Fred added. "We can stop by here on the way back, can't we?"

"I'm not sure you're going to have the choice," Angel said, backing up slightly and reaching for the wickedly tipped halberd he'd grabbed from the basement storage on the way by. "If you take a look around it might occur to you that this thing isn't going to be happy to find you here."

"It didn't kill us before," Wesley said staunchly. "It almost certainly could have, to judge by what little I remember of our behavior."

"That was before you tracked it into its own home territory," Angel said, and winced at the sound of an angry, coughing growl as it built its way to a roar.

"It sounds big," Fred said, sounding small.

"It *is* big," Angel told her. "You wanted it? It's all yours." *Let them be scratched and stupid for a few days . . . by the time they come out of it, I'll have the Giflatl taken care of.*

"Keep a safe distance," Wesley suggested. "We just want to test our theories with minor—"

The Giflatl came charging around a corner, racing along on its stumpy legs with its tail sticking straight out behind it and every single one of its many little arms reaching for them. The boils on its shoulders and back looked bigger, and seemed to pulse and ooze with mucus.

"Fred," Wesley said, as fast as any man could speak and still be comprehensible, "write it down. Angel's to come with us. I don't want him left behind here with the—yaugh!" He threw himself against the sewer wall, ducking down low to avoid the Giflatl's arms; Gunn did the same, swiping at a thick scaley leg on the way by. "Don't hurt it!" Wesley said. "We need it alive!"

"By all means, don't hurt it," Gunn muttered, rolling to his feet and flicking a wayward bit of nastiness off his arm as Fred gave a gasp and did what Angel wished he could—turned and ran.

"Fred!" Wesley shouted after her. "It's all right! If you *are* hurt, you'll heal. It's what we want!" But as the Giflatl made an astonishingly agile turn, pivoting on its tail, Wesley himself could not help but scramble away. And then they were all in it, harrying the creature from four sides as Cordelia joined in, almost as reluctant as Fred. Fred crept back, close enough to give the Giflatl a quick boot in the behind—close enough to take a slap from one of those lightning fast arms. And then Gunn, harassing it with the machete without intent to land the blows and taking a bad score of cuts across his arm; bright blood spurted.

And Angel watched, standing out of the way of the skirmish, halberd in hand. Hating himself for it. *They'll heal. And I can't afford to be out of the game right now.* Not until he could move in with Kluubp backing him, ready to transport the creature as soon as it had been weakened.

Wesley went down, and then finally Cordelia, neither with anything more than minor cuts. Fred giggled in an uncontrolled way, a scary not-quite-sane way. And Gunn, his bright green shirt soaked with blood but no longer actually bleeding, cried something frighteningly close to, "Yee-ha!"

Wesley clung to Cordelia as she cried, "Barney arms! It has Barney arms!"

In the center of it all, the Giflatl hesitated. It tasted the air with a long, globby tongue, checking each of them—each except for Angel, who had apparently escaped its notice with his quiet stillness and his distance.

"Oh, look," Cordelia said, her voice dreamy. "I've got a card on my chest. Have you guys got cards on your chests? Of course, they wouldn't look like my card, because, I mean . . . *my* chest, what can I say?"

"Bart's Gym," said Wesley, reading his card upside down with some effort. "Stop glomming demon."

"I remember that!" Fred said, shouting with the enthusiasm of a drunk.

And none of them noticed that the Giflatl gave a satisfied sounding snarl and contemplated them with intent—as expected, unwilling to tolerate invaders so close to its lair. The evidence of that coated the sewer walls.

"Run," Angel said suddenly, realizing that the bulging, swiveling eyes were no longer moving independently, but had focused fully on the sprawling, venom-drugged demon hunters. "Run *now*."

"Say," Fred said, pulling index cards from her back jeans pocket. "Angel has a card, too. It says he has to come with us. Or is it that we have to stay with him?"

The Giflatl snarled and pounced at Gunn, just as Gunn lurched away without care.

God, they're useless. Worse than useless. Angel considered the halberd, hefted it; balanced it . . . "Will you get *out of here*?" he urged them. "It's going to kill you!"

"What is?" Wesley asked, looking at the Giflatl just as the thing bounced off the wall behind where Gunn had stood and whirled in snarly anger to launch itself at Wesley. He gave a high, surprised yell of surprise and threw himself aside, more offended than alarmed.

Angel cursed soundly under his breath and launched the halberd like a javelin, hoping they wouldn't remember they didn't want the beast hurt and hoping beyond that they'd be distractable if they did remember.

"Hey!" Cordelia yelped, ducking as the weapon flew past. "Watchit, mister!"

"Just run, dammit!" he yelled back. And then, when it seemed they would scatter in every possible direction, "*This* way!"

Like a galoomphing herd of independent cats, they sorted themselves out and ran toward Angel, overtaking him without slowing. Behind them, the Giflatl howled in pain and fury, its mouth open wide to reveal every row of teeth. The halberd shaft bobbed at its haunches. *Damn. A better throw would have killed it.* And right then Angel didn't care what the keeper wanted and didn't care what his friends wanted. He himself wanted that monster out of his life, and if that meant killing it . . .

He wished he'd had more time to aim.

"Take it home!" he shouted into the tunnel, hoping it was weakened enough so the keeper would be able to net it. A wry little voice in his head told him that would be too easy, but . . .

He turned and discovered the four Giflatl

venom-affected demon hunters waiting for him, arms crossed. However far they'd run, they'd come back, and they looked determined. Wesley's headlamp, back in position, lit him like a road flare. Fred thrust an index card at him and said, "See? We're not going anywhere without you."

"This *is* vaudeville," Angel muttered. *Or at the very least, a circus. Candid Camera. A really annoying new reality show.* "Take your pick," he said out loud, eyeing the gang. Blood-spattered but healed, and so full of energy he thought they might literally start bouncing off the walls.

"And here," Cordelia said, waving another card. "Here's where we're supposed to be. This gym place. Some glomming demon. So are you coming?" Beside her, Gunn merely crossed his arms and raised an eyebrow, although he spoiled it a moment later by taking the card away to read and remind himself what they were up to.

Angel plucked Fred's index card from her hand and examined it. "All right, then," he said. "Let's go."

She might have asked for the card back if she'd been thinking straight. But she wasn't. And as much as he wanted Cordelia's latest round of visions resolved, Angel wanted the Giflatl gone more—and knew his chance when he saw it.

By the time they were halfway there, he trailed them by a significant distance. And moments after that, he was gone—along with the index card that would remind them he was supposed to be along.

The four glomming-demon hunters clustered together outside Bart's Gym, under the single incandescent bulb by an unprepossessing front entrance. "Private kind of gym," Gunn observed of it as they'd approached. "Private as in . . . you're not welcome here."

"We'll be too conspicuous inside," Wesley decided with much importance, as Cordelia and Fred put their heads together and let out a particularly conspicuous peal of giggles, as though they were and had been best friends for ages instead of being two people who seldom reacted the same way to any given situation.

After a moment of confusion, together they huddled over the index card in the only available light, with Wesley's headlamp faltering after the use of its bright halogen bulb. They peered at the index card. "What's that?" Gunn asked, pointing to the drawing in the corner. "Looks like a lump of oatmeal with legs and arms."

"It *is* a lump of oatmeal with legs and arms," Wesley proclaimed after studying it a moment.

"No, silly!" Fred said. "Look, see the little arrow? It's the glomming demon! That's what we're looking for."

"It's going to take all four of us to deal with

that?" Gunn said, and scoffed. "I'll step on it and we'll be done."

"It's not drawn to scale," Fred explained.

"Then what *is* scale?" Cordelia asked, but as soon as her gaze met Fred's, they burst into giggles all over again.

"What I want to know is where's the action?" Gunn asked. "We're here, aren't we? Right where our notes said. But no action."

"And I for one would like to point out how well this system is working," Wesley said, finger poised for pontification. He looked back at his own index card. "One: find whatever demon. Two: get wounded. Three: heal. Four: invincibly go forth to conquer the demon in Cordelia's vision. All very neat and mannerly, and here we are right at number four."

"Invincibly go forth . . ." Gunn said, trying the words on for size and clearly liking them. "Invincibly . . ."

"Well, unless you go get your sodding head cut off," Wesley told him, leaning close in quite a confidential manner. He turned to address no one in particular—a soliloquy mode. "*Sodding!* Ha, I'll say it again. *Soddin—*"

Cordelia glanced down the alley beside the run down little gym, startled to find a figure at the far end of the building. It slumped against the wall in a posture of defeat, huge water bottle by its side, made sexless by the oversized hooded sweatshirt and astonishingly baggy jeans. "Probably a guy," she decided out loud.

"What guy?" Fred asked, peering around the edge of the building. "Oh! Do you suppose it's *the* guy? The one you saw in your vision?"

"Ooh, that's a thought," Cordelia said, beaming. "Hard to tell, though—with the darkness and the clothes being designed to hold two or three people instead of just one."

"Let's ask, shall we?" Wesley said, and marched straight down the alley. The others followed.

The figure in question straightened as they approached, and even with fizzy giggles running up and down her spine, Cordelia recognized the despair on his face. Some part of her even knew they were too late, though it wasn't a part that truly cared right at the moment, even though his handsome Hispanic face drew other parts of her attention quite strongly.

"Excuse me," Wesley said, "by any chance are you a boxer? That is to say, by any chance were you a boxer up until a few moments ago, and now you mysteriously find yourself unable to box your own shadow?"

The young man's features hardened suspiciously. "Get outta my face, man. I don't know you."

"Oh, but we know you!" Fred said. "Cordelia saw you in a vision, which is how we knew you'd lost your ability to box. And now we're after the demon that stole boxing from you, so can you tell us if you've seen anything around here that looks like a giant lump of oatmeal with legs?"

"And arms," Gunn added.

"You people are messed up," the young man said, full of scorn. "I got enough trouble without you babblin' at me. Get lost, or I'll . . ."

"What?" Fred said, as helpfully as possible. "Considering the boxing thing is gone, now."

The young man made a terribly rude gesture in her direction and took off, not with any true hurry, his shoulders hunched in his oversize sweatshirt and no life in his jogging gait. He didn't look back, not even to notice he'd left his water bottle.

"How sad," Fred said, deeply affected. "That poor young man, he . . . what are we here for, again?"

Wesley tapped his index card. "Step four! Conquer the demon in Cordelia's vision."

They stopped, taking stock of the area. The alley appeared empty, and the small lot behind the gym—enough for two cars, a garbage bin, a certain amount of accumulated junk and plenty of prickly-looking weeds—seemed innocuous enough. The single bulb that lit the area from behind a protective cage put out only a sullen light, but it was enough to take in the nature of the area and even, with their eyes adjusted to the darkness, some of the detail.

"Not seeing a demon," Gunn declared after a moment of the taking-stock silence.

"According to my notes, it has the abilities of a chameleon," Fred said, holding her index card up to the faltering light on Wesley's forehead. Close up to the light, so she herself was only inches away from his face and didn't seem to notice.

"Fred . . ." Wesley said tentatively, taking her face between his hands.

She didn't seem to notice. "And it might sing. Or it could read our lips, which would certainly be handy for it if we were standing out of earshot and one of us said, 'Let's find that glomming demon and kill it right now!'"

"Fred . . ."

"Oh, here." She reached up for him and for a moment Cordelia thought she was returning his fumbling affection, but in the end she only shifted his head slightly so she had better access to the dimming light as she checked her notes. "Soccer . . . so it can kick. And now it boxes. I suppose that means it's a kickboxer."

"Fred . . ."

"Enough of this!" Gunn said, and loudly. He grabbed up the abandoned water bottle and spoke into the apparently empty space. "Read my lips *this*—you are outta here!" And he squirted the water in streams that crisscrossed over the garbage bin, the junk, and the back of the building.

As one, they pointed in triumph. Up against the brick, there was a dry spot. Directly in front of the dry spot, what had looked like dirty old brick shook itself off and suddenly became discernible as a lumpy demon who, while not as big as some, came up to Cordelia's waist and struck her as quite big enough.

"Now," Gunn said with satisfaction. "*Now* we can kick butt."

"Now we can *find* butt, then kick it," Cordelia said, fighting the impulse to wander away after the cute boxer. *Concentrate. It's just the goofy juice from the thing with all the arms, playing with your head.*

"There," Wesley said, pointing in a most decisive manner. "That's its butt, right there."

"I think we should try to talk to it." Fred moved in closer, bending over the glomming demon; it watched her warily from its flat, black little eyes, and otherwise didn't budge. "Look here," she said to it. "You're causing all sorts of trouble, Cordelia's getting visions, and we want you to stop. You've got tons of stolen abilities already, right? Can't you just be satisfied with those?"

The demon stared up at her a moment with no discernible reaction, and then as swift as a young Muhammad Ali, popped Fred in the face with an expertly delivered punch. She gave a little shriek and tumbled backward, and Cordelia rushed to her side as Gunn and Wesley stepped forward, equally fierce and furious. The demon didn't hesitate, leaping at them with a grace that was just *wrong* for a blobby being with little stick arms and legs. It landed a series of telling blows that neither Gunn nor Wesley was able to counter before it retreated to the corner of the lot, up against the building like a boxer against the ropes.

"I'm okay, I'm okay!" Fred said, flailing awkwardly to get herself upright while Cordelia—*let's be honest now*—hindered as much as she helped. Finally sitting, Fred wiped at the blood beneath her nose and then gingerly felt her nose itself . . . and then giggled. "All better!" she announced.

Wesley, who'd been bent over and turning that peculiar shade of green Cordelia had noticed guys often turned when kicked in very tender areas, slowly straightened, looking both astonished and relieved. "Oh," he said. "Heh. Well, enough of that, then!"

It's working. It's really working. We're healing as fast as it can hurt us. The problem is . . .

They hadn't managed to hurt *it* at all.

Gunn recovered first, clashing with the glomming demon to exchange a flurry of kicks, blocks, and punches. He took a few hard blows, staggered back, and let Wesley pick up the fight. Fred muttered to Cordelia, "Why are we fighting it again?"

Cordelia snagged the now-battered index card

from Fred's back jeans pocket. "And could those get any lower?" she said of the jeans, sticking the card in front of Fred's face. This wasn't quite like last time . . . when they'd all gotten such a big dose of the venom that they couldn't function at all. This time she had little whispers of common sense flitting around in her head, but they were just so hard to grasp. . . . And meanwhile the urge to roll over on her back and watch the stars was almost undeniable. "Now that *is* crazy," she decided. "The stars? In L.A.?"

"Ohh, right," Fred said, but not in response to Cordelia. She climbed to her feet and shoved the card back in her pocket. "All right then! Let's get down to it!"

"Fred," Wesley gasped, backpedaling under a flurry of furious blows, all of which were too fast to see and very few of which he blocked, "we *are* getting down to it. Would you care to join us?"

But the glomming demon backed off to its corner, and although Cordelia had a hard time discerning where its face was, never mind its expression, she would have said it grew more thoughtful. That it studied them. And just as she got a glimmer of alarm, she felt suddenly strange all over. A cold wind blew through her body, through every bone and muscle and organ . . . but somehow stirred nothing else in this back alley. No one's hair, none of the weeds, no one's clothing . . .

Fred gasped slightly and looked down at herself, and Gunn gave a highly annoyed, "Hey!" as Wesley sucked in his breath and turned his gaze immediately to the glomming demon.

With sudden clarity, Cordelia realized that she could think again. She *was* thinking again. Here they were in a back alley fighting a bratty little pudge of a demon and it was whipping their butts. Gunn had never even tried to use his machete on the thing, and Wesley's tactic seemed to be to allow the glomming demon to beat itself to death against his own body.

Waitaminute . . . if I'm thinking clearly again—

The demon giggled, a high-pitched, near-hysterical sound that made Cordelia want to slap it. It charged at Gunn, ran up his body like all the heros in the latest action films were running along walls these days, and when Gunn slapped at it in surprise, latched on with its demony mouth and its demony teeth. And it still giggled, muffled though it was.

"Didn't anyone ever teach you it's not polite to giggle with your mouth full?" Gunn asked, both seriously cross and seriously taken aback; he finally seemed to remember he had the machete at his side, and he snatched it free to repeatedly bonk the demon on the head with the hilt protruding from his fist.

If we're all thinking clearly again—

The glomming demon bled freely from the top

of its head, leather skin split and weeping. It released Gunn and retreated once more to its corner, still making snuffly self-pleased little noises. After a moment it broke into full-throated song, kicked up a rock with its foot, and bounced it off its knees in a way that just had to hurt. It was emulating a soccer ball dribble, Cordelia realized.

And Gunn bled. They all looked at him, bleeding. They all looked at the glomming demon . . . no longer bleeding.

"Hey!" Cordelia said suddenly, loud enough to be heard over the operatic singing. "It glommed our ability to heal!"

Fred scowled fiercely at it, not an expression Cordelia had seen before. "It glommed everything the venom was doing for us—and *to* us."

Gunn looked at his arm—no worse than a small dog bite, more bruising than bleeding. "It stole from us all those things we hunted so hard to—"

Wesley finished for him. "To steal from the creature in the sewers."

Startled, they all turned to pin their stares on him instead of the glomming demon. He shrugged ever so slightly. "When one comes down to it, that is the essence of what we were doing, is it not? Willing to harm something else to take from it something we thought would benefit us."

"Don't go getting all philosophical on me," Gunn said, deepening his scowl—and then aiming it at the glomming demon instead of Wesley. It sang, and had added shadowboxing to its showing off. Not a mean feat with the rock-bouncing still in play. Gunn said, "I'm ready to go back to kicking butt."

"Not without a strategy," Wesley said. "Now that we're capable of thinking of one. I had no idea how poorly we'd fight under even the mildest influence of that venom."

"What strategy?" Cordelia said bluntly. "If it stole the venom's effect from all of us, then isn't it four times as invincible? What can we do against that?"

"Ohh, I'll come up with something," Gunn said. "Anything to stop that noise."

I wish we'd come more heavily armed," Wesley admitted. "I didn't think we'd have that much trouble with this thing."

"Our best chance is to keep it distracted," Fred said. "Don't ever let it concentrate on any single one of us, or it could steal our ability to fight—however modest that might be. But if we attack in pairs—"

"Pairs are good," Cordelia said, barely audible against the volume of liquid notes pouring from the demon's mouth. "But . . . this glee club thing it's got going might never wear off. Mr. Lumpy really doesn't seem like much of a problem anymore."

"Hello, ow?" Gunn said, pointing at his arm. "It might not look like much, but I'm hopin' that thing's had its rabies shots."

"Attack in pairs," Fred said again, raising her normally soft voice over the demon's singing. "Charles and I, and Wesley and Cordelia. Before it gets a notion to run off!"

They all looked to Wesley; he gave a short nod. Cordelia shifted to position herself opposite him, and they rushed the demon. It never stopped singing as it engaged them, except for those moments it interrupted itself to giggle. An instant later they both stumbled backward, on the defensive; Fred and Gunn jumped in. *I fought the lard, and the lard won,* Cordelia thought in a daze, watching Gunn take a chunk from the demon with the machete. If the demon felt the wound, it gave no sign.

She and Wesley leaped in again, and this time Cordelia began to get the rhythm of it, relaxing enough so to her significant surprise, she applied some of the blocks Angel had taught her, and did so with good effect. *Precision,* she thought, and lashed out with a side kick to catch the demon squarely in the middle of its under-furnished face with her toe. "Ow!" she cried, when the toe crumpled every bit as much as the face. "Ow, ow, broken!" But when she glanced up it was to see Fred and Gunn headed into the fray, so she threw herself aside, rolling with her momentum, and popped upright again just in time to see Gunn relieve the glomming demon of its head. Maybe even some of its shoulders. Hard to tell with the lumpy factor mixed in there.

The angelic, soaring voice cut short. The head fell to the ground with a splat, not rolling conveniently away or even rolling at all. The body collapsed where it was, in mid-kick and all.

Cordelia regarded it sadly.

"What?" Gunn said, protest in his voice. "Killing it's what we came here to do."

"It's not that," she said, and sighed; she considered wiggling her toe to see if it was really broken and then thought better of it. Oh, for just a tiny bit of that sewer creature's venom . . . "I was hoping that when it died, the things it stole would be returned. You know, that that girl could sing again. And the boxer would, well, box. And especially the woman who read lips . . ." *And my* toe, *dammit!* She sighed again, and this time Fred sighed along with her.

Wesley cleared his throat. Bruises had come up on his face; no doubt there were more beneath his neatly buttoned shirt. "I think we've learned a valuable lesson here today."

"Yeah, yeah," Cordelia said, not interested in a moralistic life lesson lecture just then. "Nothing is free, the venom took things from us that were important not only in our work, but to who we are as people, yada yada yada."

Wesley raised a single eyebrow at her over one puffy and blackening eye. "I was going to say that perhaps calling the effects of the venom 'invincible' was overstating the case somewhat."

A silent moment passed.

"Oh," Cordelia said brightly. "Well, that too."

"Angel," Fred said, looking at them all as if she could find some kind of answer on their faces. "Where's Angel? He's supposed to be with us, isn't he?" She searched herself, patting herself down to reveal only more index cards—all blank—and her marker.

"Here, let me do that," Gunn offered, but quickly held up his hands in a "just-kidding" gesture.

"I thought I remembered . . ." Wesley started, but glanced at Gunn and Cordelia for confirmation.

"Don't look at me," Cordelia said. "Though I think he *was* with us, and now isn't."

"Just like the last time," Gunn said. "We lost him somewhere between here and the venom creature, though. . . . I'm sure of it."

"We'd better go back." Fred sent an uneasy look in the direction of the sewer.

"I do believe he intends to harm it," Wesley said by way of agreement.

Fred stuffed the blank index cards away in her back pocket. "That's not what I meant."

"Oh, you mean more like he was hurt last time so what if he's hurt this time?" Gunn asked, not sounding particularly concerned. "Hey, *he's* the one who left *us*."

"He could have had good reason," Cordelia said, shooting an angry look at Gunn. "We'd never know it if he did, either, because we were all juiced up on demon venom. I'm with Fred." She held her hand out, looking pointedly at Wesley. "If you're not coming, then at least hand over the headlamp."

"Oh, I'm coming," Wesley said. "I have quite a few questions I'd like answered, if nothing else. Explanations I think he owes us. And . . . as you say . . . if he's gone up against this particular demon, he might well be hurt." And then, although his mouth didn't say it, his expression and his eyes spoke clearly enough: *Or worse.*

CHAPTER TWELVE

Angel strode back toward the Giflatl territory, fast enough so anyone human would have to run to keep up but slow enough so all his second thoughts crept through and around his mind.

It's going to hurt.

No two ways about that. He wouldn't get away without more slow-healing injuries. Time during which he'd be unable to protect Connor or respond to Cordelia's visions. Not to mention the way his body recoiled at the physical memory of the last time.

His feet didn't mind the path he'd put them on, but his legs had a firm notion to turn around and go the other way. Or at least to hesitate. To think this through.

I've done that. Kluubp said the thing was about to spawn. Angel didn't know what a pregnant Giflatl looked like, but he believed Kluubp's anxiety.

And he sure didn't want any more of these things running around L.A. The time was *now*.

It could do more than hurt. It could dust me.

Fine, then this struggle to overcome fears he couldn't remember having for the last two hundred years or so would be over. And Cordelia would look after Connor. So would Lorne.

Not the same way I would. Not with a father's love.

And his feet kept moving.

His feet, he decided, knew best. And deep inside, behind what would have been a wildly pounding heart, so did he. Without fighting, without *risking*, he could no longer work toward the unattainable redemption that drove his every decision. He could no longer follow the mission. Even Connor would understand that fact eventually.

He'd have to.

He came upon the area of intensifying gick factor and finally slowed. There was no sign of the Giflatl, but he drew the long sword at his side and groped behind a set of pipes to claim the crossbow. On the ground not far away lay the broken shaft of the halberd. That meant the Giflatl still carried the steel of the weapon itself. Not a bad start.

And again, he heard the keeper approaching— lighter of foot than the Giflatl by far, with an accompanying swish of robe. He double-checked the set of the crossbow bolt and waited.

Kluubp came within view, his expression first anxious—and then, as his less acute dark vision saw Angel, relieved. "Thank the Powers you're back," he said. "I'm afraid it might be too late, but . . ."

"But let's take care of it anyway," Angel finished for him. "You have a plan?"

"Easy plan," Kluubp said, already back to his assertive self and probably unaware that Angel had seen either the worry or the relief—or unaware that those things had been just as convincing as all his words put together. "I wish I could avoid this, but it's simple enough in the end. I need you to fight it."

You wish you *could avoid it. . . .*

"When it's weakened enough, I'll net it and return it to my own dimension. We'll nurse it back to health there. It is, after all, a valuable resource."

"Right," Angel said. "So it's just a matter of who's using it for their own means . . . but one way or the other, it's being used."

Kluubp's upper lip stiffened in his offense. "You know very well why it can't stay here, and that keeping it in my own home, where it allows us to live safely, is a much better alternative than being forced to kill them off in this dimension where they would cause terrible havoc in this now densely populated area. They were not meant for these circumstances any more than they are meant for living on my world."

"Relax," Angel said. "Just making the point. I want it gone just as much as you do." As little as the gang might understand . . . He hefted the crossbow, shifted his grip on the sword, and said, "Show me the way."

"I'll do better than that," Kluubp said. "I wouldn't ask you to brace it in its actual lair—it's far too territorial." He opened his mouth wide to emit a strange twinned piercing sound, somewhere on the scale between only-a-dog-can-hear-this and you-just-pierced-my-eardrums. He repeated it a few times while Angel did a head-tilting wince, one eye shut as if that would do any good, and then he called, "Gerfluudey!"

"It has a name," Angel said flatly. *Dogs* had names. Pets and loved ones had names. He wasn't so sure about laying into a pregnant Giflatl named Gerfluudey.

Gerfluudey made the decision for him. It roared its angry battle cry and came pounding into view, bent on killing the intruders. Kluubp not only moved against a wall, he found an access ladder and climbed up out of reach. "She remembers the last time I called her!" he shouted down at Angel, barely audible over the Giflatl's angry challenge.

"Don't tell me," Angel said, not caring that he probably wouldn't be heard. "She holds a grudge." And didn't fail to note that the creature had suddenly become a *she*. As he lifted the crossbow and braced it against his biceps, aiming again at the thick haunch muscle, it occurred to him that Kluubp, a master at getting what he wanted, had deliberately depersonified the Giflatl up to this point by failing to refer to her as anything but "it."

He pulled the crossbow trigger.

Gerfluudey's roar turned to a squall of pain and anger; several of her arms clutched ineffectively at the deeply sunk bolt, tugging and squalling and spilling more of a mucuslike substance than blood. In that instant of her distraction, Angel reloaded the crossbow with the single extra bolt attached to the side—and he had the time to realize she looked different. The slimy coating still streamed over her body, but the boils didn't pulsate as they had; from here they looked more like craters than boils at all—though he'd have to get closer to be sure it wasn't a trick of the light.

He didn't particularly want to get closer.

The second crossbow bolt took her higher, at the base of one of her many arms. She didn't waste any time trying to remove it this time. . . . No, this time she went after the source.

Angel stood in the middle of the sewer, balanced on the balls of his feet, facing her straight on. Holding his ground. As she closed in on him, committed to her straight charge, he leaped up against the side of the sewer, using it as a kick-off for a flip that took him over the Giflatl's head. Though she couldn't react in time to turn on him, her startling eyes swiveled independently to watch him. When he landed on his feet those eyes were still watching him, even though she faced the other way.

Ugh. That's just not right.

He brought his sword down across her halberd-wounded haunch, ducking the arms that reached back for him. The edge bit into her flesh—but mostly it just bounced back again, repelled by a scaley exoskeleton that proved much more vulnerable to pointed punching weapons than straight edges. He leaped backward, giving the sword an annoyed look and adding one in for Kluubp as well—and then saw that Kluubp was as surprised as he. No doubt the keepers were more used to preserving the creatures than exploiting their vulnerabilities.

A long broadsword wasn't exactly a great weapon for poking. Nonetheless, he drew his arm back and took a stab at Gerfluudey.

Gerfluudey was having none of it. She tucked her rump, turned her stumpy tail into a tripod, and pivoted in a snarling move that turned her arms into many little blurs and whipped her toothy maw around much closer than he'd thought possible. Even though he whirled around to turn the momentum of his follow-through into another slashing blow, taking off at least three of those little arms, she still unleashed her powerful hind legs at his chest, smashing him backward with such force he lost the sword, lost his thoughts, lost anything but the deep knowledge that this would be bad.

He slammed into the wall, and what hadn't cracked at the blow she'd given him cracked at the impact against the concrete block. He had an instant of déjà vu, and almost expected to find himself sticking, impaled, as he'd been not so long ago. But after that instant he slid slowly down the wall, his legs folding beneath him with no resistance whatsoever.

And it was bad.

He reached for the sword, only inches away but way too far; pain seized his ribs like a constrictive band, triggering spasms in every muscle along his back and torso. He cried out, startled by the intensity of it, and the Giflatl swung its heavy head down to huff gaggingly putrid breath at him. All those teeth, no toothbrush . . .

She clearly considered him down for the count. *Hell, I am* down for the count. Limping closer, tipping down to tilt her head so one of her eyes could look him up and down, she opened her mouth wide, her remaining claws opening and closing with eager readiness and her body crouching ever lower until he realized she was working herself up to pounce with all her formidable personal weaponry at once.

Oh God, this is going to hurt.

Without giving himself any more time to think about just how much it would hurt, Angel threw a blurringly fast punch, sinking his hand deeply into the Giflatl's eye. She gave a horrible screech, whipping her head back and forth and whipping Angel along with it—until his hand came loose from the edge of the bony eye socket holding it in place and flung him back up against the wall.

Oh God yes it hurt.

Gerfluudey threw herself back and forth in the tunnel, making it suddenly too small for anything but her huge flailing body, a giant creature in the throes of a terrible temper tantrum. Kluubp shouted something; Angel couldn't tell what. There was no such thing as thinking, not in a world made of so much pain; it filled his mind and forced away everything but a heartfelt and gasping groan.

Kluubp's hand landed lightly on Angel's shoulder and he could have killed the keeper for that alone. "Excellent job, most excellent," he said. "I can take it from here. Get yourself home if you can. I'll check up on you later."

If he could. If someone or something else didn't seize an opportunistic moment to get rid of him.

"You can make it," Kluubp said, pulling out a netting of some sort from beneath his robe, a netting big enough that it couldn't have ever fit there in the first place. It glowed faintly blue. "Go on. You can make it."

Damned right he would. He had a son to protect. And a mission to follow.

An odd shimmering blue light reflected in a distant tunnel, barely enough to notice.

Fred noticed. She glanced around to see if she was the only one and found everyone else wearing a squinty look that made it clear they'd seen something too. "It's gone, now," she said softly. She hesitated as Wesley's headlamp flickered against the sewer floor. He made a quick adjustment, switching from the brightest setting on the headlamp back to the soft moonglow of LED light.

"Batteries don't last long on the bright setting," he said with apology.

"Geeze, you'd think we could manage a run to Costco for one of those giant packs of batteries," Cordelia said, limping slightly on her bruised foot. "You know, so we could have flashlights that aren't attached to your head?"

"It's that busy demon-fighting lifestyle." Charles moved a little closer to Fred in the dripping darkness, who found herself grateful for the gesture.

Cordelia said, "Yeah, or else someone keeps ignoring the to-do list."

"Weapons," muttered Wesley.

"Right," Charles said. "We've been over this. Should have brought more. Didn't."

"Well, we *were* thinking in terms of acquiring

the happy healing venom," Fred said with uneasy guilt. "And then I guess we weren't thinking much at all."

"No," Wesley said, and pointed to a faint glimmer at the very edge of the light. "*Weapons.*"

Cordelia ran ahead, crouching briefly at the glimmering spot. When she rose, it was to hold out a substantial sword. "This is one of Angel's. His big Camelot sword."

Wesley cleared his throat. "Not actually—"

"Oh, be quiet!" Fred snapped, drawing again on that remembered confidence. The under-the-influence Fred. "The point is, it's Angel's. He was back here, and he was fighting something."

Beside her, Charles hunkered down, drawing Wesley's attention and thus the light. He pointed at a dark splatter. "Big fight," he said. "That light plays with the color a little, but I'm betting it's red."

"I don't think you'll find any of us willing to take that bet," Wesley said softly.

Cordelia gave them all a grim look. "We'd better look for him."

Angel made it as far as the Hyperion stairs. Through the tunnels and the basement and up into the lobby, and not at all sure how he'd managed that far. Blood dribbled from his mouth down his chin and splattered the front of his shirt; if he'd needed his lungs to breathe he'd be dead. As it was the habitual camouflage breathing, the involuntary gasps of pain . . . they'd been enough to allow the blood from rib-punctured lungs to rise in his throat and mouth.

The ribs grated when he moved. They grated when he sat on the stairs, leaning his head against the wall and promising himself a moment's rest. They grated when he suddenly came back to awareness some unknown time later, his mouth full of his own blood in a way that made him ravenous and nauseous all at once. He resisted the urge to swallow; he leaned over slightly and spat on the deep burnt orange carpet covering the middle of the stairs.

"Charming," said a deep, unfamiliar voice. "I can see why you make friends wherever you go."

Angel gave a bleary squint down at the lobby, where a large bald man in bad polyester, and emitting vampire vibes leaned casually against the reception counter, looking like a poorly dressed James Bond villain. *This is so turning out to be a not-good day.* Out loud, he started to say, "Amazing, isn't it?" but found his voice choked with blood and coughed at the intense tickle of it. Blood sprayed across the back of his hand, already raised to wipe the corner of his mouth. *More stainage.*

"I'm beginning to think everything I've heard about you has been an exaggeration," the big man said. "Like playing telephone. Someone says, 'Did you hear about Angel? He's a wuss,' and by the time it makes the rounds it turns into 'Angel's tough' and somehow everyone believes it." The man cocked his head, considering, and his fang-face made a sudden appearance as his voice turned angry. "Or maybe it's just my lucky day. Here I'm figuring I'm going to be all noble and face off with the notorious turncoat Angel, and I find you leaking blood all over the place—and if I'm not mistaken, in a great deal of delightful pain. Delightful for me, that is. I might even be tempted to wonder why you're not healing even the ittiest bit if it didn't give me so much pleasure to see it."

Angel looked at him again, more carefully this time. Still big, shaved bald, badly dressed . . . totally unfamiliar. "Do we know each other?" he asked with difficulty, still managing an I've-got-better-things-to-do undertone.

"Not yet," the vampire said, evenly enough. He brushed at something on his suit jacket, but it turned out to be a worn nubby patch and he only made it worse. "And even now, only for a few short moments. You killed two of my friends today, did you know that?"

"Fashion police," Angel croaked, trying to remember if he had any stakes stowed away in this pocket or that and finding only a smallish knife. "I'm afraid you're going to have to go, too."

The vampire looked down on himself and smiled. "This?" he said. "Oh, please. This is just a little something I stole to wear to messy killings. I'm quite the natty dresser, really." He moved a little closer, a smooth, stalking glide that immediately identified him as an aged vampire, and not just some throwaway punk. This was a vampire who knew how to survive, and he took an arcing path through the lobby to close in on the stairs with an expression both curious and satisfied. "Not healing," he murmured to himself, and he reached into the broad, flapped pocket of his polyester suit jacket to withdraw a stake. "Not in the least."

"It's catching," Angel warned him in a raspy voice once more clogged with blood and pain. He tried to gather himself as the vamp moved up on the stairs, but knew with desperate certainty that pure willpower wouldn't be enough. Not this time. And to judge from the vamp's slow, malicious pleasure, he knew it too.

All right then. Let's bring the fight to my level. Angel's foot flashed out, taking the vamp in the side of the leg and bringing him crashing down on the stairs, surprised but hardly alarmed.

"As if," the vamp said, while his polyester suit soaked up the pools and splashes of Angel's blood. Without concern, he splayed his hands against the stairs, pushing off—

Angel slammed the knife through the vamp's

hand and into the stairs, into the bloody carpet. He gave the blade a fierce twist, making the vampire snarl with pain, and pushed down hard, grinding the hand, mixing the blood. Still snarling, the vamp jerked his hand free and backhanded Angel so hard as to knock him down the stairs, leaving him stunned with the agony blazing through his ribs as he coughed up a fresh surge of blood. Moving on sheer determination and grinning thinly through dripping lips, he made it to his hands and knees and looked up at the vamp, who yanked the knife free and threw it across the room with nothing more than annoyance.

"As *if*," the vamp repeated.

"You've eaten one too many valley girls," Angel told him, barely able to draw enough breath to fuel those words. "Pay attention. *It's catching*."

The vamp looked at his hand again. It bled sluggishly . . . but it still bled. For the first time, uncertainty flickered across his features.

It wouldn't last. Whatever small amount of venom had been smeared into the wound from Angel's blood on the stairs, it definitely wouldn't last. It was only an instant's respite, one he should be taking advantage of by grabbing a stake from the weapons cabinet or from behind the counter or from beneath one of the seat cushions or in a potted plant where it had been carelessly dropped or any of the dozen other places they kept the things on hand. Not that he had the strength to drive it home, but . . .

There was no *not* trying.

He didn't waste time getting to his feet; dragging himself to the short bottom tier of the stairs and fumbling his way down toward the weapons cabinet seemed to be his best option.

But suddenly the other vampire was there, looming over him, leaning against the cabinet door with his palm splayed against the glass, deliberately smearing blood on it. He said, "Maybe it is. Catching, I mean. But one of us is broken and one of us isn't." Abruptly, he smashed his hand through the glass, grinning around his elongated canines. "You would be the broken one. When you move, you sound just like that glass. Should I see just how broken you can get before you fall to pieces?" He picked up a handful of glass, crunching his fist closed around it, and then opened his fingers to let the bloody pieces fall to the floor.

Angel gave him a look of pure annoyance. "Now you're in for it," he said. "We just replaced—"

The vamp grabbed Angel by the throat, lifting him to his feet and shoving him against the wall beside the cabinet. Angel clawed at the hand with little effect. "Handy thing, the throat. Perfect size and shape for gripping, and did you notice how the squeeze gives you that instinctive panic, even if you don't actually need to breathe?"

As a matter of fact . . .

Angel drew on all his remaining speed and lashed out for the bald vamp's exposed ear—not boxing it, but snatching it, yanking hard. Something ripped audibly. The vamp shrieked in an amazingly high pitch and dropped Angel, who crunched to the floor like the broken glass around them and went right for the weapons, knowing he had only an instant before the vamp came back at him.

He almost missed the sound of running feet, the very human gasps of dismay—even Gunn's muttered, *"Damn,* didn't we just fix that?" For the vamp grabbed him by the back of the shirt and agony ripped through his torso and Cordy shouted "Hey!" and Fred gave an outraged yell and threw herself on the vamp and eventually Wesley and Gunn yanked the bemused interloper free and Wesley used a familiar-looking broadsword and a mighty two-handed stroke to take the vamp's head off in spite of crowded conditions.

In the instant of silence that followed, Cordelia said, "Don't you think my hair's short enough?" in the kind of tone that should have made Wesley wince as she brushed a short hank of hair from her shoulder.

"Angel," Fred said breathlessly, falling to her knees by his side and putting her hands on his shoulders as if she'd turn him over.

"Uh-uh," he told her. "Just . . . leave the wounded vampire be. For now. Shall we?" It wasn't as effective as he'd hoped, not with frothy blood still sliding down his chin and a voice barely into the hoarsely audible range, but she hesitated.

"God," she said. "You look terrible."

"That's the truth," Gunn agreed. "You look like Hell."

"Don't, actually," Angel said, wincing as he tried to gather himself and decided rolling over to lean against the wall and face them was the best he could do. "Take it from someone who knows."

"It's just . . ." Cordelia hesitated and knelt beside him, using her sleeve to wipe the corner of his mouth. He would have caught her hand and stopped her, but . . . it felt nice. "We don't see you like this. We never think about you being hurt like this. Even last week . . . well, we were kind of out of it. I barely remember. . . ."

Fred gave her a sober look, and then met Angel's gaze head on. "I remember what you said in the courtyard the other night. That we take you for granted. I think . . . you're right." She looked back over her shoulder at the guys, both of whom looked equally awkward in their own way. "He's always getting hurt this badly, because this is how hard he fights out there. We just never really knew it."

"We took it for granted," Wesley murmured in a soft echo of her earlier words.

Gunn said with studied casualness, "Look, epiphany's great and all, but someone's got to sweep up this glass."

"Epiphany?" Cordelia repeated.

"Hey, I can use the big words too." Gunn gave her a look that dared her to deny it, and she instantly gestured surrender. "Guess I'll just get a broom, then. At least it's not goo or slime or some other nastiness. Glass, I can deal with." And he leaned his machete against the stairs and headed back to the basement.

"I'll get you some blood," Fred said to Angel. "You must need it."

Wesley picked up the machete and hefted the sword, hesitating long enough to give Angel a nod, one that acknowledged the truth of Fred's words. Then he said quite matter-of-factly, "I'll just put these in my office so no one trips over them until we can get cleaned up."

That left Cordelia beside him, sitting back on her feet to regard him with a critical eye, but one that held a worried softness. She tucked her short hair behind her ear, looked at her hands as though she didn't know what to do with them, and ended up wiping away more blood. She stroked back the short hair at the side of his face, then gave a little laugh and stopped herself. "How cliché," she said, and then looked at him and quite deliberately did it again. "But . . . it makes me feel better."

Angel said, "Yes. It does."

Lorne made a sudden and startling appearance on the balcony, freezing the action below into a tableau of the aftermath—Gunn sweeping, Fred kneeling by Angel, and Cordelia with a carefully microwaved glass of O-pos, the good stuff from the blood bank. Wesley headed from his office to the weapons cabinet, determination on his face—a definite impending quest for information. But when Lorne looked down and blurted out "Good golly, Miss Molly!" they stopped what they were doing and looked up at him, all with various states of lifted eyebrows and unspoken, sardonic, *"And?"* comments.

Angel thought he was probably the only one to notice Lorne's eyes dart his way and then back behind again; he was certainly the only one to know why. Kluubp was here. Somewhere. Again.

"Oh, look," Lorne said, a weak recovery. "You all had a party and you didn't invite me. Let me just extend my gratitude—"

"You've been here?" Wesley said. "And you didn't happen to notice anything amiss?"

Lorne hesitated, then admitted, "I had company."

And before anyone could question *that*, the

company itself came out on the balcony to look down at them. Kluubp.

I don't need this. I really don't need this.

"Yoda?" Gunn said, sounding put out. "You had Yoda in the hotel and you didn't tell us?"

Kluubp made an impatient noise and stomped his foot. It didn't make much noise, but inspired the smallest smile on Angel's part. In his reedy double voice, Kluubp said, "My name is Kluubp. K-L-U-U-B-P, which is not pronounced *Yoda*. Have you people even *seen* the movie? You'd note some terribly important differences if you had, distinct flaws in that character's appearance. And the ego! Did you even notice the ego?"

"Okay, okay, we get the point," Cordelia said. "And no disrespect, Mr. Kluubp, but we're kind of busy here. The mayhem and bleeding and wounded friend and all. You know how it goes. Maybe we could chat another day?"

"We most certainly can not. And I know all about the mayhem and bleeding and even the wounded friend. You might say—"

"It's his fault," Angel inserted, easing himself just a little more upright. Kluubp wouldn't be here, wouldn't be revealing himself, without good reason—and with the Giflatl gone, Angel didn't want to think about what that reason might be.

Cordelia looked down at Angel. "What? You know this Kluubp person?"

"'Mr. Kluubp' didn't last very long, I see," Kluubp grumbled, making his way to the stairs and then down to them with Lorne at a reluctant distance behind him.

"And you knew about this," Wesley said, looking directly at Lorne.

Lorne looked right back at him. Angel would have winced at the impending conversation if he . . .

Well, if he'd had the energy to care. But in light of all that had happened already, of what he had faced from within and without, he left the wincing for those unavoidable moments in the future during which he was going to have to move from this spot.

Lorne said, "Yes, I knew." Wesley rarely garnered any of Lorne's spontaneous pet names, and this time was no exception. Nor did Lorne go wishy-washy on the facts; as ever, he either told the truth or refused to, without implying he didn't have the knowledge. "The Cliff's Notes version, anyway."

"I asked him not to say anything," Angel said, in case it wasn't obvious.

"But you told him," Wesley asked, with the clear if unspoken corollary—*and you didn't tell us*.

"Actually, I stumbled onto the situation," Lorne said, and his voice had taken on an uncharacteristic edge. "It was during a Connor moment, I believe, when I was the only one around to take care of him. And oh, yes, while I was checking on Angel after something tried to slash him into little pieces, but the rest of you were off hunting for the fountain of healing and couldn't be bothered with bandage changing and brow-soothing."

In the silence that followed, Angel looked at Lorne and raised an eyebrow. "Brow-soothing?" he mouthed, trying to look offended but aware from Lorne's dismissive wave that he hadn't mustered it.

Fred said suddenly, "He's right. We all know it, too. I think we should just skip this part, don't you? Because I for one want to hear about the rest of it *now*."

"You know, I don't generally think on the same wavelength as Fred," Cordelia said, "but I have to agree. Even though this looks pretty hinky, what with the demon team and the human team and especially with the demon team having all the secrets—"

"Not helping," Angel said, figuring she would think his gritted teeth came from a fresh onslaught of pain and thus not bothering to hide them. In fact, the pain was not fresh at all. It was quickly getting very, very old.

Cordelia didn't even bother to glance at him. "Yes, well," she said. "The point being I agree with Fred. Let's hear the goods from our visitor. After all . . . it's his fault."

Kluubp pursed his nearly lipless mouth in

annoyance, his ears flattening briefly. But as if wisely sensing this silence would not last long, he took center stage. Literally. He walked out into the lobby, robes swinging as much as robes so short could swing, and turned to face them all. "The creature you've been hunting is called the Giflatl. I am responsible for it, and it is responsible for both the unusual injuries Angel has received and your . . . fountain of healing, as you might well call it. However, the Giflatl does not belong in this time and place, as events proved. I convinced your friend of this and after a time, he helped me to trap the Giflatl and return her to my world."

Gerfluudey, Angel remembered.

"At great and obvious cost to himself," Kluubp reminded them all when no one broke into spontaneous cheers at his revelations.

"So it's gone? This ji-floo thing?" Gunn looked between Kluubp and Angel.

"It's gone," Angel said simply.

"And it never occurred to you to simply tell us what was going on?" Wesley asked, not looking at Kluubp at all.

Angel cleared his throat and spat blood. Beside him, Cordelia winced. "You know," he said, "by the time I understood the situation, you were dead set on finding the thing for your own means. Obsessed with it—and not all of that was the effect of the Giflatl venom. And me . . . I had my own problems to deal with. So no. It never occurred to me to simply tell you all what was going on. You tell me—would it have made any difference if I had? Or would you have maybe only changed your plans and gone after Kluubp as the potential source for even more Giflatl?"

Unexpectedly, Gunn said, "We *were* pretty far gone. I mean, I know I was. The way I let you and Fred get into trouble that night . . . the goof juice was great, but man—no use being that way if you can't stay with the program while you're at it."

"We could have worked on that," Wesley said, almost automatically—and then pulled himself up short, giving his head a quick shake. "It's insidious, isn't it? We all wanted what you have. We wanted to put the fear behind us."

Angel said, "Doesn't work that way. You think I don't have fear? We've all got our soft spots. We just have to deal with them in our own way. With our own resources."

"Like hanging around unsavory alleys to bait 'n' stake a few vamps," Cordelia offered dryly, looking over at him.

He looked back at her and said nothing, and eventually she gave him the smallest of knowing smiles and looked away.

"Wait a minute," Fred said, getting to her feet to think out loud at full pace. "We ran into the Giflatl, and you knew we'd forget it—most of it, anyway—

and that Angel wouldn't. So you came to him for help, but he had to heal up first—the normal way. Or almost the normal way."

"He had to be convinced. I needed all the time it took him to heal and more," Kluubp said, with a sour tone in both voices and an irritable flick of his ear. "I saved him that night, but was he grateful enough to grant the one little favor I needed?"

"Oh, get off it," Cordelia said dismissively. "You used him as much as you saved him, don't you think?"

"It was to his benefit. And yours, as little as you want to believe it."

But Fred was still pacing, biting the edge of one finger until she stopped in front of Kluubp and said, "You're not done yet."

Angel had an instant trepidation that told him Fred was right.

She said, "You got what you wanted. Angel kept things from us and then he helped you take the Giflatl away, which is why he's a great big fat mess over there."

"Hey," Angel protested weakly. "Not fat."

"Leaving you with no reason to show yourself now. You could have slunk off back to wherever you sent the Giflatl and we'd never have seen you."

"Fred's right," Cordelia said, then stopped to give her head an amazed and frowning shake. "God, I said it again. That's kind of scary. But . . .

you don't have to be here, surrounded by angry humans. Confessing your sins."

"Angry, well-armed, demon-killing humans," Gunn added.

"But not fat over here," Angel said, shifting oh-so-carefully and with Cordelia's instant help. Then he added, "Not stupid, either. Why *are* you here, Kluubp?"

"To take responsibility for the strife I've created between friends?" Kluubp suggested.

They all looked at him.

Kluubp muttered something that could only have been vile. "I told you she was about to spawn. I *told* you we had to hurry."

Angel's trepidation returned full force. "She did it," he said. "She did look . . . different when I saw her that last time. All those boils—"

"They weren't boils," Kluubp said, with a certain terse annoyance. "She was incubating her spawn."

"In her own skin?" Cordelia made a face that said, *Ew*.

"Under all that snot?" Fred followed up with an *I-don't-really-want-to-know* face.

"Yes, yes, and yes," Kluubp said. He gave them a look of utter impatience and said, "Do you realize what this means? I don't have the capacity to round each young Giflatl up and send it home. They must be killed, and they must be killed before their presence causes damage beyond repair."

"He means," Angel said, "before someone other than us actually realizes what they are and what they can do."

"I *mean*," Kluubp said, shooting Angel a dark look from his big Yoda eyes, "before they bring this city down."

"Yeah, right," Gunn said, and snorted. "What's so dangerous about people feeling no pain?"

Lorne walked over to the reception counter, picked up an abandoned newspaper, and waved it in the air. "Hello? Do you read anything besides the comics? Those people feeling no pain also have no inhibitions and no common sense. Did you or did you not see Homeless Hannah leap through Angel and Fred to reach Connor? Do you think she's been the only one? Were you not just moments ago lamenting your own sorry behavior under the influence? And let's not get into what happens if some scientist actually separates the silly juice from the healing juice. Does everyone get it when they need it? Or only the entitled? How about Homeless Hannah? Or you, for that matter?"

"That's enough," Wesley said shortly.

"Is it? Because really, I'm only getting started. I'm thinking, for instance, how many secrets and suspicions and hard feelings have filled this hotel over the last few weeks—"

"No, really," Wesley said, his voice without

undertone. "That's enough. We see your point."

"The venom's an amazing resource," Fred said wistfully, sticking her hands in her back pockets and rocking back on her heels. "But we're not ready for it. None of us is. The price is too high. *All* the prices."

Cordelia sighed, sticking out her bruised foot to give it a wishful eye. "So you want our help," she said to the foot, and then glanced over at Kluubp.

"I came for Angel's help," Kluubp corrected her, looking as if that had been quite a reasonable thing to say. "He's the only one of you fast enough to deal with a young Giflatl."

Cordelia gave him a disbelieving look, then shared it with Fred. "Excuse me," she said, not acting like she cared if Kluubp excused her or not, "but have you looked at him lately?"

"Definitely looking whupped to me," Gunn added. "Which I might as well say, because hey, how often does the chance come along?"

Angel himself might have taken offense if he hadn't been busy aiming a narrow-eyed stare at Kluubp. Then even that seemed like a little too much effort, and he gave up, closing his eyes altogether to let everyone else hash this one out, tipping his head back slightly to rest against the wall and wishing he was somehow somewhere else. Up in his room. Connor at his side, gurgling and cooing and even crying. Because now the others

would argue over what was to be done with the Giflatl spawn, they'd argue over who was to do it,
they'd . . .

They'd . . .

They were silent.

Never a good sign.

Angel opened his eyes again just in time to see
Kluubp reaching for him with intent; the others
seemed frozen—except for Cordelia, who first
moved out of Kluubp's way and then moved in
close again so there was no mistaking her close
scrutiny of his actions. Her short hair was mussed
from the day's travails, and there was a smudge of
something nasty on her high cheekbone and again
on her well-defined chin. Definitely at the end of a
day that had not been easy on her—or on any of
them. Fred's long sloppy braids looked like they'd
been dipped in something, Wesley's beard stubble
somehow shadowed his whole face—looking pale
even for a Brit—and Gunn's rich dark skin had a
gray undertone. Whatever journey they'd taken
had not been an easy one.

Nonetheless, they had the look of a closely knit
group not to be taken lightly. And to judge by
Kluubp's expression—the tightened mouth and
flattened ears—he knew it. But he didn't hesitate
as he put his stumpy little hands on Angel, merci-
fully choosing an arm and shoulder, two spots that
were basically whole. "My request is not wholly

without merit," he said, and gave a serene little squint of concentration.

Angel grunted as it hit him, a surge of painfully prickly warmth suddenly coursing through his body. From head to toe and back again, until he felt full and more than full, his whole body numb and trembly and out of control—so when his head tipped back and his mouth dropped open and his eyes stared blankly upward, there was nothing he could do about it and still it went on.

Gunn suddenly stepped forward, grabbing Kluubp by the back of his robe to lift him right off the ground and out of contact with Angel. "Whatever you're doing, you've done enough," he said, his voice with that low, hard edge that occasionally popped out and reminded them all that until recently, Gunn had lived an entirely different life about which they knew very little.

"I have not—," Kluubp started, only enough to prove that both voices were being choked by his robes. "Put me down!" he squeaked in outraged harmony.

Gunn obliged.

Kluubp glared up at him, rubbing his nearly non-existent neck and the discreet side-by-side voicebox lumps. "I wasn't done," he said with much resentment. "You shouldn't have interfered."

"No?" Wesley said. "You seem to have acquired a nasty habit of making decisions for all of us. Perhaps next time you'll remember we don't take kindly to it. Now, what was that all about?"

Kluubp gave him a good hard glare, a look not nearly as effective as it might have been had he been anywhere near Wesley's height. "Look at him, why don't you, and ask yourselves that question. Had you not interrupted . . ."

Angel felt all pairs of eyes turn toward him as much as he saw it; he was too busy looking at himself, dazed but . . . suddenly feeling much, much better. His arms and legs still tingled, but in his ribs and chest, those places that had been so heavy with pain and blood and crunching broken parts, he felt only light relief.

It lasted until he moved, the most cautious of movements to bring himself to a full sitting position. Then the aches bloomed and he felt stiff enough to creak out loud, but . . .

"Nice," he said, and patted his own sides just to double-check. He climbed to his feet. "Very nice."

"You're okay?" Cordelia asked cautiously. "As okay as a dead person with an evil alter ego could ever be, I mean?"

He gave her a look.

"He's okay," she announced to the rest of them.

Naturally, they all turned back to Kluubp. Even Angel, who felt a blooming resentment. "You could have done that the first time, and didn't?"

"It is not effortless," Kluubp said, a little offended in return. "I had yet to track down the Giflatl, and needed the strength to return it home."

"And this time you have no choice," Wesley said. "Now you need him to kill the young Giflatl before they grow and scatter."

"Hold on, hold on," Gunn said. "Are we just glossing over that part where Angel goes from drooling blood to leaping to his feet?"

"I was not drooling," Angel said, quickly checking his chin.

"Yeah, what about that?" Cordelia looked at Kluubp with a frown. "Can you all do that? Can you show us—"

"Drooling, not my thing," Angel said, more assertively this time.

"No I cannot," Kluubp said, "And please stop looking at me like that. It was a simple, but exhausting manipulation of electromagnetic forces combined with a localized time-shift of . . ." But he trailed off, and Angel took note of just how they were looking at him. A gang well used to destructive and apocalyptic magic, looking at Kluubp in disbelief, entirely unwilling to hear a technobabble explanation.

Kluubp threw his short arms in the air, flattened his ears, and rolled his Yoda-eyes. "Oh, all right. I confess. It was the Force."

"That's better," Gunn said. He went over to the weapons cabinet, threw the doors open in spite of the broken glass. "Now. Let's go get rid of some Giflatl pups."

CHAPTER THIRTEEN

"This place is starting to look too familiar." Cordelia put her hands on her hips and glanced over at Wesley's headlamp. "I sure hope that thing lasts."

"It should," Wesley said with ultimate confidence, but Cordelia gave him a look anyway because she had learned that these moments of ultimate confidence were usually hiding moments of ultimate bluff. Sure enough, he added, "As long as I keep it on this setting," and she wasn't even sure how much stock she put into that.

"This setting" meant the moonglow effect—enough light to avoid walking into walls, but she wasn't sure how much help it would be in spotting zippety little Giflatl demons. Kluubp, the strange little Yoda clone, had already described the things as coming from so-called boils on Gerfluudey's back. They'd incubated within her skin itself, creating little craters.

How gross is that? Even in a demon-hunting world of grossness . . .

But Gerfluudey was gone, and she'd left behind the pups. Chihuahua-sized, zippety pups, with fewer arms and a longer tail but otherwise just miniatures of mom monster. And just as effective with their venom.

As if I need another dose of airhead Cordy to put on my resume.

Cordelia blinked at that sudden thought, surprised by it. Or rather, surprised that it hadn't been an eager desire for invulnerability. *Temporary healing,* she corrected herself, adding silently, *temporary healing that makes you an ineffective idiot as long as it lasts.*

Nothing came without a price, it seemed. Even Angel's usual fast healing . . .

Cordelia glanced at him; he led the group with Kluubp struggling to keep up, and if she hadn't known him as well as she did, she might have failed to notice the natural fluidity of his stride had a subtle hitch to it—or that for once he wasn't holding back so they could keep up. Whatever Kluubp had done for him, it had been enough . . . but it hadn't been everything. So here he was, doing what he always did and what they barely ever noticed—pushing that vampire's body to the limit, taking hits that would kill a human and not only failing to curl up into a little ball of *ow*, but fighting on.

It made her feel a brief surge of guilt for her own disgruntlement over her sore foot.

But only a brief surge. Pain was pain, and in general she wanted nothing to do with it no matter how heroic Angel was being at any given time. Though things could be worse—at least she'd gotten rid of the agonizing migraines that came with the visions. Not yet certain of the ultimate ramifications of that decision, but, hey, another day without migraines was another day of sunshine in her book.

Ahead of her, Angel stumbled. *Like that ever happens.* Quick to move up with a steadying hand, she said to Kluubp, "It's too soon for this. We'll come back later. Maybe by then we can *all* have flashlights."

"Later will be too late," Kluubp told them. "We're almost there."

Fred said, "Then we'll come with you, but Cordy's right. Your big healing scene wasn't big enough."

"Whose fault is that?" Kluubp asked. "And please, give me some credit. I wouldn't have wasted energy with the—oh, fine, call it a healing—if I hadn't needed Angel. The pups are more wary than the adult Giflatl. They'll only emerge from hiding to attack a demon."

"How about using you as the bait, then?" Gunn suggested.

Affronted, Kluubp stopped the procession to turn back to Gunn and put his hands in the vicinity of what might be hips. "Did I ever suggest I was a demon?"

Angel interrupted, sounded tired but as inexorable as ever. "Let's just get this over with."

"Very sensible." Kluubp nodded with approval. "Just around this corner."

They turned the corner and ended up at what had been a homey wooden door, carved with a pleasing mushroom motif. Skewed away from the door was a welcome mat that echoed the door's mushrooms, but it was stained and crusty.

Distressed, Fred said, "This was someone's home. Some nice little old couple, I bet, and they probably carved it themselves." The sewers and storm tunnels were full of such places, homes of shy and retiring demons who were more like the underworld version of *Leave It to Beaver* than anything else, a natural and well-integrated part of L.A.

The Giflatl had taken over this one for her den. Not tough to guess what had happened to the original occupants.

Wesley flicked his headlamp to the high beam and looked around the interior of the home. Unlike many of the snug little homes of the underground, this one was huge and nearly cavernous; the furniture had been splintered and shoved up against the walls, and the shredded remnants of a carpet lined the floor.

"Bet she pays a lot in hotel cleaning fees," Gunn muttered.

"Look!" Fred gasped, pointing.

Cordelia looked up from the welcome mat—she'd been trying to puzzle out its message—and immediately saw what had startled Fred. *Eyes. Many pairs of bulgy little eyes, glaring back out at us in the light. Cute.* They came from the corners, from niches up near the ceiling, from beneath folded-over scraps of carpet. They glared not at the group . . . but at Angel.

"Batter up," Cordelia muttered, swinging her weapon of choice for the evening—a nice weighted aluminum baseball bat. Gunn had a mace, Fred carried a crossbow, and Wesley had chosen a weird old sword that broadened out near the point and could probably be used for both whacking and cutting.

Angel seemed to be counting on skewering rather than whacking. He carried a light but sturdy rapier with a rather fanciful guard, and he didn't raise it from alongside his leg as he regarded the Giflatl-filled room.

One of the pups growled, a little falsetto noise that should have been funny but so wasn't even close.

And then Wesley's lamp flickered.

He instantly switched it back to the LED light; all the swiveling little eyes winked out—but a flurry of snarling threats joined the first.

"They don't like your moonlight," Angel murmured, his voice completely failing to reflect the way Cordelia's heart had started pounding, her panicky second thoughts about killing the pups. *Why not catch some and raise them and keep their venom on hand just in case, in case one of us is really hurt and might even die—that'd be worth a few days of goofy juice effects.*

From the sudden stark silence within the group around her, she suddenly knew she wasn't the only one. Second thoughts and third thoughts and fourth . . .

Quite suddenly, Kluubp said, "You can't capture them without my help. And I will not give it to you."

We could too. They all thought it, loudly enough to echo silently in the sewers.

"Or mine," Angel added.

We could if we had time to get ready, time to build a trap or two and make a plan and—

"No," Wesley said. "I don't suppose we can."

"Let's go, then," Gunn said, sounding determined enough to make up for all their hesitation and wishful thinking. "Kluubp said they won't go for humans right now. We should go on in there and be ready."

"One of us should watch the door," Fred said, her voice full of that uncertain tone she often got even when she was fairly certain about something.

"I'm quite capable of that," Kluubp said, and cleared his throat with a double-voiced sound. Cordelia took it for a hint. She straightened her back, reminded herself she couldn't really be hurt here anyway, and marched into the room.

The vibrato snarls faded, and an anxious chittering took their place. "Good," she said into the darkness of the room. "Be afraid. Be very afraid. We're here to kick your baby butts."

Something about that just didn't seem right. But if Kluubp, who had gone to great lengths to capture Gerfluudey, didn't think they could be caught . . .

Gunn slipped into the room behind her; she knew him by his confident movement. And Wesley, who moved more quietly if with no less assurance. And then the brave hesitation that was Fred. Wesley's light glowed in the roomy space, bouncing off the walls just enough to impart a dim illumination. The swiveling, bulbous baby Giflatl eyes winced and blinked, and their chittering intensified. Cordelia eased along the wall, Wesley by her side; Gunn and Fred moved to the other side of the door to do the same.

"Come on in," Gunn said quietly to Angel. "The water's fine."

"Great," Angel said, an undertone. "As long as it's not a blood bath."

Quite normally, Fred said, "That's kind of strange, really, because as a vampire you think you'd enjoy a—oh. You meant *your* blood."

"Right. I meant my blood." Angel moved to the doorway, hesitating there to test the reaction of the Giflatl spawn.

Cordelia winced in spite of herself as the newborn Giflatl pups launched into a veritable frenzy of snarling. Wesley jerked in reaction, turning to check Angel as his headlamp light tracked across the wall, leaping wildly and making the interior of the cave resemble a dim Lava lamp with traveling light, traveling reflections, frantically leaping Giflatl babies . . .

"I think I'm motion sick," Fred said, not quite a moan.

But Cordelia stared at the glowing eyes of the ferocious little Giflatl pups and said abruptly, "Do that again."

"What—," Wesley started.

"The light," Angel said, and his voice held the alert note of a hunter suddenly on trail. "Sweep it across the wall on the same level as most of the eyes."

"You're on to something," Wesley guessed, but didn't wait for an explanation before doing as asked.

Repeat performance. Cordelia relaxed her guard somewhat as the little Giflatl sprang out of the path of the light.

"The first time you fought the Giflatl, you wore that headlamp," Angel said.

"I don't recall," Wesley said, keeping the light steady, opposite the door. "But I imagine I did."

"And you really pissed Mama Giflatl off, too," Angel said. "She was winding up to remove Wes parts when that light shone in her eyes. Not the bright one, the LED you've got on now. That's when she left."

"You seem to remember quite a lot about that night after all," Wesley said softly, a reminder of the times Angel had told them all he didn't.

Not now, Cordelia thought. They had enough to think about, standing in the middle of a Giflatl swarm. A Giflatl swarm riled by Angel's presence and Wesley's light. She said, "I don't suppose our friend Kluubp knows anything about their sensitivity to this light?" and put the conversation firmly back on track.

"He does not," Kluubp said dryly from the doorway behind Angel, his voice somewhere down near Angel's knees. "We have no such light on my world. I can but tell you that they most definitely don't like it."

"News flash," Gunn muttered.

Fred said, "If we got them all in one place, could

you create the interdimensional net thing you talked about earlier? Get them all at once? And then we wouldn't have to kill them?" Her voice rose on a hopeful note.

"Yes," said Kluubp, sounding a little surprised himself. "If they were close enough to me. I've never had the means . . . you propose to . . . *herd* them? Using the light?"

If they're close enough?

"What's close enough?" Gunn asked, a suspicious tone in his voice for which Cordelia didn't blame him one bit. Kluubp had quite clearly played games with their little family grouping right from the start. All the same . . .

"Try it," she said. "If it works, we never touch them, they never touch us . . . what do we have to lose?"

"My equilibrium," Wesley responded, and the light bobbed wildly as he removed the headlamp and turned it into a hand lamp. "That's better."

He started at the edges of the room, the parts closest to Cordelia and, on the other side of the door, to Gunn. The Giflatl spawn scolded him fiercely, their eyes glowing like sapphires in the diffused LED illumination as they rolled in this direction and that to track the light. As it neared any single one of them, the barely discernible Giflatl leaped away.

"Hey!" Gunn protested as one of the creatures

jumped for freedom, heading straight for him. He swept it out of the air with his mace; it hit the rock with a dull crunch and slowly slid down to the floor. The other young Giflatl went utterly silent, then rushed Gunn en masse. A terrifying bundle of arms and claws and bounding, glowing eyes, and Gunn crouched slightly, solidifying his stance and raising the mace even as he said with cool calmness, "Backup would be nice here."

"On it," Wesley said, dashing over to join Gunn and turn the headlamp directly on them; they emitted little falsetto chitters of horror, knocking each other over in the attempt to escape the light.

"Guess they saw the light," Gunn said with some satisfaction. "Now let's get 'em rounded up and herded out."

The headlamp flickered and died.

In the moment of utter silence that followed, even the Giflatl spawn held their tongues. Cordelia stiffened, holding her breath—so was everyone else, to judge by the total absence of such noises. Then Gunn spoke matter-of-factly into the darkness.

"Bound to happen."

And Angel, who could still see perfectly well, said, "Here they come."

His voice alone was enough to give Cordelia a perfect mind's-eye picture of him. He stood by the door, braced and waiting, that grim but determined look on his face, ever ready to face the impossible. And as aware as any of them just who the Giflatl would go for now that they'd been invaded, pushed around, annoyed to the breaking point—and released. Their chittering turned to temper-tantrum snarling; their claws scraped rock.

Angel stood firm.

As one, the Giflatl charged. Cordelia didn't need eyes to know it, not with the snarling built to the breaking point and the sudden scrabbling of claws and the rush of movement . . .

Of all of them, Angel was the one they could hurt. *Again.* The one who'd faced his fears down just to be there, just as they'd had to let go of their own fears to come help destroy the source of healing venom. Angel could be hurt . . . and she couldn't. Not really.

With great desperation, Cordelia threw herself in front of Angel. In quick succession, Fred landed beside her, Gunn on top of Fred, and Wesley on top of them all—all moving in simultaneous and independent decision in the darkness. They scrabbled to untangle and arrange themselves for blind defense, with the Giflatl charging onward in great fury, leaving Fred just enough time to mutter, "Here comes the snot," before the cave lit with another sort of light, an intense neon flash in a shade of blue Cordelia would have just moments before sworn didn't exist. Her eyes shrieked at the sight of it and so did she, squinching them shut with just enough time to see the Giflatl descending upon them. Fred cried out in her ear and Wesley yelped and Gunn gave what would surely later be considered a manly shout of surprise.

Cordelia had no illusions about her shrieking. *Terror.* Anticipation of severe shredding—and knowing she wouldn't remember it later did nothing to alleviate the shock of *run away* that tingled down her arms and legs and left her more or less helpless on the ground even if she hadn't been on the bottom of the pile. *Run away* and the knowledge that she couldn't, wouldn't—not and leave Angel alone before the little beasts.

Then the unearthly light flared wildly, and Kluubp gave the most triumphant of shouts. Everyone in the pile shouted back at him in wordless protest that he should sound so pleased at the moment of their shredding.

And suddenly the light died and there was silence again.

Extended silence.

No scrabbling of claws. No chittering. No snarling.

"That," Kluubp said in the most satisfied of voices, "was close enough."

CHAPTER FOURTEEN

Angel came down the stairs to the lobby, Connor ensconced in his arms like a prince. He made no attempt to hide the silly grin on his face as Connor essayed an especially loud burp. Fathers had dispensations for silly grins. Especially fathers who had every reason to think they might not ever have babies, and yet again a father who had just put behind him a serious threat to his ability to keep his son safe. Or to see his son grow up. Or even to see this particular burp . . .

Back to normal, all healed up, and no more Giflatl venom on the scene.

Back to normal—Cordelia waiting for another vision while she tended some paperwork, Fred paging through a book with doodle-heavy notebook to hand as she stretched out on her stomach in front of the shelves in the reception office area, Gunn absorbed in his Game Boy but ready to leap up at an instant's notice and grab some action, Lorne off to see a private client, and Wesley . . .

"Aha!"

And Wesley immersed in research in the office, china teapot set not far away and tea just about oversteeped if Angel's nose told him right.

No one took special notice of Wesley's *aha!* Cordelia worked, Fred read, Gunn attacked something virtual with ferocity, and Lorne still wasn't there. Angel sat on the landing where the split stairs met and made faces—all of the human variety—at Connor.

After a moment, Wesley's somewhat peeved voice followed his exclamation. "Isn't anyone just the least bit curious?"

Without looking up from the invoice form she was frowning over, Cordelia said with complete disinterest, "Please, oh please, tell us why you've gone all aha-y."

Wesley emerged from the office, a particularly aged and hard-worn book in his hand. It was about the size of a checkbook—and in fact Wesley had inserted it into an old checkbook cover to protect it—and the pages were yellowed and cracked. "Two sisters from Pennsylvania wrote this little guide to supernatural occurrences in the mid-1800s," he said. "Naturally it was received with some horror, and there was quite a scandal.

I believe they ended up institutionalized, and then performed a great escape and ran off to Canada."

"Are we getting to the 'aha' part any time soon?" Cordelia asked, resting her chin in her palm to look over at him.

"Hey, this is great," Angel said, glancing down at Connor. Nap time, and Wesley's recitation was just about doing the trick. "Don't stop now."

Gunn gave a meaningful grunt. Fred wiggled her feet in the air and doodled.

Wesley gave them all a look of great forbearance. "I found the Giflatl."

This time Gunn glanced up. "So did we. A few days ago, if I remember right. The case is solved, English. No more invincible us."

"No more extremely silly us is more like it," Fred muttered, and then looked up, startled, as if she hadn't quite meant that to be out loud.

"That's not the point," Wesley said, tucking the book in the front pocket of his pale blue button-down shirt. "Before Kluubp left, he told me I would never have tracked down the Giflatl through my own resources. His kind have long made a quest of expunging any reference to the creature from any written record. But I felt I was on to something with the scavengers that were cleaning up after the thing, so I followed up on it. I . . . wanted to see if I could. Because when all is said and done, that's a skill I can call my own."

Gunn hesitated in his game-playing. "I'll give you that," he said. "I guess we all got to just count on what we have. Do the best with it."

Silence fell in the wake of his words. Angel didn't have to guess what they were thinking about; it showed on their faces. Cordelia's uncertainty about her new demon aspects, and what they would mean to her in the end. Fred's obvious consideration of looking for a place to hide. And Angel knew the things that weighed on Gunn and Wesley had little to do with fear of the physical, and more to do with what they'd left behind in their lives; their disquieted and uneasy expressions confirmed it. The Giflatl venom had given them a solution for all their concerns—fixing some of them with healing, obliterating others with days of altered behavior.

And now it was gone. And like Gunn had said, they had only themselves to count on.

And each other.

Cordelia sighed, the first to come out of introspective silence. She said, "I still wish those people had gotten their skills back when we killed that greedy little lump."

"I suspect its unusual activity was tied into the Giflatl as well," Wesley said. "It became suddenly active at the time we first encountered the Giflatl, as I recall. And if it had any notion what the Giflatl was doing to the resident demon population, it might well have been spurred into collecting skills for its own defense."

"I think it went a little overboard," Cordelia said dryly.

Angel thought so too. But he was happy enough to sit on the stairs watching everything be normal, with his normal son in his arms. Well, okay, as normal as things got around here and his son was actually the impossible progeny of two vampires, but one took what one could get.

And he was perfectly aware when Kluubp emerged from the basement and hesitated just outside the lobby before striding in with his apparent usual overbearing confidence. "Look who's not gone yet," he said, quietly for Connor's sake, and nodded at the archway as Kluubp passed under it.

Kluubp stopped where he was.

Gunn said, "I hope you don't have some other lame-ass errand for us to run for you. Stop the Giflatl, round up the Giflatl babies . . . we've got real work to do, you know." He made an especially emphatic jab at the Game Boy and muttered, "Yes!"

"Actually, the stop the Giflatl thing was mine," Angel said, all modesty.

"Indeed," said Kluubp. "No, I'm merely readying

for my final departure, and I came by to say . . . thank you."

"Well, may the Force be with you, too," Cordelia said, but there was a pleased smile lurking behind her rejoinder.

"You're welcome," Wesley told him, more solemnly. He absently touched the book in his pocket but remained silent on the subject.

"I wanted to say, too . . . perhaps I should have known I could trust you all with the Giflatl's secret, once I grew to understand you. I did not give you enough credit, and I hope you don't hold any grudges." He made a *tsk* noise, presumably at himself. "I would understand, however, if you did."

"Oh, I don't know," Wesley said, reluctant but honest. "It seems to me we had as much struggle with the situation as anyone might have. There's no guarantee we would have made the right decision had we truly been given a choice."

"I want you to understand," Kluubp said. "What I've done has made no difference to your fountain of healing. The Giflatl does not produce the venom in captivity; it doesn't survive in captivity well at all. So had you managed to get even that far in your plans, ultimately you would have failed."

"You knew that all along," Gunn said, accusation in his voice. Angel said nothing, but raised an eyebrow at Kluubp to echo Gunn's words. "And you had to get in the way anyway? Set us against each other?"

"I did," Kluubp said. "The road to that failure would have been long and difficult. It would have created chaos for both our worlds—and for nothing. Yet . . . I think I underestimated you. Had I told you the facts and allowed you to make your own decision, perhaps it would have been easier for all of us. For you did make the right choice when it counted." Kluubp wiggled his fingers against one another in what appeared to be an abashed gesture. "Without you I could never have saved the young Giflatl, all of which mean a great deal to my people's survival. As I should have known you would. After all," he added, and waved vaguely around the lobby, "this is what you do."

"Apology accepted," Wesley said, although no direct apology had been offered.

Angel exchanged a long, silent look with Kluubp, a more private look. He still found it a bemusing process to read those familiar, yet not familiar, features, especially with the fresh dusting of Dorito seasoning evident to both eye and nose, but he saw clearly enough Kluubp's apologetic regret. And yet he knew what it was like to make the hard decisions, the ones few beings had the strength to make, and then to follow through on. He said, "You did what you had to . . . and you'd do it again."

"Yes," Kluubp said, musing over the frank notion. "I suppose I would. But nonetheless."

Angel said, "Apology accepted. So long as you don't walk away with the notion that it was all right."

"No, no," Kluubp murmured. "And now, I must contact the editors of this fine guidebook of mine. They say nothing of your hotel—"

"Um, no offense," Gunn interrupted, "but we'd rather keep it that way."

The keeper hardly skipped a beat. "Your snack food, then. And the tolerance of the city occupants for the inexplicable. And let's not forget the reality shows!" He rubbed his hands together. "So much to see! I'm sorry to be leaving so soon. But as I said . . . I'm here only to thank you. And wish you well." And he departed in a swish of robe that was meant to be dramatic and . . . wasn't.

"There's something to that," Angel said, thinking back to the night he'd had a perfect view of charging Giflatl spawn, goaded by Wesley's LED round-up tactics and eager to rip Angel to tiny, painful shreds—and an equally perfect view of his night-blind friends simultaneously diving to his defense. "About that night," he said, and looked down at Connor's perfect little face with his perfect little nose, sleep-droopy eyes, and rosebud mouth before glancing up again to find them all watching him. "Thank you."

"Well," Cordelia said, her matter-of-fact tone not quite hiding the smile in her voice, "watching each other's backs, leaping into the fray . . . after all, that *is* what we do. And as long as we do that, what is there to fear?"

ABOUT THE AUTHOR

After obtaining a degree in wildlife illustration and environmental education, Doranna spent a number of years deep in the Appalachian Mountains riding the trails and writing sci-fi and fantasy books. She has since published an eclectic variety of titles, from the award-winning *Dun Lady's Jess*, and contemporary *A Feral Darkness,* to creating the no-holds-barred heroine in *Wolverine's Daughter.* She enjoys the chance to dabble in established worlds like Star Trek™ (*TNG: Tooth and Claw*) and Angel (*Impressions*).

Doranna has moved on to living in the northern Arizona mountains, where she still rides and writes, focusing on classical dressage with her Lipizzan. There's a mountain looming outside her office window, a pack of dogs running around the house, and a laptop sitting on her desk—and that's just the way she likes it. And if she happens to use a dorky headlamp for nighttime barn chores, she's not telling.

You can contact her at:
dmd@doranna.net, www.doranna.net, or
PO Box 31123
Flagstaff, AZ 86003
(SASE please)

> "Well, we could grind our enemies into powder with a sledgehammer, but gosh, we did that last night."
>
> —Xander

As long as there have been vampires, there has been the Slayer. One girl in all the world, to find them where they gather and to stop the spread of their evil and the swell of their numbers.

LOOK FOR A NEW TITLE EVERY MONTH!

Based on the hit TV series created by
Joss Whedon

2400-01

When I was six months old, I dropped from the sky—the lone survivor of a deadly Japanese plane crash. The newspapers named me Heaven. I was adopted by a wealthy family in Tokyo, pampered, and protected. For nineteen years, I thought I was lucky.
I'm learning how wrong I was.

I've lost the person I love most.
I've begun to uncover the truth about my family.
Now I'm being hunted. I must fight back, or die.
The old Heaven is gone.

I AM SAMURAI GIRL.

A new series from Simon Pulse

The Book of the Sword
The Book of the Shadow

BY CARRIE ASAI

Available in bookstores now

. . . A GIRL BORN
WITHOUT THE FEAR GENE

FEARLESS™

A SERIES BY
FRANCINE PASCAL

PUBLISHED BY SIMON & SCHUSTER